THE
OATHBOUND BLADE

FRACTURE PACT BOOK TWO

MEGAN O'RUSSELL

Ink Worlds Press

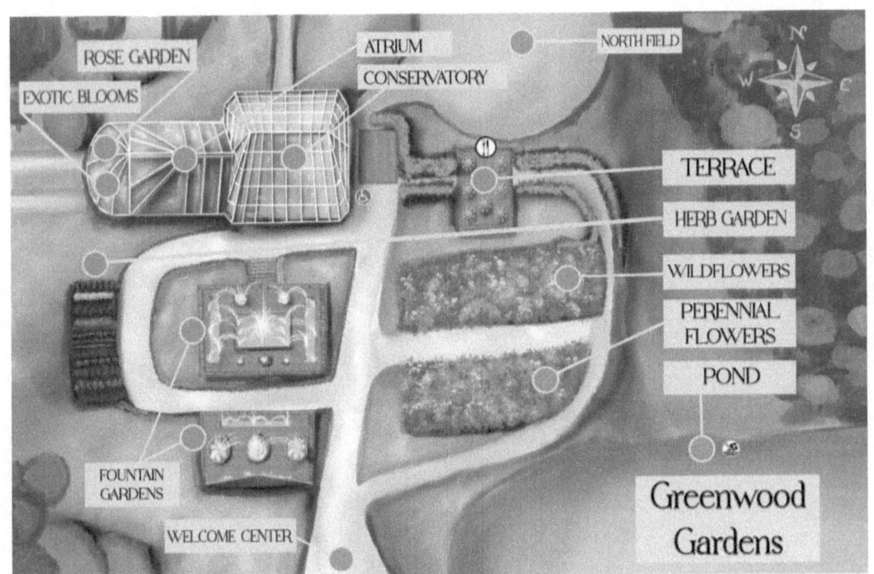

ROSE GARDEN
ATRIUM
CONSERVATORY
NORTH FIELD
EXOTIC BLOOMS
TERRACE
HERB GARDEN
WILDFLOWERS
PERENNIAL FLOWERS
POND
FOUNTAIN GARDENS
WELCOME CENTER
Greenwood Gardens
N
W
E
S

THE OATHBOUND BLADE

Ari

The blare of the horn sliced through Ari's thoughts, shattering the shred of reason she'd been clinging to.

"Move, dammit!" Ford stomped on the gas, racing toward the three Maree blocking their path.

The Maree leapt aside at the last moment, barely avoiding being added to the casualty count from the evening's disaster.

"What happened?" Ford gripped the steering wheel, his knuckles white as he swerved the VW van around the corner.

"Everything went wrong." Lincoln yanked off his white tux shirt. He balled the fabric up and pressed it to the wound on Eve's stomach.

The sword had sliced straight through her gut. Even a werewolf might not be able to heal from a wound that bad.

"The incantation?" Ari tore her gaze from the blood seeping through Lincoln's shirt and looked to Grace.

"I didn't know." Tears streamed down Grace's cheeks. She

sat on the floor between the front seats of the van, trembling and gripping her stomach like she was the one who'd been stabbed.

"Jerek used an amplifier," Lincoln said.

Amplifier.

The word sank through Ari's thoughts, shifting to a horrible stabbing pain around her heart.

"What?" Jack wiped the blood from his forehead with his sleeve.

"It's like feeding speed to magic." Ari crawled to Jerek's side. She laced her fingers through his, daring him to wake up and cringe at her closeness. He didn't flinch. "At the best of times, it's dangerous. But with the heliostone projecting the spell and the Fracture blocking him, there's no way he could have been stupid enough to believe he'd survive."

"I didn't know," Grace whispered. "I didn't know."

"Then we did all this for nothing?" Jack leaned back in his seat. "We didn't mend the Fracture. Eve didn't get to kill Chanler."

"I don't think Chanler was the one to cast the curse," Lincoln said.

"What?" Ford swerved onto the oceanside road.

"Mariah." Lincoln looked to Ari. "I asked her where you were. She said LeBlanc ran the place. The house, the museum. Chanler's name is on everything, but it's LeBlanc who's in charge. Who would destroy the feu only to hand the power they'd gained to someone else?"

Ari dug her nails into the back of Jerek's hand.

He had to wake up. That was the only option.

Jerek Holden had to wake up and explain how every pain they'd suffered had been worth it if Louis Chanler wasn't the villain. If Chanler hadn't been the one to rip magic from the world—

How many people died tonight?

"Where do you want me to go?" Ford asked as the lights of downtown Newport came into view.

"We have to find a place for them to rest," Lincoln said.

"And then we plan. We figure out a new way to mend the Fracture." Ari let go of Jerek's hand.

"Jerek is close to dead." Grace's voice cracked. "Eve is bleeding out. They could both be dead by sunrise. We failed. It's over, Ari."

Don't give up. You can't give up. You've already sacrificed too much.

"No. We made a promise," Ari said. "Things went to shit today, but that doesn't mean we get to be done. Our world is still broken, and there's still no one else to fix it. So we come up with a new plan. It's what Jerek and Eve will want."

"Jerek was willing to die for the feu," Lincoln said. "I'm not giving up."

"I'm too deep in to climb out now," Jack said.

"I'm with Ari," Ford said.

"I..." Grace shrank in on herself, cowering like she wasn't the most dangerous person in the van. "Okay. Okay. We'll find another way."

She held the Blood List and heliostone out to Ari, passing off the objects they'd shed so much blood for.

Ari set the stone and scroll on Jerek's chest.

It had been his idea to mend the Fracture. His plan to bring magic back into the world. He'd wanted to use the heliostone. He'd chosen the spell that had almost killed him.

The heliostone shimmered with a faint light that danced around the dark interior of the van.

Jerek Holden had no right to let the weight of the magical world come crashing down on Ari's shoulders. That was never part of their deal.

"Should we go back to the beach house?" Ford asked.

"We can't," Lincoln said.

"We don't have a choice." Ari pushed herself up onto one of the bench seats that ran along the sides of the van. "My laptop's at the house. Jerek's bag is at the house."

"We can buy new things," Lincoln said.

"You can't replace my laptop," Ari said. "Ford's either. Not if you want us to be able to find a place to hide a wounded werewolf and comatose magician."

"I'll take us to the house," Ford said.

"Ari, let's go to a motel." Lincoln shifted, piling more of his blood-soaked shirt onto Eve's wound. "Get Jerek and Eve inside, then Jack and I can go back to the house—"

"Don't fight me on this." Ari gripped the edge of her seat. "We go to the beach house."

Lincoln looked up at her. His face still had the alterations Jerek had made. His hair, his lips, his nose were all wrong. But the worry in his eyes was distinctly Lincoln Martel.

He had a streak of blood on his cheek.

Maybe it was his. Or Eve's. Or Jack's. Or another Maree's.

Too many people had bled at the museum.

It's worth it. I'll make it worth it.

Ari grabbed one of her daggers from the floor. She lifted the outer layer of her dress and sliced away a piece of the lining. She wiped the blood from her hands, scrubbing at the deep red that had matted around the sides of her nails.

The sound of the road beneath the van's tires changed as they reached the bridge that would carry them away from Aquidneck Island.

Far below the steel and concrete, the waves of the Atlantic lapped at the shore.

The vast darkness of the ocean offered peace and calm. If only Ari could jump out of the van and dive into blissful nothing...

"Eve's still bleeding," Lincoln said.

"I don't know how much more blood she can lose." Grace twisted to her knees, kicking the length of her black gown behind her. She pressed her fingers to the inside of Eve's wrist. "We need to take her to a hospital."

"People like us don't get to go to hospitals," Jack said.

"But she might need a blood trans—"

"Either she'll make it, or she won't." Jack spoke over Grace. "Handing Eve to somb doctors doesn't help anybody."

"We can't just watch her bleed to death!" Grace shouted.

Ari dug at the blood lodged under her nails. She should have taken the time to paint her nails before the opening of the Museum of Magic. Red polish could have hidden the blood.

But no one was supposed to bleed. Easy plan. In and out. Save the feu.

Go to the opening gala for the Museum of Magic. Steal the Heliostone. Buy Jerek and Grace enough time to use the Heliostone and the Blood List to undo the curse that had stolen magic from the world twelve years ago.

Bring magicians back to their full strength. Rebuild the world of the feu into something better than it had ever been before.

But something went wrong. Someone knew they'd planned to steal from the museum.

And Jerek—

Ari started to shake. She twisted the scrap she'd been using to clean her hands. The trembling didn't stop.

Jack slid forward from the back seat to sit beside Ari. He wrapped an arm around her shoulders, pulling her close. He kissed the side of her head and whispered, "I've got you," quiet enough the others wouldn't hear.

Ari unfurled her fingers, letting the bloodstained scrap of fabric fall to the floor.

"Jack, take over keeping pressure on Eve's wound. Lincoln, Ford, and I will grab what we need from inside," Ari said.

"What about me?" Grace asked.

"You've already done enough." Ari reached for the door as the van skidded to a stop beside the beach house.

Grace

Ari shoved the van doors open, sprinting for the house before Lincoln and Ford had leapt out of their seats.

Grace braced herself between the front seats as the van bounced from the sudden flurry of movement. Her muscles tensed, and her heart lurched into her throat, sending energy crackling through her limbs as instinct screamed for her to run.

"You should lie down." Jack knelt beside Eve, only using one hand to keep pressure on her wound.

"I'm fine." Grace loosened her grip on the seats. "I can take over for you."

"You're shaking," Jack said.

"I can take care of Eve." Grace managed to get to her knees. "You should get some fresh air. Stay away from the blood."

"Excuse me?" Jack's jaw tensed.

"You're a vampire."

"And that means I'll see my wounded werewolf friend as a snack?"

"I didn't—"

"Or are you worried I'll go after Holden's blood?" Jack nodded toward Jerek.

"I'm not implying—"

"Bats don't eat wolves," Jack said. "Not our vintage. And drinking your boss isn't a good idea, even if a job's gone south."

"How am I supposed to know how you'll react to blood? You've been hurt. You've been fighting."

"I'm not the one who almost killed a member of this crew." Jack's fangs pierced his bottom lip. A bead of blood trailed down his chin.

Grace scrambled back between the seats.

"If you can't be helpful, at least be quiet. I'm trying to hear Eve's heartbeat."

Grace pulled her knees to her chest and fixed her gaze on the soles of Eve's bare feet.

Eve had stepped in blood. A Knight Maree's probably. Eve had wounded a Maree, and they'd bled. She'd gotten their blood on her feet.

An easy path. Fighting, to wounds, to blood.

Grace hadn't been in a fight, hadn't attacked anyone.

She'd been performing a spell meant to save the feu. A pure, ecstatic energy had surged through her body, expanding everything that was Grace Esther Lee-Weiss beyond the terrified girl into something bigger and stronger than she'd ever thought she could be.

And that wonderful, euphoric moment had almost killed Jerek. Might still kill Jerek.

Eve had earned the blood on her feet fighting an enemy.

Grace had nearly murdered a friend during one of the best moments of her life.

Lincoln

The back of Ari's red dress disappeared into her room before Lincoln reached the top of the steps. He glanced through the open door as he ran past, needing visual confirmation she hadn't been dragged into her room by an unknown enemy.

She tossed her pink backpack onto the bed and grabbed her laptop from the bedside table.

Good enough.

On her feet. Moving. No knife at her throat.

Safe enough for now.

He grabbed the knob on the door to Jerek's room, twisting it open even as the flutter of panic that fought against his heartbeat whispered Jerek must have locked the door with some type of magic Lincoln didn't have a hope of breaking through.

But the door just opened.

Jerek had left the light on. He'd made the bed, carefully

smoothing the sheets as though wanting to be sure whoever went into the room after him wouldn't miss the bag he'd left packed and ready in the center of the seashell-themed quilt.

Lincoln threw open the closet doors. The hangers were empty.

He yanked out the dresser drawers and looked under the bed. Empty, everywhere.

Jerek had gotten rid of everything except his bag.

Anger stifled Lincoln's panic as he grabbed the pack.

A slip of torn notebook paper had been tucked behind the straps. The paper had been crookedly folded, like it had been a last-minute addition to the display of Jerek's pack.

Lincoln's fingers shook as he unfolded the note.

Pet's Paradise.

Cas Emergency Contact ~ Ariel Love

"Did you find his bag?" Ari ran into the room, her pack over her shoulder and a stack of towels in her arms.

"I have it." Lincoln put his hand behind Ari's waist, guiding her into the hall before handing her the note.

"Jack doesn't have a stash of blood, right?" Ford called from down in the kitchen.

"No." Ari opened the note.

Lincoln tightened his hold on her as her whole body started to shake.

A gasp of a swallowed sob caught in her throat.

"I think I have enough for tonight." Ford ran into the hall carrying two grocery bags. "Is there anything else we need?"

"We're done here." Ari crumpled the note, shoving it into Lincoln's pocket. "We have to find a safe place for Jack before sunrise."

Ari

The steady rhythm of the crashing waves quieted Ari's temper as the soothing sound carried up from the rocky shore far below the stilted beach house.

She took a deep breath, tasting the salty tang of the sea air that swept in through the balcony door.

Calm. Never fussed. The water didn't care how many hours Ari had spent poring through the books in Jerek's pack.

She'd started with the journal. A worn notebook filled with pages of scrawled words. The entries started in Mr. Holden's handwriting. Jerek had made notes in the margins of his father's research, questioning his father's reasoning, inserting his own ideas. Half the time, the letters were so cramped Ari couldn't tell if Jerek had been writing in English, or shorthand, or if it was all some sort of incantation.

Mr. Holden's notes ended before he'd run out of pages. His last few entries were full of determination.

He had found a way to mend the Fracture and return magic to the feu. He would be the one to put the world back together so his son's generation could have a chance to thrive.

Jerek hadn't even left a blank page between the end of his father's writings and the start of his own notes.

Two blank lines. That was the only space Jerek had allowed to mark his father's death.

The breeze picked up, fluttering the pages of the journal.

Ari pressed her fingers to the passage she'd been reading, not allowing the scent of the waves to lure her from the words Jerek had underlined, like the heading of a new chapter in the tale of his race toward martyrdom.

Death Begins ~ *I have finally given up my childlike hope that I had misunderstood my father's final words. A curse strong enough to block the connection between magician and magic cannot be looked upon as an ordinary incantation. The caster did not alter the state of something that already existed, but rather planted themselves as a barrier to sever the connection between magician and magic.*

A reasonable person could not hope to survive standing against a force as great as the mystery that grants magicians their power. Creating the stopper would require more magic than a person could safely use in a lifetime. For the caster, death is the inescapable sacrifice.

Likewise, a reasonable person could not hope to survive removing the stopper and freeing magic to cascade back into the world. The incantation would burn through the magician, and even if they should survive the casting, greeting the flood of magic racing to freedom would provide a terrible death.

Despite what many may believe, my father was a reasonable man. He knew mending the Fracture would cost him his life, yet he continued down the path to his destruction. He had me speak the words, knowing my incantation would cause his death.

Even through the storm of fury at my father for making me his killer, I've found myself resolved to follow his path. The world needs magic. The Fracture must be mended. I willingly work toward my doom knowing the salvation of the feu is the prize to be bought with the end of my sorry life.

Death began this terrible curse. Death must end it.

But before I pull the stopper and greet the flood of magic, I need to find where my father went wrong and find someone I know will continue my quest if my life isn't a worthy enough sacrifice for victory to be found.

Ari tightened her grip on the journal as a stronger wind whipped through the balcony door, like a specter had come ripping past Jerek's and Eve's beds, making sure it still wasn't time for death to claim the two who'd fallen in the battle at the Museum of Magic.

Ari held her breath, staring first at Jerek's chest then Eve's, making sure they were both still breathing, before looking back to the notebook.

In digging through my father's earlier records, I've found myself wondering what began his fascination with the schism within the early Knights Maree. Such long ago trials—

Ari didn't bother turning the page. She'd already read the passages Jerek had scrawled right after condemning himself to die on behalf of the feu.

"You were condemning me, too, you know." Ari looked to Jerek. "You were so set on abandoning me with this mess."

"It would be better than just sitting here!" Grace's shout carried from the living room.

The low rumble of Lincoln's voice answered.

"We've been waiting for three days! We could be on the other side of the country by now," Grace said.

"So we lay Eve and Jerek on the seats in the van and just hope we don't hit any bumps that might toss them around?" Jack's voice cut through the wall behind Ari's head.

"At least we'd be harder to find," Grace said.

Lincoln spoke again.

"Should I really trust the person who insisted our hideout have ocean views?" Grace said.

Ari looked out toward the water. The late afternoon sun sparkled off the waves. The curtains flanking the balcony door swayed in the breeze, as though wanting to highlight why the shore was the perfect haven.

"We have to be patient." Lincoln finally spoke loudly enough for Ari to hear. "Magic has been broken for twelve years. We can take the time to let Eve and Jerek heal."

Bang.

The bedroom floor shook as someone slammed the living room's door to the balcony.

"Grace, you can't leave the property," Lincoln shouted.

The door slammed again.

Ari looked back to the journal.

Death Begins ~ *I have finally given up my childlike hope that I had misunderstood my father's final words. A curse strong enough to—*

A gasp came from the corner.

Ari leapt to her feet, dropping the journal and grabbing the dagger she'd kept tucked by her side.

Eve's chest shook as she gagged on air.

"Eve." Ari reached the bed in two steps.

Eve rolled onto her side, hacking out a cough.

"You're okay." Ari sat next to her, reaching toward Eve but not knowing what to do that might actually help. "Just breathe."

Eve gripped the sheets as she dragged in a bigger breath.

"That's good. Keep going." Ari touched Eve's back, waiting a heartbeat before daring to rub gentle circles. "Nice and easy. There you go."

Eve's breathing slowed.

"Where are—" She started coughing again.

"Careful." Ari set down the dagger and grabbed a bottle of water from the bedside table. "Can you take a sip?"

Eve nodded.

Ari slipped her arm beneath Eve, easing her up just enough to drink. "Not too much."

"Where are the others?" Eve asked as soon as she'd swallowed.

"We're all here." Ari tipped more water into Eve's mouth. "Jerek is still out, but everyone else is up and moving."

"Did we get Chanler?"

"No."

Eve tensed.

"We're not done with Chanler," Ari said, "I promise."

"I should've torn his throat out the minute I saw him."

"Maybe, but you have to rest up for round two."

"I'm fine." Eve sat up and shoved the covers back.

"You almost died."

"I'm a werewolf. It happens." She grabbed the water bottle from Ari.

Ari dodged away as Eve swung her legs over the side of the bed. "You've been out for three days."

"No wonder I'm starving. Whose underwear am I wearing?" Eve frowned at the tank top and panties.

"They're new." Ari took Eve's elbow, steadying her as she stood. "It was either that or leave you in a bloodstained gown."

"Underwear is great." Eve pulled free from Ari's grip and headed toward the door.

"Be careful."

Eve flung open the door and stepped into the hall.

"You need to rest." Ari followed, keeping her hands out in case Eve fell. "Get back in bed, and I'll bring you some food."

"Glad you made it," Jack called from the bathroom. "I was starting to worry."

"I'll try to heal faster next time," Eve said.

"Make sure there's not a next time. If I'd seen..." The bathroom door creaked like Jack had leaned against it. "Just don't abandon me, okay? I can't be the only creature feature in this mess."

"You're stuck with me until Chanler bleeds out at my feet." Eve braced her hand against the wall, steadying herself as she kept walking.

"That wouldn't be comforting coming from anyone but you," Jack said.

"She has a special flare for vowing vengeance," Ari said.

"Give me a sandwich, and I'll go after Chanler right now." Eve stopped where the hall met the living room. "What the hell is that?" She pointed to the far wall.

"A giant mess." Ari stepped around Eve.

"It's our timeline." Ford leapt to his feet, his face instantly flushing as he pointed to the left side of the sticky note-paved chaos. "We're all color-coded." He ran his finger down the line of pink notes. "This tracks Ari's movements from the moment we arrived at the museum."

"What color am I?" Eve headed toward the open kitchen at the back of the room, reaching for the handle of the refrigerator in a way that could have either been starvation or the floor tipping beneath her feet.

"You don't have a color yet," Ford said. "We had to wait for you to wake up. You can choose orange or white."

"Great," Eve said.

"The more exciting portion of the wall is the villain tracer." Ford pointed to the picture-covered, right-hand side of the wall where strings weaved between pushpins, linking all the pieces of the disaster together. "We started with the more common name of *murder board*, but there's no need to add darkness to the situation."

"A creepy name would really crush my spirit." Eve pulled a packet of sandwich meat, block of cheese, and bag of apples from the fridge.

"It's not quite as bad—"

"Can you go sit with Jerek?" Ari cut across Ford.

Ford held Ari's gaze for a moment too long. "Sure."

He took his laptop and headed down the hall that led to two of the bedrooms and the larger of the rental's bathrooms, which had become Jack's hideout.

Eve shambled to the couch nearest the villain tracer, already reading the notes on the wall as she collapsed into her seat and tore open the package of sandwich meat.

"Start from my eyelevel in the web." Ari sat beside her. "Then go up to your eyelevel and start circling down."

Eve shoved a slice of meat into her mouth, studying the notes as she chewed. "What the hell does it mean?"

"I'm not sure," Ari said.

"Then why tack a portrait of Chanler to the wall?" Eve devoured another slice of meat.

"Not everyone in our group enjoys digital flow charts, and we needed something large enough for us all to look at anyway."

"Don't dodge the question." Eve bit off a corner of the cheese block.

"Do you want me to make you a sandwich?" Ari started to stand.

Eve grabbed Ari's wrist, gripping almost hard enough to bruise. "Talk. Now."

"Things went sideways at the museum." Ari sank back into her seat.

"I know. I got stabbed."

"And the Fracture didn't get mended. And the Knights Maree were all over our asses."

"If you're trying to figure out where things went wrong, I'm pretty sure it started with Jerek lying to all of us and using an amplifier." Eve finished the cheese and moved on to an apple.

"But why did the security cameras turn back on when my program should have kept them blanked out for another hour? And sure, we expected museum security to be tight since we'd already stolen the Blood List from the Council of the Feu headquarters, but why were there enough Maree to start a siege? And who set off the museum's alarms?"

"We did," Eve said.

"Not the last time. Someone else tripped the alarm to clear everyone out of the building. And all that might not even be our biggest problem." Ari tucked her feet beneath her. "Eve, we think Chanler might not be the one who caused the Fracture."

"What?" Eve froze.

"Lincoln talked to Mariah Chanler. From what she said, her father doesn't even have control over his own estate. Why would Chanler rip magic from the world just to hand over control of his life to Callen my-hand-is-attached-to-a-clipboard LeBlanc?"

"Chanler is a murderer." Eve set aside the remains of her apple. "Chanler is a butcher who deserves to die. I get to be the one to kill him."

"What if we were wrong? If there's any chance Chanler is innocent—"

"Louis Chanler is the butcher of Blood Mountain." Danger glinted in Eve's eyes. "That monster murdered my family."

"It could have been someone else."

The world tipped as Eve leapt to her feet and hoisted the arm of the couch, sending Ari toppling to the floor.

Eve screamed as she rammed the couch against the wall over and over again.

5

Grace

The yellow van waited at the bottom of the long flight of stairs that led down from the front door of the stilted house to the shell-covered driveway. The van hadn't been used since Ari had sent Ford into town for clothes, food, and a printer—the bare essentials for seven teens on the run from knights and murderers.

Ford's supply run hadn't taken that long, only a few hours. Some kind of civilization had to be close by.

Just a quick drive. That was all Grace needed.

Get out of the house and away from the others and not worry about anyone smashing anything. At least for a little while.

Grace gripped the knees of her too-baggy pants.

You're not asking for the world. Just some car keys.

Another awful crash came from inside.

Taking a drive is better than destroying the furniture.

A door on the far side of the house slammed shut.

Grace's fingers ached as she unclenched her fists and ran down the steps.

The warmth of the day still hadn't reached the shadowy open area below the house. The chill tickled the back of her neck, like something more menacing than the broken shells beneath her feet lurked in the shadows.

Lincoln stood on the deck at the foot of the stairs on the ocean side of the house, his hands tucked behind his back as he stared out at the waves.

"Lincoln." Grace slowed her steps, giving the Maree time to process that it wasn't an enemy running up behind him. "Do you know who has the key for the van?"

"Ari." Lincoln didn't bother looking at her.

Grace's fleeting hope for potential escape popped and vanished. "There's not a chance in hell she's going to give it to me. Is there?"

"I doubt it."

"Could you ask for the key for me?" Grace stepped in front of Lincoln, willing her face to stay calm as she looked up at him.

"You can't leave the property. None of us can. The best thing for us to do is stay out of sight while we regroup."

"Ford went to town."

"For supplies."

"I'll get more supplies. More sticky notes, or printer paper, or juice boxes, I don't care what. I'll do whatever errand you want. I've just got to get out of here."

"That's not possible."

"Because Ari said so?" Grace clamped her mouth shut, rocking back on her heels as she waited for someone to stomp outside and shout at her for yelling.

"Because every time one of us is spotted creates another chance for Chanler or the Maree to find us."

"Then I'll just drive around. I won't stop anywhere."

"No."

"I can't just stay trapped here!" Grace backed away from him. "Jerek isn't awake and Eve is smashing things and it's just too much. There isn't enough air in that house. I need to breathe."

"And Jack needs to feed." A wrinkle pinched between Lincoln's eyebrows. "And I need to run ten miles to burn off some anger. And Ari needs to sleep for more than two hours. And Eve needs to—"

"So we all stay stuck here suffering together?"

"We all accept discomfort for the good of the group."

Grace dug the heels of her hands into her eyes.

"Breathe, Grace," Lincoln said.

"Or the house might catch on fire, yeah I know." She sank to the ground, her eyes still closed. The heat of tears pushed against her eyelids. She took four deep breaths before lowering her hands. "Can I—may I please borrow your phone?"

"No."

"I just want to make sure my dads are okay."

"I lost my phone a while back. Jerek, Ari, and Ford have the only phones left."

"Ari won't let me near any of them." Grace swiped the tears from her cheeks. "She'll keep me cut off and trapped here."

"You said you wanted to help us find another way to mend the Fracture."

"I do, but—"

"You can't say you'll stand against Chanler or whoever else caused the Fracture if you're not willing to stay on lockdown in a beach house for a few days. This isn't a bad place to hunker down, and we aren't going to be here forever."

Lincoln pointed to the sun glimmering off the water. "Enjoy the view. Work on controlling your magic. Help Ari research

Chanler's connections. Get some extra sleep. Do whatever will keep you calm. We made it out of the Museum of Magic and are lucky enough to have a chance to regroup. Be grateful for the quiet, Grace. It's not going to last."

Lincoln patted her shoulder and headed to the far end of their house's secluded stretch of shore, leaving Grace alone as tears streamed down her cheeks.

She pulled her knees to her chest, not bothering to hide her shaking hands as she tried to think of a way to wake up from this horrible nightmare.

6

Jack

The buzz of the bathroom light sliced into Jack's ears, but he couldn't convince himself to flick the switch off and end his suffering.

Spending the daylight pacing between a toilet and a shower was bad enough. Pacing in the dark felt worse somehow. Sadder. More desperate.

He'd be able to see plenty well with the light off, but lurking in the darkness was the habit of monsters.

He dug his hands into his pockets, resisting the urge to bite his thumbnail.

The thumbnail's not the problem.

The stench of burned coffee carried over the scent of the ocean. The stink of dead fish tainted the air, too. The bottles of cleaner tucked under the sink completed the aromatic disaster.

Ari, Ford, and Jerek were still in the house.

Eve had stormed outside. From the distant cracking of wood, she was working through her rage one smashed tree at a time.

But Jack hadn't been left alone.

Nope. Three people still in the house. Burning coffee. Researching. Ari's and Ford's heartrates steady and slow as they pored through information. Jerek's slower still as he lay helpless in bed.

The taste of blood seeped into Jack's mouth as his fangs pierced his lip.

He leaned closer to the buzzing light above the sink, letting the sound slice deeper into his thoughts.

Safe in hiding. Rallying. Regrouping.

Planning a way to save the feu.

Pounding thumped through the buzz in a rhythm that didn't fit a human heartbeat.

"Jack?"

The thumping came again.

"Jack, it's Ford. Can you get under the blanket?"

"The house has another bathroom." Jack stared into the mirror, holding his own gaze.

"I know. I just need to talk to you for a minute," Ford said.

"Now's not the time." Dry pain scratched down Jack's throat. He gripped the edge of the sink.

"I'm going to come in," Ford said. "Please get under the blanket so you don't get sun burned."

"I told you, now's not the time."

"It's life or death."

The edge of the sink crackled as it cracked in Jack's grip.

"Jack?"

He lifted his hands from the sink. His fingers didn't tremble. He willed the rest of his body to stay as calm.

His fangs wouldn't comply.

"This better be quick." Jack stepped into the shower and tossed the heavy wool blanket over his head like he wanted to be a winter-chic ghost.

He mashed himself beneath the showerhead as the doorknob turned.

Ford closed the door behind him. "All clear."

Jack tossed the blanket off his head.

Ford stood with his back pressed against the cracked sink. "This is bigger than the other bathroom."

"Well, I don't get a bed, so I guess it evens out." Jack barely moved his lips as he spoke, muddying his words to keep his fangs hidden.

"You're right." Ford glanced toward the door. "Absolutely."

"You can flee as soon as you tell me why you had to barge into my bed and bath combo."

"You don't need a bed." Ford squared his shoulders and met Jack's gaze. "Not like the rest of us."

"Thanks."

"You can't eat like us either. We're all going to have dinner, and you'll be trapped in here."

"I'm aware." Jack pressed his back to the wall, as though the tile might be able to swallow him whole and offer the blissful salvation of nothingness.

"You were hurt in the fighting. You lost a lot of blood."

"Get to the point." A weight pressed on Jack's lungs.

"You haven't fed in days, and you can't leave the house. It's not safe."

"Then lock the bathroom door from the outside, and have Eve stand guard," Jack growled. His fangs sliced into his bottom lip.

Ford flinched, shifting his stance as though preparing to flee from the horror of the fanged monster with blood-tainted lips.

"I'm doing my best." Jack looked up at the light above the sink, willing its buzzing to bury the screaming in his head. "I'm sorry."

"Don't be. It's what you are."

"I'm trying. I swear."

"You have nothing to apologize for. You're a vampire. You have to drink blood to survive."

Jack's breath hitched in his throat as the weight of his hunger pummeled his stomach.

"And I'm a human. Pure, uninteresting somb. No feu treaty or lineage to worry about. Just lots of perfectly good blood."

"Get out." Jack hunched in on himself, trying not to feel the hollow in his gut.

"You need to eat. I have blood. Let me help you."

"I didn't know blood play was your thing."

"It's not." Ford leaned over and locked the bathroom door.

"I can't—" The pounding of Ford's heart drowned out the buzzing of the light. "I can't ask you to do this."

"You're not." Ford reached for Jack's hands.

A sob hitched in Jack's throat.

Ford took his hands, gently guiding Jack toward him. "It's okay."

Jack's whole body trembled as he stepped out of the shower, leaving only a breath of space between him and Ford.

"I'm not sure how this goes." Pink crept into Ford's cheeks. His pulse thundered in his neck.

Jack slid his hands up Ford's arms, taking his shoulders to close the gap between them.

Ford tipped his head to the side, willingly offering ecstasy.

A painful, raging wanting clawed through Jack's chest. He brushed his lips against Ford's neck, using the last bit of restraint he had to offer Ford a chance to run.

Ford took Jack's waist, anchoring himself to the moment he'd chosen.

Jack shut his eyes and pierced the side of Ford's neck.

7

Eve

"That's not a good enough answer." Eve paced behind the surviving couch where Grace and Jack sat with Ford crammed between them like a willing sacrificial lamb.

"I don't like it either." Ari tapped the barbecue fork she'd been using as a pointer on the black and white picture of an older woman. Then she reached past the woman, tapping the picture of Louis Chanler, the monster Eve should have killed when she'd had the chance.

"That doesn't change the fact that Louis Chanler and his mother Gladys Chanler"—Ari slid the pointer back to the woman —"were known to be on bad terms. But he still inherited her fortune when she died less than three months after the Fracture."

"Why would you rip magic from the world just to get rid of

one old lady?" Jack leaned forward. His arm brushed against Ford's.

Neither of them flinched or pulled away. Like Ford had forgotten he was a somb a vampire could easily kill and Jack had achieved perfect self-control. Like he wasn't ready to claw his way out of this beach-themed prison.

"Horrible people do horrible things," Lincoln said from his post just inside the hall that led to Jerek's room.

Eve didn't look at him. His still-altered face was too much of a reminder that they'd lost.

Their shot at fixing magic. Their shot at Chanler.

Her shot at revenge.

"Whoever caused the Fracture chose to do something evil," Grace said. "Does why they decided to destroy magic really matter?"

"Yes, it does." Ari gripped the barbecue fork in both hands. "I didn't risk Ford's life getting us a printer and spend hours making this chart just so we could muse about our villain's back-story. If there is any chance that Chanler might not be our guy, we have to know."

"We have the heliostone," Lincoln said. "Priority one needs to be mending the Fracture."

"I don't know—" Grace began.

"Chanler is the priority." Eve rounded on Lincoln, fists clenched, ready to punch his unfamiliar face. "He cast the spell, he comes first."

"We can't be sure it was him," Lincoln said. "And we can't afford to get this wrong again. If it wasn't Chanler, we could drive the one who really cast the curse underground."

"Or one of us could end up underground," Jack said.

"Chanler is a part of this." Heat flared through Eve's limbs.

"I'm working on both. I'm looking for a different way to mend the Fracture and trying to nail down who, besides

Chanler, could've caused it," Ari said. "I can multitask and Ford is helping. There's no point in arguing about what we should do first before we have enough information to do either."

"We can get information from Chanler." Eve dug her nails into her palms, resisting the urge to scratch her arms as the heat beneath her skin began to squirm. "We find Chanler. We take him. I make him tell us everything he knows about the Fracture."

"And then you'll gut him while he's still tied to a chair?" Grace asked.

"Yes." The word rasped in Eve's throat.

Grace was smart enough to flinch.

"If it wasn't Chanler, my money is on LeBlanc," Jack said.

"Then I'll have a chat with him, too." Eve gripped the silver pendants around her neck. Both of them—hers and her mother's hanging together.

Because Chanler killed her.

"Let's figure out who to gut before commencing said gutting," Ari said.

"Are you really going to be able to find out anything more than what you already know? You and Jerek were so sure you had all the answers." Something like panic raised the pitch of Grace's voice. "What if there isn't another way to break the curse? What if whoever caused the Fracture has nothing to do with Chanler?"

"It was Chanler!" Eve pounded the back of the couch.

Jack grabbed Ford's arm, yanking him out of Eve's reach while Grace squeaked and tumbled to the ground.

"Please don't break another couch," Ari said. "I know Jerek promised you vengeance, but you need to breathe."

"Breathe?" A laugh rumbled in Eve's throat. "All I want is to tear out of my skin. I'm a wolf. I don't belong trapped in this cage waiting for the internet to spawn some vague clue. Let's take Chanler and be done with it."

"Do you need to run?" Lincoln kept his tone even and his hands by his sides, his fingers relaxed and his palms facing Eve.

"Afraid I'll snap, Maree?" Eve prowled toward him. "Breathe, right?"

She took a deep breath, digging for the scents beneath the overcooked eggs, dead fish, and salt. Through it all, the musk of misplaced pride and cowardice tainted the room.

"Were my claws too much for you? Did you tally up the Maree I sliced open at the museum?"

"Those Maree were following orders." Lincoln flipped his palms as the muscles in his arms tensed.

"Enough." Ari stormed over, planting herself between Eve and Lincoln. "He's right, Eve."

"Atrocities don't matter as long as they were committed under orders?" Eve shifted her hold on the pendants.

"You need to run." Ari pointed to the balcony door beside the villain tracer. "You haven't shifted since you were hurt."

"You banned us from leaving the property." Tension dragged down Eve's back.

"If anyone sees you, kill them before they can call for help," Ari said.

"Why can she leave while I'm trapped here?" Grace said.

"She doesn't start fires," Jack said.

"It's different for crypted feu." Ari held Eve's gaze. "Vampires feed. Wolves run. It's not a cliché, it's what they were made to do. Go tear through some miles. We'll talk in circles more when you get back."

"If the Maree come while I'm out there"—Eve backed away, her fingers already sliding to the clasp on her pendant—"shift-starved or not, I'm the muscle here."

"We'll scream real loud," Jack said. "Promise."

Eve nodded, turning her still-bare feet toward the door.

The glass panes let in the light of the moon. The moonlight glistened on the water, luring her out of her skin.

She flipped her pendant open, revealing the moonstone set into the silver as she stepped out onto the balcony.

The heat that crawled through her flesh brightened, surging down to her hands as her fingers lengthened into claws. The tension raking down her spine blossomed out into her shoulders, giving her strength beyond her pure human form. Pressure kneaded through her jaw as the magic within the moonstone gave her the teeth of a predator.

Someone gasped.

The sound didn't matter, not as sweet, heady relief melted through her.

She took two long strides, then leapt up, her feet barely touching the balcony railing as she pushed off and flew out into the night.

She landed on the rock wall a story below. The day's warmth still clung to the stones beneath her feet.

Bats flew to the right. A racoon scrambled through the bushes on the far side of the house. Birds nested to the left.

Deer behind and to the left, far past the birds and raccoon.

An owl fled as Eve bolted into the trees, beginning the hunt.

8

Lincoln

Lincoln sat on the second bed in Jerek's room, staring at the cartoon dinosaur print pajamas Ford had bought for him.

"Not the right size?" Ari looked up from the journal she'd been reading since their meeting had fallen apart.

"They fit." Lincoln turned the pajamas, tipping the dinosaurs on their heads. "I'm just not sure if we should've spent more time on natural history in the compound's school. I don't recognize any of these species."

"They're from a kid's TV show." Ari closed the journal and set it on her lap, keeping her finger between the notebook's pages to mark her place. "It's Ford's version of brutality. Nice comfy jammies with annoying, singing dinosaurs all over them."

"Why would Ford want to be brutal with me?"

"Strong, handsome, literal knight—too bad you're not quick on the uptake."

"What?" Lincoln set the pajamas aside.

"You're intimidating," Ari said. "You're the second person Jerek pulled onto this team. And you're a Maree. You're a human born into the world of the feu. If we all walked away from this right now, you'd still be a Maree. Ford would be tossed back out into the somb world with no connection to the feu."

"Except you," Lincoln said.

"I don't think that helps."

Lincoln looked to Jerek as a flutter grazed his heart like he'd spotted someone eavesdropping. "It was good of you to send Ford to Jack."

"I didn't send anyone. I mentioned Jack's issue to Ford. Ford followed up on the information all on his own."

"Then came to you to get patched up with a pink band aid?"

"What did you expect? I was in charge of packing the van's first aid kit."

Lincoln picked the pajamas back up, unfolding the full length of their garish pattern. "I would've gone to Jack. If it had gotten worse."

"It was worse. He needed to feed."

"I could've been the one to do it."

"Vampires aren't allowed to feed on Maree." Ari gave up holding her place and set the journal on the floor beside her chair. "Ford was the only option. It had to be done."

"You sound like Jerek."

"No, I don't. I didn't lie to Ford. I told him the truth and let him make a choice."

"I'm sorry. You're right. Not like Jerek at all."

The tag in the pajamas said *Made in Turkey*. They'd crossed over Italy to reach the U.S., flying right past the place where Lincoln should be.

In the Maree compound, orders were given and followed.

He knew precisely what was expected of him, and no one ever asked him what choices should be made.

"You're safe to put them on, you know," Ari said. "I promise not to tell the Knight's Council."

"You can sleep first."

"I'm fine."

"You need to rest."

"Are you afraid to undress in front of me?" Ari cocked her head. Her hair shifted with the movement, the blond tresses shimmering against the pale pink of her top. "You've already flashed your fancy Maree tattoo."

"If you're sure you're comfortable." Lincoln turned away from Ari. That left him facing the balcony windows. He angled himself toward the corner as he pulled off his shirt.

"You can take off your briefs, too. I promise you don't have anything I haven't seen before."

Lincoln froze with his hand on the zipper of his pants.

"I'm teasing," Ari said. "Times are tough. I have to find joy where I can."

Lincoln checked the waistband of his briefs, making sure they were firmly in place before pulling down his pants.

"Rwarrr," Ari purred.

Heat rushed to Lincoln's face.

"Kidding again. My eyes are closed," Ari said. "I'm not a voyeur. Making you squirm is just too easy."

"Does modesty only exist in the Maree?" Lincoln pushed his shoulders back, taking his time as he folded his clothes.

"Modesty exists everywhere. I'm just immune."

He abandoned his unfolded socks to yank on his pajama pants.

"I promise I won't attack," Ari said.

"That's not..." Lincoln shut his eyes.

Don't make things worse.

"I can hear my mother and grandmother lecturing me." He turned around. "In a room with a girl. Door closed. Half-dressed. This sort of thing could see a Maree scrubbing floors for months. It's hard to know when what's expected at the compound isn't normal to everyone else."

"If it makes you feel any better, I think most parents give their kids the *keep your pants on* speech. And we have a chaperone." Eyes still closed, Ari nodded toward Jerek.

"Even if he were awake, I don't think Jerek would be a good chaperone."

"Believe me, he's terrible." Ari laughed. The gentle sound faded as her grin sank. She opened her eyes, turning her gaze toward Jerek. "What the hell do we do if he doesn't wake up?"

"He will."

"I don't like comforting lies. You and I both know he might not make it." Ari unfolded her legs and stood.

"He's strong."

"What if that made things worse?" Ari stepped past Lincoln to stand beside Jerek's bed. "If the force he fed into the amplifier surged back through him to create the stupid, shitty spell he thought could save the feu—" Her voice caught in her throat. "I don't know how to help him."

"We're keeping him safe. That might be all we can do."

"I can't lose him." She looked up at Lincoln. A tear trailed down her cheek. "I know you're his best friend, but he's mine. And I don't have a whole flock of Maree family to fall back on. My world is chaos and Jerek. That's it. If I don't have him as an anchor, it's all just noise."

"That's not true."

"Please don't say I have Ford. He's a good friend, I adore him, but he's not like Jerek. Ford feeds the chaos. Without Jerek…I'd disappear."

"Ari, that's not true."

"It is. I promise you it is."

Lincoln's heart stuttered as he reached out and brushed the tear from her cheek. She leaned into the touch, letting him graze his fingers past her silky hair. "Then what about me? I'm the opposite of chaos. I'm so anchored in the Maree ways, I won't undress in a room with a girl without getting teased into it."

Another tear spilled down her cheek.

"I'm here, Ari. Whatever happens with the Fracture, or Jerek, or anything else with the feu, you have an ally. I don't have many friends. And I don't abandon the people I care about."

Heat flooded Lincoln's face as she placed her hands on his bare shoulders and leaned in, brushing a gentle kiss on his cheek.

"Promise you won't let me disappear," she whispered.

He raised his hands, teetering on the edge of daring to touch her hips.

"I promise." He locked his arms at his sides.

Ari stayed close for another moment, her hands on his bare shoulders, her hair cascading down his bare chest. "I'll hold you to it."

She stepped back and swiped the tears from her cheeks.

It seemed odd that the air around Lincoln could suddenly feel so empty.

"Get some sleep." Ari nodded toward the empty bed. "I promise not to take too many pictures of you drooling."

"I can take first watch."

"I won't sleep anyway." Ari curled back up in the chair, holding the journal like it was another anchor to cling to. "Sleep. Now."

"Wake me up when you get tired." Lincoln climbed into bed and rolled to face the wall.

"Goodnight, Maree."

"Goodnight." He closed his eyes.

It only took a few breaths for his neck to start prickling with the fear that she might be looking at him. His arm was over the covers, his Maree tattoo in full view.

She's seen the tattoo.

He adjusted his head on the too-fluffy pillow.

If she could see his arm, she could see his shoulders. His upper back, too.

He pulled his shoulders back, flexing the muscles his years of training had earned.

A sudden jolt of panic pummeled his gut.

She'd know what he'd done.

If she caught him trying to show off—not that he'd wanted to show off—he'd never be able to look her in the eye again.

She's reading. The last thing she cares about is your stupidity.

He exhaled, forcefully relaxing his back in a vague mockery of a bedtime routine.

As he dragged himself into sleep, a strange scene played out in the far back of his mind.

A storm raged around a rock rising from the center of the sea. He stood on the rock, his arms wrapped around a girl. The wind whipped through her blond hair as she clung to him. He held her tighter, shielding her from the wrath of the sea.

9

Grace

The chill of the night still clung to the shade beneath the stilted beach house. Grace rubbed the goosebumps on her arms, pretending they'd been born of the temperature and not the anxiety gnawing at her gut as it pulled the band around her chest tighter and tighter.

She shook her hands out and planted her palms on the picnic table, locking her gaze on the small crystal ball sitting in front of her.

Look deeper into the sphere. Channel your energy.

Grace's leg started bouncing as the tightness in her chest rose to her throat.

The rhythm of Eve's steps as she paced through the shade slowed.

Channel your energy.

The ground beneath the house had been covered in broken seashells that cracked as they were crushed beneath Eve's feet.

Each tiny pop and crack was the sound of something being broken that would never be made whole again.

Channel your freakin' energy.

"Should I worry about you having a panic attack?" The cracking of Eve's footsteps got closer.

"Magic isn't easy," Grace said.

"I didn't say it was," Eve said.

"I just need to focus." Grace dug her nails into the weathered wood of the table.

"Okay."

"You talking isn't helping me focus."

"I can shut up," Eve said.

"Thanks."

"But your heart is racing so fast, I thought I should make sure you weren't going to pass out."

Grace crushed the shells beneath her feet as she dug her heels into the ground to stop her leg from bouncing. "Keep your werewolf hearing away from my internal organs."

"It's not something I can turn off. Wolves are meant to hear racing hearts."

"Just my luck."

"You're right, you are lucky." Eve sat on top of the table, towering over Grace. "Werewolf, vampire, magicians, even a knight, all piled into one overpriced vacation rental."

"I didn't pick the house. I didn't ask to be here."

Eve grabbed the crystal.

"Put it back," Grace said.

Eve rolled the sphere between her hands. "None of this was your choice. I get it."

"You really don't."

"Shitty things happened, you're stuck with the fall out, and all you want to do is scream."

"Are you trying to make things worse?" Grace snatched for the sphere.

Eve lifted it out of her reach without seeming to have seen Grace move. "When shitty things happen, it's okay to feel shitty."

"Wise words from the couch smasher."

"Exactly." Eve looked down at her. "Shit happened, and I had to rip out of my skin. I had my freak out. Now I can think."

"Good for you."

"I don't know anything about how magic is supposed to work, but if you stay this twitchy, you're going to light the house on fire before you make the crystal glow. Scream, throw things, curl up and cry, whatever you have to do. We're not done with this thing, and when we walk into the next fight, we'd be better off with no magician than one who might light us all on fire."

"I'm trying—"

"No. You're panicking and wallowing. Get it out and get your shit together, or I will chain you up and lock you in a closet before I walk into a fight beside you." Eve set the sphere on the table and hopped down to the ground, landing with a crackling crunch.

The crunching followed her back to her pacing place.

Tears blurred Grace's vision. She couldn't fix her gaze on the center of the sphere.

She didn't have any magic to funnel into the crystal anyway.

The crunching rhythm of Eve's pacing didn't change as Grace laid her head down on the table and dissolved into silent sobs.

10

Ari

IVs of fluids, a catheter, liquid nutrients, bed sore prevention—Ari scrolled through the articles on her laptop. Pages and pages of doomsday prepper advice for handling someone in a coma.

But Jerek hadn't shown any signs of dehydration or malnutrition. She'd even made Lincoln help her check for bedsores.

"A magical problem needs a magical solution, Ariel Love." She pressed her knuckles into her eyes.

Old lore, new lore, Maree lore, back-alley-might-kill-you lore—she'd dug through it all. And the only healing spells she'd been able to find were more complex than Grace had a hope of managing without Jerek to guide her.

She clicked away from the prepper site and over to her second favorite fake social media profile.

Two clicks later, Mariah Chanler beamed back at her from a

photo that was definitely taken by a skilled photographer carefully staging a candid pic.

A boat ride a day keeps the worries at bay ;) was the most recent post.

In a photo just below, Mariah gave a thoughtful frown as she considered a row of strategically concealed dresses. That post read: *Greenwood Gardens Gala Friday night. What color should I wear? Red? Maybe I won't be the only girl in red prowling through the shadows.*

"It's a bad idea. A Jerek Holden-level bad idea."

"Most of my ideas are brilliant." The soft words came from the far side of the room.

Ari stood. Her laptop slid off her lap, hitting the ground with a thump. She stepped over it, unable to look away as Jerek's hand shifted on top of his sheets.

"Jerek?"

He turned his head, wincing as a tired smile reached his eyes.

"Jerek." Ari knelt on the bed beside him. She pushed his hair away from his still-altered face. His skin held a healthy warmth. "Are you okay? Wiggle your toes or something."

"My toes are fine."

Ari leaned down, draping her arm over Jerek's chest in the gentlest hug she could manage. "Okay. You're okay."

Jerek brushed his hand against her arm. "Where are we? What happened?"

Anger sliced through Ari's relief. She sat up, brushing the tears from her cheeks and her hair out of her face. "What happened, Jerek Holden, is that you almost died. I've spent days hovering over you, desperately trying to find a way to wake you up. Because you, Jerek Holden, decided to sacrifice yourself to mend the Fracture."

"Did it work?" Hope lit Jerek's eyes.

"No, it didn't work. Even though you lied to me, lied to all of us to get us to play into your psychotic plan to indulge your death wish."

"What went wrong?" Jerek gripped her hand.

"Nothing went wrong!" Ari pulled away from him and stood, backing out of his reach. "You were doing a really great job of dying. Lincoln had to rescue you."

"He did what?" Jerek grabbed the sheets, trying to pull himself to sit up.

"He saved you. We saved you."

"I didn't want to be saved."

"Of course," Ari laughed. "You're the great Jerek Holden. You have a plan to fix the world and we're just supposed to trot along at your heels. I trusted you. I never questioned you. You almost made me an accomplice in your suicide."

"Suicide was never my intention."

"You plotted your own death!"

"To protect the feu."

"So you die and magic rushes back into the world? Great, as long as you don't care about the people you leave behind. Did you even once think about Grace? Did you even consider you'd be destroying her if you made her kill you?"

"I didn't have a choice."

"Yes, you did! You were the only one with a choice. You stole the decision from the rest of us."

"It was better if you didn't know." Jerek rolled onto his side. His arms shook as he pushed himself up onto his elbow.

"Better for you or for us?"

"For everyone. For the feu." He shoved his sheets away.

"For me too, Jerek?" Fresh tears burned down Ari's cheeks. "Would my life be better if things went back to the way they were before the Fracture and I didn't have a Holden as an ally?"

"You don't need me."

"Yes, I do! You make me fight for a better world, then try to abandon me with the shit world I was stuck with before the Fracture *and* your blood on my hands."

"You're strong enough. You don't need me beside you." He gasped as he shifted his legs toward the edge of the bed.

"That's not true and you know it."

"Magic, Ari. We made the choice to find a way to restore magic to the world."

"To a new world you promised *we'd* build."

"You'd build a better one without me. The hope of a new beginning—if anyone could mold that joy into change, it's you."

"And you'd get to be a martyr for the cause. Did you set aside money for them to build statues in your honor?"

"Don't be ridiculous." His face tensed in pain as he lowered his feet to the floor. "I never cared about being remembered or anyone even knowing how the Fracture had been mended."

"You just wanted to throw your life away."

"It's my life, Ari." He met her gaze. "I get to choose what sacrifices I'm willing to make."

"Not anymore." A cold calm trickled through Ari's body. "You're done making decisions. For you, for our team, for the feu."

"Ari—"

"You are no longer in charge of anything." Ari held up her hand, silencing Jerek. "You are the money behind the operation, nothing more. And don't even think of threatening to stop paying our way through the shit storm you landed us in. I will strip your bank accounts if you push me."

"Will you steal Holden House as well?"

"Why not? You already tried to give me your cat."

Jerek opened his mouth, then closed it, still holding Ari's gaze with no hint of regret in his eyes.

"One of the others can check for bed sores on your ass. I

don't even want to look at you anymore." She grabbed her laptop and the journal from the floor.

"The feu won't survive if we don't mend the Fracture."

Ari wrenched the door to the hall open and slammed it shut behind her.

Everyone but Jack waited in the hall. Grace tearful. Eve glowering. Lincoln stern. Ford wide-eyed.

"He's awake." Ari cut through the cluster. "Someone else can feed him."

11

Eve

"The mountain remains secure." Mrs. Holden's voice filled the hall like she was as big and powerful as Eve's father.

He stood behind Mrs. Holden, letting her talk to the pack. His face so calm while he listened to the broken magician go on and on, even Eve didn't know what he thought of Mrs. Holden's speech.

"Whatever problems arise within the Council of the Feu will not affect your ability to stay in your homes," Mrs. Holden said. "This mountain is the property of the Holden estate. We never have, nor ever will sign the mountain over to the Council or anyone else."

Eve tensed her chin and widened her eyes, trying to make her face as unreadable as her father's. She tucked her feet beneath her, sitting up on her heels so Mrs. Holden could see Eve in her seat all the way at the back.

"Don't fidget, Evelyn." Eve's mother gave her a warning glance.

"Sorry." Eve fidgeted more to get back to sitting the way her mother wanted.

"My husband and I gave you our word," Mrs. Holden said. "We intend to keep it."

"How?" Finlay stepped forward from his normal place in the corner. "Your magic is gone. You can't protect yourselves, let alone your claim to our mountain."

"Enough," Eve's father said.

Finlay scratched his half-gray beard, staring at his alpha for a moment before stepping back to sulk in the corner.

"I'm afraid the Holden estate's claim on this mountain is much more mundane than you might imagine, Finlay," Mrs. Holden said. "There is no spell work involved in our ownership of this land. It was paid for in cash. The deed is registered with the somb government."

"So the somb police will be sent to toss us out of our homes?" Karen laughed. "At least we have some fun to look forward to."

"No one is going to try and force you out of your homes." Mrs. Holden stepped closer to the rows of listening werewolves.

She didn't shake or look scared. Mrs. Holden faced the pack like she still had her magic.

Eve glared at Mrs. Holden, willing her to glance over and cower at Eve's fierceness.

A hand grabbed Eve's wrist, tugging her sideways.

"Stop." Eve wriggled her wrist free.

The hand grabbed her again.

"Stop it." Eve glared down at Mark.

He crouched beside her chair, bouncing like he might explode. "Come on."

Eve glanced to her mother, who watched Mrs. Holden with

her lips pursed. Eve wondered if Mrs. Holden knew that meant her mother was going to give Mrs. Holden a lecture later.

"Please, Evie." Mark shook her arm.

Eve slid out of her chair and onto the floor beside her little brother.

"Come see." Mark crawled toward the window behind their mother.

Eve looked at her mother one more time before squeezing between the seats to follow Mark.

"There is no reason for contention," Mrs. Holden said. "Fighting amongst ourselves only pushes us further into the chaos and destruction caused by the Fracture."

"Look, Evie," Mark whispered.

Eve looked out the window onto the slope alongside the meeting hall.

In the back where Mother kept Eve and Mark, the ground was forever far away. So far away, the stilts that held up this side of the building were slanted enough that Eve could climb them. Mark could, too, but not all the way to the top. Mother said he was too little.

A robin swooped through the trees. There were squirrels, too.

A latecomer sped up the road in a black truck.

Father wouldn't like that.

"No, look." Mark jabbed his finger against the wall beneath the window.

A crooked picture of four stick wolves had been drawn in blue marker.

"What did you do?" Eve tucked her hands behind her back, keeping them away from the picture.

"It's us." Mark smiled as he pointed to the wolves. "It's Mama and Daddy and you and me! I'm going to put in Grammy, too, but I want her to be human so she can cook."

"You're in so much trouble." Eve looked back to her mother.

"I cannot overstress the importance of strengthening our alliance," Mrs. Holden said.

The door at the front of the room opened.

Hannah slipped inside, keeping her head down like she wanted to hide from her alpha even though Eve's father didn't look Hannah's way.

"I'm not gonna get in trouble," Mark said. "It's a picture of us!"

"Mark, hush." Eve's mother glared their way.

"This land cannot and will not be sold in individual parcels. The mountain has to stay under one deed to preserve the integrity of this sanctuary," Mrs. Holden said. "Together, we can defend ourselves, no matter what weapons or knowledge our enemy may possess. If even one acre of land on this mountain is sold to a person who wishes to harm this pack, we lose the very advantage this mountain—"

"Mama look!" Mark pointed to the picture.

Eve backed away as her mother's eyes got wide.

"Mark Gibbs, get over here. Now," Mother said.

Mark scurried backward, cramming himself under a chair.

Eve froze, trying to escape notice as her mother got out of her seat.

Mother bent low as she cut around to the window, like she didn't want people to know it was her kid who'd ruined the wall in the hall.

"This is not the time to sever alliances," Mrs. Holden said. "If we can't find a way to—"

Bang!

The floor bounced, and heat knocked Eve onto her back.

"Evelyn!" Mother screamed.

It sounded muddy, dull.

The other screams sounded funny, too.

Eve tried to get up, but her head was too swoopy. She rolled onto her stomach.

The floor was crunchy and sharp. And the front wall was on fire. And broken. Right in the middle where her father had been.

"Daddy!" Something sliced her hands as she pushed herself to her knees. "Daddy!"

Crack!

The ground tipped.

Mother grabbed her under the arms, lifting her. Eve reached out, ready to hold onto her mother, even though it should've been Mark kept close in Mama's arms.

Mother turned toward the window, keeping Eve too far away for her to cling to.

Crack!

The floor tipped again.

Mother flung Eve away.

Bang!

Pain sliced through Eve's back as she flew out the window.

Her gaze was still fixed on her mother, her pale skin smeared with red, the orange of the fire sparkling on the silver of her moonstone, but then the flames swallowed her.

Eve screamed as she hit the ground and tumbled down the slope, crashing into a tree.

"Mama!" Eve clawed at the ground, trying to get up, but the ground was too wobbly, and her arms wouldn't help her. "Mama!"

Crack!

The stilts beneath the hall buckled.

The building tipped and crashed to the ground, flipping over on itself and sliding down the hill.

"Mama!"

The hall smashed into the trees and the flames got bigger, eating the whole building.

"Mama!"

Lots of people inside the hall screamed. But none of them called for Eve.

"Mama!"

The smoke burned her throat.

"Mama!"

She choked on her scream, gasping for air until the whole world went black.

———

"Eve."

Something pressed on Eve's foot.

"Eve, wake up."

The thing tapped her.

"Eve."

Eve tossed back the covers and leapt to her feet, the mattress bouncing beneath her.

"Please don't hurt me!" Grace stood at the foot of the bed, holding a spatula in front of her like a shield.

"What's wrong?" Eve pushed away the curls that clung to the sweat on her forehead.

"Nothing." Grace backed away.

"Then why the hell did you wake me up?"

"You were having a nightmare."

Eve jumped off the bed, landing on the solid, unmoving ground.

"At least, you sounded like you were having a nightmare," Grace said. "Maybe I was wrong, but it sounded like you needed to wake up. I was trying to help."

"With a spatula?"

"It was the longest thing I could find on the kitchen counter.

I didn't want to get too close to you." Grace gave an apologetic smile.

"Smart."

Grace rocked back on her heels. "So, are you okay?"

"Other than being awake, yeah." Eve grabbed her blankets off the floor.

"Good."

Eve spread the blankets out and crawled between her sweat-dampened sheets.

"It's just that...if you aren't okay, you could tell me," Grace said. "About the nightmare. Or if you just wanted to talk."

"I'm fine."

"Whatever's bothering you, I promise I won't judge." Grace went to her own bed, still clutching the spatula. "And I've been to so much therapy, I know all the steps of trauma counseling."

"Good for you." Eve twisted her hair behind her and rolled to face the wall.

"It's just...well, with everything that happened at the museum with you and Jerek and the fighting, you can't just shrug something like that off. It's like you said, it's going to mess with your head for a while. Maybe ripping out of your skin wasn't enough. Maybe the nightmares are your brain's way of trying to sort through everything in a non-feu way. Believe me, Eve, I understand."

"No, you don't." Eve rolled back over and sat up, fixing her glare on Grace. "You don't get it now and you never will. While you were growing up in your safe little somb life, the feu lost everything. Homes, friends, family, our entire world got torn to shreds while you were coloring pretty pictures and having play dates.

"Whatever happened at the museum, whatever *trauma* your little stint as a magician might have caused, it is nothing, *nothing*, compared to what born feu have survived."

"I was born feu," Grace said. "Being adopted by somb parents doesn't change that."

"Yes. It does."

"What about Jack?" Grace gripped the spatula. "He wasn't bitten until a few months ago."

"And he knows his place. Learn yours before you insult someone with a temper."

"You helped me before. I was just trying to return the favor." Grace bit her cheeks like there was a chance in hell Eve might not notice her lip wobbling.

Eve held Grace's gaze, letting the danger of her rage dance through her eyes. "The last thing I need is your help. Your leaving me alone so I can sleep, sure. Your help? You're a magician. Not a therapist. Not a friend. Worry about trauma on your own time. The only thing I want from you is decent magic. I've already been stabbed. I'm not bleeding to fix any more of your messes."

"Right. Sorry." Grace kept the spatula in her hand as she got into bed and rolled to face the wall.

Eve flopped onto her back. She stared up at the shadows on the ceiling.

Nightmares didn't claw their way out of the corners to torture her.

"Fighting amongst ourselves only pushes us further into the chaos and destruction caused by the Fracture."

Mrs. Holden's words rumbled through Eve's mind.

They needed allies. They needed to work together to mend the Fracture. Incompetently erratic or not, Grace was the only untainted magician Ari and Jerek could dig up.

Eve's mother would want her to be nice. She'd be horrified at Eve's being rude to a poor little girl who was too lost to understand the damage the butcher had done.

It wasn't Grace's fault she'd been spared.

Eve pictured her mother scowling, giving Eve a silent warning to apologize or face the consequences of tarnishing the Gibbs family name.

But then the orange light of the flames flickered across her mother's face as Eve flew farther and farther away.

Hot tears leaked onto her cheeks.

She pictured Mark instead, beaming with pride at the picture he'd drawn.

She didn't see him again after the first blast. He'd been hiding under that chair. He'd been so close to the window.

Mother could have grabbed one kid in each hand, tossed both of them out the window.

Or just Mark.

If mother had just grabbed Mark, saved him instead—

Pain dug into the front of Eve's throat.

The butcher.

The butcher had set the bombs that murdered the wolves. The butcher had caused the Blood Mountain Massacre.

All of it was his fault.

Eve pictured the butcher standing in front of her, a knife in each hand as he foolishly tried to defend himself.

The butcher's face shifted—Chanler's, to LeBlanc's, to the old woman from the picture.

The face didn't really matter much as Eve leapt into the air, slicing her claws through the butcher's throat before she'd even landed.

12

Jerek

"Which circles us right back around to being screwed." Ari tapped on the image of Chanler. "At this point, we're spinning our wheels digging through twelve-year-old info."

"I've spent the past day sifting through Chanler's, LeBlanc's, and every other suspect's emails from the time of the Fracture on." Ford inched sideways, keeping himself just behind Ari's shoulder, using her as a shield while they presented the awful facts.

Jerek kept his hands on the arms of his chair as he weighed the group. Lincoln stood near the kitchen, behind the path Eve kept pacing as though she were waiting for someone to give her an excuse to scream.

Grace sat on the floor against the far wall, as separated from the rest of them as she could manage without fleeing to her room.

Jack sat on the couch, his gaze flicking to the pink band aid on Ford's neck, while Ford stared at Ari's left ear as though hoping he might be able to crawl into her brain and devour the majesty of her thoughts.

Ari watched Jerek with a look of cold detachment that would have carved a hollow into his gut if it had stopped feeling like his organs were sparking and squirming with the memory of amplified magic ripping through his body.

"We're working a cold case, Jerek," Ari said. "We need more information and, since betrayal and disappointment are the themes of the moment, the internet has let me down. We need a different resource."

"Like torturing Chanler," Eve said.

"I know that's your favorite option," Ari said. "But we can't just charge after him."

"I don't mind going in alone." Bloodlust glinted in Eve's eyes.

"Not gonna happen," Ari said.

"It'll be easier to get in on my own," Eve said.

"But if the danger comes from within our house, you'd be left utterly exposed without any backup," Jerek said.

"*Within our house?* What's that supposed to mean?" Grace gripped her knees, keeping her gaze fixed on the wall of images rather than look at Jerek.

"It means shit went sideways at the Museum of Magic and we don't know why," Jack said. "Best case scenario, one of us screwed up and let something slip. Worst case, someone in this room betrayed us and almost got one of us killed."

"Two of us," Grace said.

"Jerek's near-death was his own fault," Ari said.

Grace flinched.

"You're right, I made that choice." Jerek pushed himself out of his seat, not allowing his face to reveal the pain that surged through his legs. "Details of the spell aside—"

Ari coughed a laugh.

"—the way the Maree responded to us, blocking Ari's code and knowing they needed to restart the security cameras—"

"They knew something was going to happen," Ari cut across Jerek.

"We had stolen the Blood List," Jack said.

"The second Chanler found out the Blood List had been taken, he knew we were coming for him," Eve said.

"I thought we weren't assuming Chanler was guilty." Ford shrank under Eve's glare, sliding farther behind Ari. "Sorry."

"I wish it were that simple." Jerek didn't meet Ari's gaze as he joined her in front of the wall. "The brutal fact is, until we know if one of us leaked information and who the culprit is, going after Chanler or anyone else is out of the question. They were prepared for us at the Museum of Magic. Next time, we could be walking into an all-out trap. It's a risk we can't afford to take."

"Who was it?" Eve crossed her arms as she looked to each member of the group with so much anger radiating from her only a fool would confess.

"I don't know any feu but you guys," Grace said.

"I only know you all and my clan," Jack said.

"Doesn't matter." Ari eased Ford out from behind her, shifting him away from the timeline of their ill-fated heist. "We were all at the Museum of Magic opening. One whisper to a guard would have been enough to screw us with the cameras and alarms."

"But look at the timeline." Jack pointed to the rows of color-coded sticky notes. "We all had moments when we were alone. When Jerek and I were playing caterers, we weren't always in view of each other. How am I supposed to prove I didn't whisper sweet nothings in a Maree's ear?"

"Easy. We stay here talking ourselves in circles until the Maree find us," Eve said. "Just keep hiding while the butcher roams free."

"We're not hiding. We're being smart," Lincoln said.

"It's somewhere in the timeline. It's got to be." Ari scanned the rows of sticky notes. She tapped the line that marked when she'd planted the eater on the case of the Caster's Fate. "If the leak happened while we were at the museum, I don't think it could've been before Mariah and I went to the Pre-Treaty Gallery. We didn't meet any security on our way down. No one noticed we were there until the alarms went off."

"If the Maree knew we were there, someone should have been watching." Jerek studied the rows of notes. His timeline ended far before the others. He couldn't contribute anything after Grace had begun the spell. White hot pain dug into his chest. He pressed his palm to the wall, trying to seem as though he was studying the notes, not fighting to keep his knees from buckling.

"Can we..." Grace began. "I don't want to accuse anyone of anything."

"Then don't," Jack said.

"But somebody has to say it." Grace squared her shoulders, like she was fighting the instinct to cower. "Ari has the biggest gap in her timeline."

"She doesn't have a gap." Ford squeezed behind Ari to look at her column of notes. "It's all here."

"What she says happened is there," Grace said.

"I can hear you," Ari said. "You do know that, right?"

"None of us can confirm where you went after you disappeared downstairs with Mariah," Grace said.

"Because I was being held captive in LeBlanc's office," Ari said.

"But we just have *your* word." Grace stood. "And you didn't let Jerek change your face like he did for himself and Lincoln."

"My face doesn't like Jerek's magic," Ari said. "He can vouch for that."

"But you said you found a picture of you and Jerek and Lincoln in front of the Council of the Feu headquarters in LeBlanc's office. You must have known there could be security pictures of you floating around and you waltzed into Chanler's museum anyway?" Grace said. "Did you honestly never consider Chanler might have gotten ahold of those pictures?"

"It was a risk that had to be taken," Ari said.

"Because your face doesn't *like* Jerek's magic?" Grace stepped closer.

"Leave it, Grace." Jerek pushed away from the wall to stand beside Ari.

"Trust me, it's not vanity," Ari said. "I would love for Jerek to be able to give me a different face."

"You went downstairs with Mariah, which wasn't the plan," Grace said.

"It's not my fault she'd rather sneak off with me than Lincoln," Ari said.

"And then you're just gone." Grace's voice began to rise.

"I was locked in LeBlanc's office," Ari said.

"Until you mysteriously show back up with two daggers you didn't have when we got to the party!"

"Grace, stop." Jerek held his hand out to her. "Take a breath and calm down. Ari planted the daggers. I vouch for her."

"That's not good enough!" Grace looked to the others. "Why are any of you letting this slide? Are you really just going to take Jerek's word and give Ari a free pass! If she was locked in LeBlanc's office, how the hell did she get out?"

"If you want to ask a question about me, be brave enough to ask me," Ari said. "Don't try to make someone else do the dirty work for you."

"Fine." Grace rounded on Ari. "How did you get out of LeBlanc's office?"

"Smashed the window with my shoe and jumped," Ari said.

"Just jumped?" Grace furrowed her brow in mock concern. "You said LeBlanc's office was up in the cliff. So that would be a fifty, sixty-foot fall at least? Good thing you didn't even get a scratch."

"I landed in the water," Ari said.

"Your clothes weren't wet!"

"Grace, stop," Jerek said. "Now."

"Why should I stop? In case someone gets mad at me for being too pushy? I'm already the least liked person in this room. How much worse can it get?"

"This isn't the time for drama," Jack said.

"How can you not care that she's lying! You can't jump from that high, land in water, and come out dry, that doesn't work!"

"It doesn't," Eve said. "Even I couldn't have pulled off a jump from that high."

"Not all feu have the same gifts," Jerek said.

"What gift does your perfect Ari have that kept her alive?" Grace said.

"That's not your concern," Jerek said.

"Don't pull that, Holden," Eve said.

"I'm good with water," Ari said. "Landing in water. Getting water out of clothes. Need your hair dried? I'm your girl."

"That's more than trace magic." Jack kept his gaze fixed on his hands. "Maybe in a pre-Fracture world—"

"I'm a div!" Ari's shout bounced around the room. "I'm a fucking div. Are you happy now?"

"Ari—" Ford took her hand, but she yanked away.

"Filthy, little half-feu Ari can land in water and dry out her dress," Ari said.

"That still doesn't make sense," Grace said. "If you're only half-magician, why is your magic stronger than Jerek's?"

Ari tipped her head back and laughed. "I never said I was half-magician. You've been working with a half-mer. Dove right into the scuzzy end of the feu."

"Half-mer?" Grace cringed.

"Grace," Eve warned.

"How is that even possible?" Grace said. "A person having sex with a half-fish?"

The room went crushingly silent.

Ari took two ragged breaths before tossing the balcony door open and storming out into the night.

"Ari." Jerek started after her.

"Don't." Ford grabbed his arm. "Dealing with you would make it worse."

Pain clawed at the anger burning in Jerek's chest.

"I'll go." Lincoln headed toward the door.

"Don't let her run. If she goes under, I..." Jerek said. "I don't know if we'll get her back."

Lincoln looked at him just long enough to nod before disappearing into the night.

"Did I say something wrong?" Grace said. "Should I go apologize?"

"You will stay away from her. You will not approach her. You will not look at her. You will not speak to her. Am I clearly understood?" Jerek stepped toward Grace.

"But I was right. Ari was hiding something." Grace's gaze darted to the others. None of them came to her defense. "I was just trying to find out the truth."

"There are some truths you don't get to demand." Jack wiped a bead of blood from his lip.

"But we needed to know," Grace said.

Jack shook his head and walked away. The painting nearest his bathroom swayed as he snapped the door shut behind him.

"I was trying to help." Grace backed toward the wall where she'd been cowering only minutes before. "I didn't—she came back into the museum with knives. I didn't know half-mer even existed."

"Don't play victim," Eve said. "It's disgusting."

"I'm sorry." Grace tucked her shaking hands behind her back. "I'm sorry."

"Seriously?" Eve leapt over the back of the couch as a hint of smoke reached Jerek's nose.

Jerek spun toward the wall.

The edges of the pictures Ari had so carefully arranged curled and blackened as flames crackled to life on the paper.

Eve yanked off her shirt, patting out the flames with the balled-up cloth as Grace buried her face in her hands and began to sob.

13

Ari

The waves lapped around her ankles. Ari closed her eyes, trying to let that small connection with the sea be enough to soothe her.

Footsteps pounded down the stairs from the balcony.

She took another step, letting the water reach up to her knees. A painful longing dug into the back of her lungs, like a tether pulling her down into the depths where no one could reach her. She let the pull lead her farther out.

"Please don't go."

She froze at the sound of Lincoln's voice.

"Ari, please don't go where I can't follow you."

Two thumps sounded on the rocky shore.

"I know you're upset, you have every right to be, just don't leave." Lincoln slogged through the water behind her.

He stopped just far enough forward to be in her peripheral

vision, like he didn't want her to see him as a threat even though he'd placed himself close enough to grab her.

"I'm not trying to excuse what she said, but Grace doesn't know any better. If she did, she never would have asked those questions."

"She would have just thought them like the rest of you."

"Your parentage isn't our business."

"That doesn't stop you from wondering." Ari walked farther out, not stopping until her fingertips trailed through the water. Lincoln mirrored her movement. "You can't tell me you haven't thought about it."

"I never considered that you might be half-mer."

"You've known I'm a div."

"I thought you were half-nymph, to be honest."

"And now that you know?" A larger wave broke against Ari's chest, begging her to give in to the ocean's call.

"It's still not my business."

"Of course it is. I'm a rarity. You only get to read about freaks like me. And you're a Maree. Getting to question a half-mer, think of all the stories you'll be able to tell at the compound. Whisper in the shadows about the div you were forced to spend time with. Delight them all with the twisted tale of my conception."

"I don't want to know how you were conceived."

"Are you sure? It all begins with a young scuba instructor who liked to experiment."

"Ari, stop." Lincoln laid his hand on her shoulder.

"Careful, Maree. Touching a div in the dark? People will think you've stooped low enough to taint yourself with a halfling whore."

He stepped in front of her, blocking the path of the waves. "I'd punch anyone who called you that."

"Why? A child born of fornication between species, of course I'm nothing but a whore. It's what I was born to be."

"You're not."

"A pansexual half-mer?" A laugh jabbed through Ari's throat. "I'm the Maree's worst nightmare. The scum that taints the feu all because some horny, selfish people couldn't keep to their own kind."

"The Maree—"

"Know that I'm an abomination that never should have been born." The waves cut around Lincoln to wash over her.

He gripped her arms like he could hold her in place. "The Maree are wrong. You are not an abomination or scum or anything else. You're a brilliant hacker who's trying to fix the Fracture."

"So we'll pretend the div part doesn't exist?" Tears burned down Ari's cheeks. She closed her eyes, pulling the water of her tears through her skin, leaving her face dry. "You can't separate the hacker from the div."

"I don't want to." Lincoln grazed his fingers across the place where her tears had been. "I need you just as you are."

"To help mend the Fracture."

"Because I'm too much of a coward to face losing any part of you." He loosened his grip on her arm. "The pink-clad blond who stands up to Jerek Holden. And the hacker who's a little scary sometimes."

A fragile laugh managed to squeeze through the tightness in her throat.

He slid his hands down to her waist. "And the div who's fighting to fix a world that's treated her so horribly." The sea swirled as he shifted closer to her. "You plucked me out of my life and dropped me into this chaos."

"Sorry about that." She looked up at him.

"I'm not." He gave her a faint smile. "Just don't make me face the chaos without you. Don't disappear. Please. Stay with me."

She laid her cheek on his chest and let him wrap his arms around her.

His shoulders relaxed then tightened again as he kissed the top of her head.

She nestled closer, letting his strength surround her as her heart slowed to a normal rhythm.

"Jerek sent you out here to make sure I didn't run," Ari said.

"I was already following you, but he warned me you might swim away." He stopped breathing for a few seconds, like he was afraid he'd said something wrong and she'd vanish into the waves.

"I've done it before. Jerek was furious when he couldn't get ahold of me for weeks."

"Say what you want about Jerek Holden, but in his own way, he really does care about his friends."

"Even when they're far from perfect." Ari tipped her head to look up into Lincoln's eyes. "Did you tell him it was you?"

His arms tensed. "What do you mean?"

"You didn't stop messaging the Maree information until after we stole the Blood List." Ari wrapped her arms around his waist, taking her turn to anchor him in place. "Your brother was with the Maree at the museum. He recognized you, even though Jerek had changed your face. You talked to him before the plan fell apart."

"I didn't—"

"Don't lie." Ari dug her heels into the sand as the waves swirled around her. "Mistakes, I can forgive. Lies are a different story."

"I never wanted to betray anyone." He let go of Ari. His arms fell to his sides. "When this all started, I was sending reports to the Knights Maree. I didn't tell them Jerek wanted to mend the Fracture, I didn't think it could actually be done, but checking in was a part of my assignment. I sent a message to my brother, too."

"What did you tell him?"

"To get the bottom five to our grandparents." Lincoln looked up at the clouds growing to hide the stars.

"What's the bottom five?" Ari kept her arms locked tight around him.

"Joan, Ruth, Henry, Nelson, and William. My youngest five siblings. If mending the Fracture goes wrong, if things get that bad—"

"You don't want them in the Maree Compound."

"They're just kids, Ari." Lincoln looked down at her, pleading filling his eyes. "My grandparents' house would be safer for them, especially if whoever caused the Fracture decided to go after the Martels since I was helping Jerek. Once we stole the Blood List and I knew Jerek was right, I stopped messaging. I got rid of my phone.

"And yes, I spoke to Martin at the party, but he came to me. He recognized me and told me that you'd been taken. I didn't tell him why we were at the museum or that we were trying to mend the Fracture. There were more Maree at the museum than we'd planned for because Chanler asked for extra guards after we robbed the Council of the Feu. I'm sorry, Ari, I am. But I never tried to put the plan at risk."

"Then why didn't you say something days ago?"

"I didn't think it could've been me. I sent in reports and messaged my brother, but no one outside the Maree should have been able to see any of it. And I told the Maree everywhere we'd been traveling, but not that Jerek was collecting a heist crew.

"I was dumb enough to hope it hadn't been me who'd

screwed it all up and almost gotten Eve killed. *I didn't mean to* isn't a great way to apologize for getting someone stabbed."

"It's not. But it'll have to do."

"Or I could leave." Lincoln reached behind his back to take Ari's wrists, easing her arms from around his waist. "Remove the problem and let you move on without having to deal with someone you don't trust."

"If I'm not allowed to bolt, neither are you. Tell the others what happened, let Eve smash some furniture, and we'll pack up and move on in the morning."

"Ari—"

"Now that we know what went wrong, it's time to make our next move. And I believe you won't let it happen again."

"They won't want me to stay."

"They won't want a div to stay, either."

"That's not true." Lincoln laced his fingers through hers. "We'd be lost without you. And if any of them think differently, we'll find a way forward without them."

"So, you're staying." Ari rested her forehead on his shoulder, wrapping his arms behind her back.

Lincoln let go of her hands and gently placed his on the back of her waist. "I am."

"And I'm staying. And we're going to figure out a way to make the rest of the pieces mash together while protecting Jerek from himself."

"We are."

A wave washed up to Ari's shoulders as a tired laugh buckled in her throat. "The heroes fighting to save the feu. If we're all doomed, I'm glad you'll be with us while the world burns."

He held her closer, not like he was pinning her in place. More like he didn't want to face the fire without her, either.

"Thanks for not letting me run." She wrapped her arms

14

Lincoln

"And I think—" Lincoln cleared his throat. "And it only seems fair that you all know." He planted himself in front of the villain tracer, his clothes still wet from standing in the waves with Ari.

Her clothes had been dry before they'd reached the steps up to the balcony. Crisp and clean like she'd never ventured out into the sea. Now she'd taken Lincoln's place, lurking where the hall met the front room. Whether she was keeping everyone in her line of sight, waiting for another chance to run, or scared of what the others might say, he couldn't tell.

"Know what?" Jack frowned at Lincoln.

Lincoln tucked his hands behind his back, keeping his chin up in a way that would have made his brothers proud. "It was me. I would never intentionally betray the group. I was trying to protect my family, and do my duty to—"

around his neck, letting him steady her on the shifting sand, giving in to the comfort he offered.

The others could wait inside—bickering or smashing or crying. Operation Snatch Cinderella couldn't begin until morning.

Eve vaulted over the back of the couch, landing a solid punch on Lincoln's cheek before her feet had even touched the ground.

15

Eve

Eve sat on the roof of the van, staring up at the still-dark sky while the others packed the few things they had. They'd thrown out the dress she'd worn to the Museum of Magic. All she had now were the clothes Ford had grabbed for her on the one trip into town Ari had let him take.

Lincoln came out of the house, keeping his chin tucked as he stalked past Eve to put his bag in the back of the van. The deep purple bruise Eve had left on his cheek showed in the moonlight.

The glow of satisfaction that should have bubbled in her chest at the sight of her handywork didn't appear.

Another Maree. Another betrayal.

Not yet. Don't slaughter the rabbit and lose the deer.

Lincoln stopped at the front passenger door. He stared at the handle for a moment, like he was trying to figure out if he'd fallen too far to claim a front seat, then opened the back doors and climbed in to sit on one of the benches running along the sides.

Grace came out next, clutching her bag to her chest, bringing it into the van with her instead of tossing it into the back.

Jack and Ford walked together, Ford seeming wide awake as he listened to Jack explain something about living in the tunnels below Las Vegas.

Eve watched the front door of the house, not leaving her post on the roof of the van as the first hints of dawn touched the sky.

The door finally opened again. Ari came out first with Jerek right behind her. Both of them still had their packs. Their things were too important to be left behind. The hacker and the Holden, setting out to save the world with backpacks and a dream.

"Should I drive?" Jerek asked as he shut both of their bags into the back of the van.

"You can drive," Ari said. "But I'm the navigator."

Eve jumped off the roof of the van, landing in front of Ari before she could reach the front passenger door.

Ari didn't meet Eve's eyes as she sidestepped to cut around her.

"I need to talk to you," Eve said.

"We can talk while Jerek drives." Ari reached for the door handle.

"Give me a minute." She took Ari's arm, just hard enough she wouldn't be able to break free, and pulled her back toward the house.

Ari didn't speak as Eve planted her far enough from the van only Jack might be able to hear them talking. Ari kept her gaze fixed on the van, like she was afraid Jerek might drive away and abandon her.

"I didn't want to wait to talk to you." Eve stepped sideways, blocking Ari's view of the van. Ari still didn't look at her. "If I'd known you were a div, I never would have pushed for answers. It was wrong for us to out you like that."

"You should've let me keep hiding my filthy little secret?"

"We should have let you do what you want with information about your own damn life." Eve leaned over, placing her face right in front of Ari's. "I just need you to believe I didn't know."

"How?" Ari finally met her gaze. "Can't you smell the mermaid in me? Can't werewolves scent out divs hiding in plain sight?"

"Honestly, I thought you had really fancy sea breeze perfume. You smell like beach, not fish."

"Fish?" Ari yanked her arm free.

"I said *not* fish. And even if you did smell like fish and had scales on your face, I'd still feel like an ass for pushing so hard. We're in this fight together."

"Don't want to insult anyone who's on your side." Ari gave a pinched smile. "Good thing I'm useful."

"You're better than useful. The Maree gave up on fixing the Fracture, so did most feu. But you didn't. You're putting your ass on the line when most people wouldn't dare. If anyone tries to insult the div who fought for the feu, I'll tear out their spleen."

"Spleen?"

"I was trying to lighten the moment." Eve shrugged.

"Does the div protection only count for me?"

"Depends on if the other divs are useless assholes. I'm not a Maree, Ari. I don't care about bloodlines. I've met too many purebred wolves who don't deserve to run with a pack. I've torn out a few of their eyeballs, too."

The corners of Ari's mouth twitched up.

"Does that mean you'll forgive me?"

"Sure." Ari poked Eve's shoulder. "But when I round up all the non-useless asshole divs, you have to have their backs, too."

"Deal." Eve clasped Ari's hand in a firm handshake then stepped out of her path to the van. "Just don't blame me for hoping it's Maree spleens I get to tear out."

"The way we're headed, it probably will be."

"Does that mean you have a new plan?" Eve opened the van door for Ari.

"Stage one of Operation Snatch Cinderella is already underway."

"Am I going to hate this?"

"That depends on how you feel about exotic orchids."

16

Jack

The vinyl of his cubby creaked as someone shifted on the bench above him.

Jack shut his eyes against the total blackness that surrounded him, trying to let the hum of the van's engine lure him into sleep.

His eyes flew open as the person above him shifted again.

And again.

And again. Then finally went still.

He took a deep breath, trying to ignore the stale scent of his cubby as he methodically relaxed his body. Toes, ankles, calves—

The rumble of the tires sharpened as they reached a hollow-sounding portion of road, like they were crossing yet another bridge.

Sleep, Jack. Let yourself sleep.

I don't need to sleep for another few days.

The person above him shifted again.

He rolled onto his side, clamping his hands over his ears.

"How much farther?" Eve asked.

"Not far," Ari said. "We can get food from town once we're done looking around."

"What town?" Grace asked from right above Jack.

No one answered.

"What are we going to look around?" Grace's voice carried over the creaking of the vinyl.

"A party venue," Ari said.

"What venue? What party?" Grace said.

"It won't matter if there's not a good way in," Ari said.

"Way in to what?" The vinyl creaked and went quiet, like Grace had stood up.

"Take a breath, Grace," Lincoln said.

Jack pressed his hands to the seat bottom above him, checking for the heat of flames.

"Ari said we should all follow Jerek blindly, and everything fell apart. Now she's asking us to follow her without question?" Grace's voice rose.

Jack couldn't smell any smoke, and the seat above him hadn't gotten unnaturally warm.

"I'm not asking you to follow me blindly," Ari said. "I need to do some reconnaissance, and since we're carpooling on this escapade, you all have the pleasure of coming with me."

"Daylight reconnaissance?" Eve said.

"Not all of us have a werewolf's vision," Ari said.

Jack knocked on the metal bracing of the seat. "One of us can't go into the sunlight."

"I'll take pictures," Ari said. "And you can go back to look around tonight."

"Thanks." Jack tapped on the metal again. "I'll just stay in here not dying then."

"Good plan," Eve said.

"There is no plan," Grace said.

"Well, staying in the dark will keep Jack—" Ford began.

"While we do what?" Grace cut across.

"Jack's safety matters," Ford said.

A smile curved Jack's lips. He shut his eyes and kneaded his knuckles against his jaw, pretending he could stop his fangs from growing.

"I'm sorry," Grace said. The seat creaked as she sat back down. "Of course keeping Jack out of the sun matters."

"Thank you," Ford said.

Jack's fangs pierced his bottom lip.

"But I still need to know where we're going," Grace said.

"I was going to wait until the well-curated and aesthetically pleasing presentation was ready, but we can do this now," Ari said. "We're going to Greenwood Gardens to kidnap Mariah Chanler."

17

Eve

"We're doing what?" Grace's shout dug into Eve's ears.

"Kidnapping might even be too strong a word." Ari moved to the floor between the two front seats, facing the group in the back of the van. "From what I can tell, Mariah might want to come with us."

"And if not, we just take her?" Grace shrieked.

Eve plugged her ear closest to Grace.

"Why do you think she'll want us to take her?" Lincoln shifted forward in his seat, furrowing his brow and cocking his head, leaving his jugular beautifully exposed.

The better to tear your throat out, you traitorous asshole.

"The honest truth"—Ari flipped her laptop open—"I think she's been asking me to."

"How?" Lincoln said.

"I've been keeping an eye on her social media," Ari said. "All her friends' social media, too, searching for any chatter about the massive diamond we stole from the Museum of Magic. No one's mentioned it. Not Mariah's crew, not Chanler, not the Council of the Feu."

"Maybe they haven't realized we took a jewel after shattering the Caster's Fate." Jerek glanced down to Ari, like she really hadn't told him everything.

Jerek didn't look upset or angry. Just curious.

"We can hope they don't know we stole a diamond, or at least that they haven't figured out that diamond is the heliostone," Ari said. "But I don't want to bank on us being that lucky."

"What did you find while you were stalking Mariah?" Grace wrapped her arms around her stomach, gripping the sides of her shirt like she was trying to keep herself from exploding in an incompetent, flaming ball of dangerous magic.

"I found Mariah looking for me." Ari turned her laptop to face the group. One corner of the pink casing had been marred by a spiderweb of cracks.

A picture of Mariah Chanler dressed in a black silk robe popped up on the screen. She was standing in front of a room filled with clothes and mirrors like a shrine dedicated to spending her rich father's money.

"Can't decide on a dress for the Greenwood Gardens Gala," Ari read the caption. "Hoping I'll meet an old friend on the dance floor."

Ari switched to another picture. Mariah held her hand in front of her face, showing off her red manicure. "Just can't forget a lady in red."

"That's flirting at best," Lincoln said. "You wore a red dress to the museum opening, but she could mean someone else."

Ari changed the image again. Mariah raced down the beach

on a white horse. "Cinderella dreaming of being swept off her feet. Blond hair, teal eyes. Waiting for a hero to whisk me away."

In the next picture Mariah leaned on a balcony railing, staring out over the sea, wearing the same dress she had on the night of the Museum of Magic opening. "Did my heart love till now? Forswear it, sight! For I ne'er saw true beauty till this night."

"Now it's getting weird," Jack said.

Ford leaned down to whisper into Jack's cubby. "And you can't even see the pictures."

"A sky of diamonds. The scent of sea in your hair. A kiss to cling to," Ari read from Mariah's next post.

"Did she write you a haiku?" Jack asked.

"She has a thing for you," Grace said. "That doesn't justify kidnapping."

"But we're stuck." Ari snapped her laptop closed. "We need more information, the internet has failed us. We need to talk to a real, live person if we want to figure out how to move forward with mending the Fracture. If we're going to talk to someone who knows anything about Chanler or creepy ass LeBlanc, kidnapping is going to be involved."

"And we should kidnap Mariah because she wants to tear your clothes off?" Grace said.

"We should take Mariah because it's about a fifty-fifty chance that she wants us to rescue her from her father and his estate manager," Ari said.

"*Maybe not kidnapping* does sound better than *definitely kidnapping*," Ford said.

"What if it's a trap?" Lincoln said. "She could be posting those things to lure you in."

"Unless someone has a better idea, it's a chance we have to take," Ari said. "Besides, it should be a much easier party to crash. It's being hosted by sombs."

18

Jack

The edge of the woods opened out to a sweeping field that led right up to the back of Greenwood Gardens with no fencing in sight.

"To the far right is the herb garden," Lincoln said. "From looking at the pictures on the garden's website, events don't usually extend that far west."

"Did you look at the pictures of the gardens or did Ari?" Jack leaned against a tree, studying the buildings in the darkness, wondering what they would have looked like before he'd been bitten. Shadows with security lights probably.

His somb eyes wouldn't have allowed him to see the paths leading from the herb garden to the fountain garden, then through rows of spring flowers to cut an arc past the forest, then hedges, a terrace, and more hedges, before reaching the massive conservatory.

"Ari found the pictures, but I looked at them with her,"

Lincoln said. "Everything should be centered around the conservatory and terrace."

"Which means I'm beyond useless until after dark." Jack chewed on his thumbnail. "I could hide in the van in the parking lot, but that seems a lot like asking to die."

"We can't chance it."

Jack looked back toward the path that bordered the woods—far enough from the party to offer privacy to anyone hoping to steal an intimate moment with a socialite.

"You should grab Mariah off the path," Jack said. "There might be cameras, but Eve can run her through the woods faster than security could follow on foot."

"Or you could run her through the woods," Lincoln said.

"Sure," Jack said. "I'll just sprint on over from the rental house as soon as it's dark and hope I make it here in time to carry a flailing heiress away."

"Eve's the better plan," Lincoln said, "but you could do it."

"Thanks for the affirmation."

"If you drove here from the rental and waited in the woods, we'd have a backup if something went wrong with Eve. We need a built-in plan b this time. We can't just assume everything will go right." Lincoln rubbed his hand across his chin. "We came too close to losing people last time."

"Agreed."

"Then you'll drive here. Have a car waiting for you in case you have to carry Mariah."

"It would be better than running." Jack pushed away from the tree, turning to face Lincoln so he could properly watch the wrinkle between the Maree's eyebrows deepen.

The wind shifted, carrying the muddled scent of herbs, flowers, and freshly turned dirt all the way up from the gardens.

Lincoln didn't react to the complex stench.

As human as a somb even if he is a knight.

"They scanned my ID when we rented the car in Newport," Lincoln said. "Even with a fake name, and Jerek messing with my face, I don't like the risk of being put into another computer system."

"Maybe Ford can rent me a car," Jack said. "At least he's not a Maree."

"He was with us at the museum. It's still too risky." Lincoln's jaw tensed as his heartbeat quickened. "Can you steal us a car?"

Jack's fangs pierced his lip.

"Two cars really," Lincoln said. "Luxury brand if possible."

"Did a Knight Maree just ask me to commit multiple felonies?"

"I don't know what other choice we have. I'd steal the cars myself if I knew how."

"It seems like a skill the Maree should teach."

"Can you teach me?" Lincoln tucked his hands behind his back like he was awaiting orders.

"I haven't said I know how. It's a big jump between slipping cash and jewelry off a drunk mark and stealing a car."

Lincoln's shoulders sank.

"Lucky for you, my criminal career has involved liberating a few high-end vehicles." Jack held out a hand, silencing Lincoln before he could speak. "No, I can't teach you. If you want the cars for the party tomorrow night, we have to steal them tonight. That doesn't leave time for grand theft auto 101. But I can get it done if I have two extra drivers."

"Jerek should go with you." Lincoln's jaw tightened again, this time causing a cartoonishly noticeable vein to pop in his neck.

"Ari can be the third."

"No. It's got to be me. If we get caught and I'm arrested, the Maree will come for me. I'll be hauled back to Italy to stand before the Knight's Council, but I won't be left to rot in prison." Lincoln rocked back on his heels. "I'm not sure if the Council of the Feu or the Knight's Council would lift a finger to help Ari."

"Grace would panic. Eve might kill people. Ford is—Ford."

"It's got to be me or Ari," Lincoln said. "Jack, I'm asking you not to bring her. Don't put her in that kind of danger."

"We're about to kidnap someone. We're all in danger."

"But she can at least be safe for tonight. And kidnapping Mariah would be harder without Ari. If she's stuck in prison and can't go to the Gala—"

"Save your justifications." Jack headed back through the woods to the place on the narrow side road where they'd left the now-black van. "You're allowed to want to keep Ari safe as long as you realize the danger is coming from the messed up state of our shitty world and don't try to diminish the incomparable queen she is."

"It'll get worse for her, you know. If we mend the Fracture and the feu go back to how things were before. The Council of the Feu wouldn't just abandon Ari in a somb prison. If she ever managed to escape, the Council would punish her for attracting the attention of the sombs. She looks close enough to a plain human—"

"But if she took a shiv to the gut and needed surgery, the prison doctors would get to play a fun game of one of these things is not like the others. What would the lungs of a half-mer even look like?"

"She's already sacrificing enough to try and mend the Fracture. I don't want her to commit any felonies she can avoid."

"Fine." Jack's fangs retracted, leaving his teeth blunt and human. "It'll be you, me, and Jerek. If things go badly, I'll sun burn and die, but at least Ari will be safe."

"Jack, I'm sorry." Lincoln stopped following him. "I know getting locked in a cell come sunrise—"

"Would mean a terrible death for me." Jack doubled back and took Lincoln's arm, pulling him toward the shadow of the van. "But I wasn't being sarcastic. I have to go steal the cars, there's no choice there. But if I'm doomed, it'd be good to know Ari would still be around to avenge my death."

19

Lincoln

The club's music blasted onto the street, calling even more drunken revelers to its door, adding to the line that stretched beneath the sign that read *Eternal Lush*.

A car stopped, letting two stiletto-wearing women out before speeding on to its next fare.

"We need to go somewhere else." Lincoln watched the women join the line to get into the club, trying to look like he was admiring the shortness of their skirts rather than fighting the urge to punch the lamppost even though he knew damn well he'd shatter his hand if he was fool enough to try taking his anger out on metal.

"Take a breath," Jack said. "You hurry a grab, you ask for failure."

Another car pulled up. This one let out a man and a woman before leaving.

"I never thought I'd be frustrated by people drinking responsibly," Lincoln said.

"There are irresponsible assholes in every crowd," Jack said. "Sombs, feu, rich, poor, criminals, saints. There's always an asshole. It's one of the sad truths of life. Just ogle the women, look put out that the rest of our imaginary party people haven't shown yet, and wait for an asshole to arrive."

"Fine." Lincoln jammed his hands into his pockets.

Pretend he was waiting for someone.

Pretend going into an overcrowded place with few exits and no way to spot danger held any appeal. Loud music pounding away as sweaty people danced, letting the shadows and sheer size of the crowd peel away their inhibitions.

Maybe, if he had the right person dancing with him, if he could brush her hair away from her sweat-slicked face and watch her laugh even if he couldn't hear the sound over the music—

Jack nudged Lincoln in the ribs. "Cue asshole number one. Stay here. Stay calm. I'll be right back." Jack shifted from a whisper to a slightly louder than normal voice as a sleek, black car rounded the corner and dove into one of the few remaining parking spots beside the club. "I'm going to check around back. Maybe they're too blazed to know where they're supposed to meet us."

He patted Lincoln on the shoulder in an almost comforting way before cutting down the side street to follow the car.

20

Jerek

The awning of the coffee shop provided plenty of shadows to hide one magician. Still, Jerek didn't let himself pace as he waited for Jack.

12:30 a.m.

After midnight, and people were still arriving at Eternal Lush.

A couple approached, keeping to the street that cut behind the club, staying on course to cross in front of Jerek's hiding place.

The smaller of the women caught sight of Jerek and grabbed her companion's hand.

Jerek offered her a nod and a half-smile, hoping that might be enough to ease her fear of the boy dressed all in black lurking in the shadows.

The women picked up their pace. The smaller one pulled out her phone, holding it with her thumb over the screen as though ready to call for help if Jerek took a single step to follow them.

You're not the people who have to worry tonight.

Jerek peered back around the corner, up the side street that led to the front of the club. At the far corner, Jack and Lincoln stood together.

A car cut onto the side street, diving into a parking spot as though the driver were trying to scratch the perfectly polished black car.

Jack patted Lincoln on the shoulder and walked down the street, heading toward Jerek and the newly parked car.

Jerek brushed his fingers against his shirt, changing the color from black to a less intimidating blue. He slipped his phone from his pocket and held it to his ear as he headed up the street.

"Grandma, I'm trying." Jerek spoke into his phone. He paused, waiting for an imagined response. "I've been wandering around for an hour, Grandma, and I still can't find it."

A woman stepped out of the black car, wearing silver pumps and a silver-sequined dress.

Jerek stopped twenty feet away from the woman, furrowing his brow as though listening to something frustrating from the other end of the line, while a man with a barely buttoned shirt got out on the driver's side of the car.

"Grandma, are you sure you were downtown?" Jerek asked. "I just—Gran—Gran, listen, I've been trying!"

The woman in silver glanced toward Jerek.

"Hold on—Gran, I said hold on." Jerek lowered his phone and took a few steps toward the woman. "Miss? Excuse me, Miss?"

The woman turned, and the man stepped in front of her, planting himself between Jerek and his date.

Damn.

"I'm so sorry." Jerek took another small step toward them. "My grandmother seems to have misplaced her car."

"What?" the man said.

"She swears she parked it somewhere around here." Jerek shrugged. "She says it was in front of a café with an awning that was purple or maybe black, and that the sign said there was street cleaning tomorrow morning, so I have to find her car tonight or she'll get towed."

"Poor thing," the woman said.

"Do either of you know of a café with a purple or black awning anywhere around here?" Jerek asked.

"Sorry, man. I don't." The man's shoulders relaxed. "Try looking at street view maps on your phone. Might be easier than wandering around."

"Thanks, I'll try that." Jerek raised his phone back up to his ear. "I've got to go, Grandma. I'm going to try looking at maps."

"Marie, that dress!" Jack cut between the man and silver-clad woman, knocking into the man before leaping away from both of them. "Oops. Not Marie. I'm so sorry, it was your hair. You look like a friend."

"I know street view is just old pictures. Gran, I kn—I know I won't be able to see your car, Gran." Jerek stepped to the inside of the sidewalk, clearing a path. "Because I'm looking for the café!"

"Just back off, okay." The man puffed up his chest, glaring at Jack.

"Honest mistake." Jack raised his hands as he backed away. "I should've known Marie wouldn't dare go for a sequined dress. You look amazing, by the way."

"Thanks." The silver-clad woman gave Jack a quick smile before taking her date's hand and leading him toward the front of the club.

The man kept glancing behind as they walked, as though

wanting to be sure Jerek was still talking to his grandmother and Jack was still on the hunt for Marie.

Jack headed away from the front of the club and cut around the corner, ducking into Jerek's hiding spot.

The man and not-Marie walked out of view.

Jerek stepped over to the curb, brushing his fingers against the man's car, turning the black to a deep, cherry red as he kept trying to explain to his imaginary grandmother that getting towed wouldn't, in fact, be the first sign of the apocalypse.

21

Jack

The line in front of the club had barely moved by the time Jack circled the full block and returned to the lamppost where Lincoln still waited.

"I couldn't find them," Jack called to Lincoln as he passed in front of the line. "Have they called you?"

Lincoln shook his head.

Come on, Maree. Give me something to work with.

"I say we give them fifteen more minutes and get in line without them," Jack said.

"There's no line jumping," a girl with bright pink streaks in her hair shouted. "We've all been waiting here."

"I never said I'd let our friends join us in line." Jack bowed to the girl. "I will leave those lagging dunces out here and go party without them. While in the true spirit of club life I believe no man should be left behind, if the bitches don't show up for the mission, that's their own damn fault."

The girl with the pink streaks in her hair began to clap. The applause carried down the line, beyond the point where the people had had any chance of hearing Jack over the pounding of the club's music.

Jack gave a grander, sweeping bow and rejoined Lincoln at the lamppost.

"What the hell was that?" Lincoln spoke in a low voice.

"An expert demonstration of how to steal a car without getting caught." Jack leaned against the lamppost, slipping the key out of his pocket and into Lincoln's.

Lincoln balled his hands into fists. "People are watching us."

"People are waiting for another bit of entertainment while they're stuck in line," Jack said. "If we'd just kept standing here, loitering like fools, as soon as two cars are reported stolen our descriptions would be given to the police as the two creepy guys lurking on the corner.

"Now we've interacted, invited the crowd into our story-line. When the police ask if anyone saw any car thieves hanging around, they'll get a big ole' *No, but maybe the two guys who were waiting for their friends saw something.* Two car thieves, the cops will hunt for. Two guys who maybe saw something in a non-violent crime? Not worth the man hours trying to find us."

"I don't like it," Lincoln said.

"Trust me. I'm a professional." Jack leaned away from the lamppost to look up and down the street.

The line shifted forward as a few lucky people were let into the club.

"We should go somewhere else," Lincoln said.

"We're fine here."

"Then we should follow someone or switch spots. See if anyone parks on the other side of the club."

"There are cameras on that street. We're staying right here."

A car pulled up, dropped two men at the curb, then pulled away.

"What if no one else parks behind us?" Lincoln asked.

"Didn't the Maree teach you patience?"

"Of course. But they also taught me that sometimes you have to switch tactics to succeed."

"Nope, you start a story, you live in it." Jack ran his tongue across his smooth teeth, waiting for his fangs to grow as panic burst through him. But there was no panic. Only a wonderful calm, born of performing a task as practiced as folding clean laundry. "Same schtick, different trick."

"What?"

"You can work the same crowd for days as long as you never repeat a grab."

A bright red car zoomed into sight, turning down the side street at a speed that would've banished any thief's guilt Jack might have felt. Not that he did.

Lincoln looked down the road in front of the club, keeping his gaze away from the red car like a good little knight. "How did you learn all this?"

"A sad, human addiction to food. Sewing gave me nimble fingers, hunger gave me the drive to learn, and upgrading to high end products, that came from pure pride. I'd rather go down as a jewel thief than a petty crook."

"I'd rather not get arrested at all," Lincoln said.

Two women got out of the red car. The driver tucked the keys into the top of her thigh-high boot.

"That's a no."

Jack took a deep breath, scenting the air, searching for something beyond the stench of sweat and too many brands of cologne.

Car fumes, trash, vodka, vomit...the blood coursing through all the people waiting in line for the club.

No time for a snack, Jack.

A blue jeep pulled up, stopping right in front of Jack as the driver peered around the corner, as though checking for parking spaces, before turning down the side street toward Jerek.

"Could that work?" Lincoln glanced toward Jack.

"I'd prefer a less distinctive body shape. But it's better than nothing."

The jeep slipped into a parallel parking spot Jack would have been too intimidated to try. Two men and two women climbed out of the jeep. The driver pressed the button on his keys, making the car's lights flash as he locked the doors, then shoved the keys into his back pocket.

"I love it when things are easy." Jack nudged his elbow into Lincoln's ribs. "Don't overplay it."

Lincoln unfurled his fists as though that might complete his façade of calm.

"This isn't even fun anymore. I'm out." Jack headed down the side street.

"Wait, what?" Lincoln chased after him.

"We've been here for over an hour." Jack picked up his pace. "By the time we get through the line and get inside, it'll be like 1:30."

"So?"

"So, I'd rather be at home, curled up on my couch, binge watching TV. Nothing good ever comes from starting to party after 1 a.m." Jack looked back toward Lincoln as he walked, listening to the approaching footsteps. Two sets of sturdy shoes. One steady rhythm of properly worn stilettos. One uneven gait of someone who'd made a poor choice in footwear.

"But you're my ride," Lincoln said.

"Then let's go."

The cluster of footsteps parted, shifting to the sides, all aiming to cut around Jack.

"But what if they show—"

"Not my problem!" Jack spun around, flinging his arms wide and taking a giant step backward as he rounded on Lincoln.

With a squeak and a shout, Jack collided with two people.

He tipped back, letting himself topple over, hitting the other two people on his way to the ground.

"What the hell!" one of the men shouted while Lincoln called, "You okay?"

"Dammit." Jack rolled onto his side, wincing as he pushed himself to sit up. "Sorry. I'm sorry."

"Just watch where you're going." One of the men, the driver, took Jack's forearm, hoisting him to his feet.

"Thanks." Jack stumbled half a step forward, bumping into the driver's shoulder as he slipped his fingers in and out of the man's back pocket. "Sorry again. You folks have a great night."

The angry man shook his head and stormed down the street, the two women and the driver trailing along in his wake.

"Now it's definitely time to go home." Jack waited until Lincoln reached him before nodding toward the newly cherry-red car. "Your steed awaits."

"Thanks." Lincoln's heart stuttered as he pressed on the key fob. The doors unlocked with a faint click and a beep.

"So little faith in me." Jack glanced up the street as Lincoln drove away, making sure the jeep people were out of sight before pressing the unlock button on the keys he'd slipped from the driver's back pocket. "I really hope you have good insurance."

He climbed into the driver's seat and edged the car out of the parking spot, checking the rearview mirror one more time before driving around the corner to stop in front of Jerek's shadowy hiding place.

Jerek climbed into the jeep, buckling his seatbelt before rolling down his window.

Jack turned down a side street, cutting away from the path Lincoln would take back to the rental house.

"So what color do you want her?" Jerek asked.

"Make her a gentle seafoam green for tonight. If we're going to risk arrest, we might as well add a nice pop of color to the police photos."

22

Eve

Eve pinned down her mound of curls, flattening their mass enough to fit under the black hat Ford had tossed her way along with the black shirt and leggings that were her costume for the party.

"I don't like it." Jack chewed on his thumbnail, watching from his chair in the corner of the windowless room, his leg bouncing in a nerve-grating rhythm. "It leaves you too exposed. We need a better plan."

"We don't have time for a better plan." Ari leaned over in front of the mirror, rearranging the bags of rice she'd used to fill her oversized bra. "Mariah's already posted that she's on her way to the party. That means we need to head out, too."

"But I could stay closer to you," Lincoln said.

Ari didn't bother responding.

Jack had shaved the sides of Lincoln's head, and Jerek had turned what hair remained a red to rival Eve's curls. Jerek had taken away Lincoln's black eye, added pudge to his face, a scar below his left eye, and a neck tattoo, which popped up over the collar of his shirt.

None of it mattered. He still stank of Maree.

"Someone should be closer to you," Lincoln said.

"Security is more likely to spot a pack of teenagers than one girl alone at a party." Ari shimmied on her dress, which hugged her fake boobs and tiny waist before flaring out into a fluffy skirt.

The poof seemed unnecessary and inconvenient but was at least useful in hiding the two daggers Ari had strapped to her thighs.

"We'll all be able to hear what's happening." Ford held out the platter of earpieces he'd dropped more than a grand of Holden's money on. He'd written the code names he'd chosen for them on slips of paper and laid their assigned earpieces on top. "Juliet, Dagonet, Firefly, Chameleon, Little Red, and DJ Cricket are charged and ready for action."

Lincoln's and Eve's looked like normal earbuds, like Lincoln was just an ass who didn't want to be at the party and was purposefully tuning out the world. And no one would have a chance to see Eve's ears.

Not if everything goes well.

"We're going to stay close enough to help Ari if she needs it." Jerek grimaced as he shoved in his earpiece. "If Mariah gets spooked—"

"Then it will blow the plan *Ari's* in charge of." Ari twisted her hair into pin curls. "I have to approach Mariah alone. If she wants to come with me, the rest of you can enjoy the party and watch my back."

"And if she doesn't want to come with you?" Grace gripped the sides of her seat. "Are you really just going to grab her?"

"Would you rather wait around and see who else Chanler

might kill?" Eve took her earbuds from the tray and tucked them into her pocket.

"One awful thing doesn't excuse another," Grace said.

"You don't have to worry about any of that," Ford said. "You just have to watch Ari's exit."

"And stay away from everyone so I don't do any damage," Grace said.

"Keep our path clear." Ari pinned on her chestnut-brown wig.

A vague anger scratched at Eve's chest. Like something had been twisted up in a forbidden way.

"Fine. I'll shut up and lurk in the corner while you kidnap someone," Grace said.

"This is a rescue mission," Lincoln said. "If what Ari says is true—"

"Then the hot girl is just waiting for Ari to show up in all the blazing glory of a mermaid in a fancy wig?" Grace stood, taking a step toward Lincoln, not shying away when he rounded on her.

"Take a breath, Grace," Jerek said.

"Sure, I'll take a breath. I'll let you change my hair and screw with my face while Ari gets fake boobs and a wig." Grace tugged on her newly mouse-brown, newly chopped hair.

Ari slipped on the round-framed glasses that softened her cheekbones. "Jerek can't change my hair."

"You're right," Grace said. "Kidnapping is fine, but your vanity must be preserved."

"He literally can't change my hair." Ari pulled off her wig and tipped her head toward Jerek.

He sighed, then pressed his fingers to one of Ari's pin curls, turning the hair an overly bright shade of pink.

"And three, two—" Before Ari hit *one*, the pink had faded,

leaving her hair its normal, perfect blond. "I've tried to have Jerek alter me before. It just doesn't work."

"Because you're half mer?" Jack took the wig from Ari, carefully brushing it out with his fingers.

"No idea." Ari repinned the curl Jerek had touched. "Maybe his magic is repulsed by the div."

The tang of stress filled the air as everyone in the room froze for a moment.

Eve held her breath for two counts, waiting for someone to act.

"Try it on me, Holden." Eve pulled a curl out from under her hat.

"Promise not to thrash me if it sticks?" Jerek widened his eyes in a way that seemed to say *thank you for stopping a mer-on-magician brawl.*

"Just not pink." Eve pulled the curl taut, holding it out in front of her so she could watch Jerek work.

He brushed his fingers against the hair, shifting the red to a bright, moonlight silver.

Everyone in the room stared at the hair for a solid ten seconds, but the silver didn't fade.

"Guess your trick works on wolves," Jack said.

"I'll fix it." Jerek reached for the curl again.

"Leave it for now." Eve tucked the hair back under her hat. "Let's see how long it lasts."

"As you wish." Jerek bowed.

"Can everyone else put in their earpieces?" Ford said. "I want to run a soundcheck."

Grace and Ari reached for the tray at the same time. Grace pulled her hand away, letting Ari take hers first.

"Now, you'll all be able to hear me," Ford said. "And I'll be able to hear all of you. And I can add Ari or other people's vocals to the mix if they need everyone to hear them. And take them out, too. But hopefully it'll just be me and Ari in your ear."

"Like a little guardian angel shoved in my ear canal," Jack said.

"Yours won't work until you're near the gardens, but yes," Ford said. "And I'll text you. Or call you. I mean—I just—I promise to keep in touch."

"Can we check the earpieces and get on with this?" Eve said.

"Right." Ford clicked a button on the side of his earpiece. "DJ Cricket to the Extreme Quest Team."

"That cannot be our team name," Ari said.

"It can for tonight." Ford grinned. "Extreme Quest Team, prepare for Operation Snatch Cinderella."

23

Ari

The weight of the rice-filled stockings stuffed in Ari's bra pressed against her chest, a scratchy reminder of all the reasons why Ariel Love, half-mer div, shouldn't be going to the Greenwood Gardens Gala. The hotel door slid open and shut behind her as a pair of somb guests meandered out to their car.

Ari checked her phone. Her ride was already three minutes late.

"Shit." She paced in front of the hotel's automatic doors, making them open and shut with a half-hearted whoosh each time she passed.

The plan is good. Stick to the plan.

They'd decided not to risk using the van. Even if Jerek changed the paint color, the vintage VW was too recognizable after their escape from the Museum of Magic. Lincoln and Grace would arrive at the party in the car Jack had *procured* for them after they'd dropped off Eve and Ford and left Jerek at another hotel.

Scattered arrivals. No hint of a pack of teenagers crashing the party reserved for the wealthy, fabulous, and likely to donate tons of money to Greenwood Gardens. A good plan. A great plan.

Unless my ride never shows.

"Shit."

The hairs of her wig tickled her neck, their unfamiliar texture and length grating the last of her nerves.

The hotel doors opened and closed again.

A man in a three-piece suit strolled out of the hotel. He stopped in Ari's path, took a moment to unlock his Audi, then looked Ari's way, giving her an apologetic nod like he'd just noticed he was blocking her path.

His gaze flicked from her teal eyes to her rice-stuffed breasts and back again.

Ari held his gaze, wishing she were capable of wearing tinted contacts.

"Waiting for your ride?" The man flipped the loop of his car key around his finger.

"Rideshare." Ari shrugged. "I should've requested the car arrive earlier."

"Where are you heading?" The man furrowed his brow. His face didn't seem accustomed to portraying worry, as though his twenty-ish years had been filled with untainted ease.

"Some greenhouse gala thing." Ari shrugged. "Mother couldn't make it and felt too guilty to cancel her ticket at the last minute."

"The Greenwood Gala?"

"That sounds right."

"I don't think the Greenwood board would have cared if she

canceled her ticket as long as she sent a donation." The man smiled.

"I tried to tell Mother that." Ari stepped closer to the man and leaned in to speak in a low, conspiratorial whisper. "She married into the social set. Twenty-some years later, she's still worried Daddy's friends won't like her."

"I've been tagging along to my father's charity board meetings since I started college." The man glanced around before taking his turn to lean toward Ari. "I promise I'm speaking from experience when I say your mother is right to worry. The board wouldn't care, but the crones might chatter. There's something about doing good works that seems to sharpen claws and speed rumors."

"Then I really will have to be on my best behavior." Ari winked.

Her phone dinged.

DJ Cricket is ready to mix. A few seconds passed before Ford sent another message. *Dagonet and Firefly coming in clear.*

Ari swiped over to the rideshare app. Her car still showed as two minutes away.

"Everything all right?" the man asked.

"I'm fine. My driver's another issue."

"Huh?"

"If the map is right, my driver's been stuck in a time loop four blocks away."

"The old time loop, eh?" he laughed. "I don't think car insurance covers that."

"Nope. I just hope the Gala won't run out of hors d'oeuvres. Mother promised I'd get snacks if I was a good little girl."

"I'll make sure they don't run out." He gave her a tiny salute.

Ari's phone dinged again.

Chameleon coming in clear.

"I'll see you at the party." The man started toward his car. "Watch out for time loops along the way."

Another message from Ford popped up on her screen. *Little Red coming in clear.*

"Actually"—Ari took two steps toward the man, feeling the heft of the daggers strapped to her thighs—"would you mind if I rode over with you? I'm starting to think my car's never going to show."

"Sure." The man turned around, offering Ari a smile. "I'm always willing to help a damsel in distress."

"Thank you." Ari cut across the parking lot, hurrying toward the man's car as he looped around to open the passenger-side door.

"I'm Regi, by the way." Regi opened Ari's door.

"I'm Juliet." Ari angled her hand as she reached for him, letting Regi choose whether he wanted to shake or...he kissed the back of her hand. "Juliet Rose."

24

Grace

Valets in forest-green vests waited in front of the Greenwood Gardens welcome center. A subtle tip jar had been attached to the side of their podium, and the man in charge of handing out valet tickets kept checking the phone he'd hidden beneath his clipboard, like people wouldn't know exactly what he was doing.

"Are you ready?" Lincoln asked.

"Yeah." Grace unbuckled her seatbelt, barely resisting the urge to jump out of the car and bolt as they reached the front of the line.

"This is DJ Cricket taking over the airwaves. Give me a *hell yeah* if you can hear me, party people." Ford's voice crackled in Grace's ear.

"Hell yeah, we're ready," Lincoln said.

"Hell yeah," Grace murmured.

A valet opened Grace's door. "Welcome to Greenwood Gardens."

"Thanks." Grace climbed out of the car, taking the valet's offered hand.

He had a faint trace of scruff on his chin and a pierced left ear. His shirt had been badly ironed. Everything about him looked so...normal.

"Enjoy your evening." The valet stepped back, ready for the next car in line.

"Shall we?" Lincoln placed his hand on Grace's back, guiding her toward the welcome center.

The doors had been propped open, like the people running the event were afraid that even the slight hinderance of waiting for a door to open might drive away their carefully selected guests.

Faint music tinkling from hidden speakers carried under the buzz of conversation in the lobby. Green-vested volunteers manned three podiums, checking guests in with their matching tablets. An archway to the left led to a massive gift shop. To the right, a small theatre offered a fourteen-minute video on the history of Greenwood Gardens.

"Welcome to Greenwood Gardens," the older woman at the podium said, her voice cheery even though her smile faltered as she stared at the tattoo that peeked up over Lincoln's collar. She ripped her gaze from Lincoln to smile at Grace. "May I have your last name?"

"Dagonet," Lincoln said.

"Of course." The woman gave up on looking at them to lock her eyes on her tablet. "Here you are. Have a lovely evening, Mr. Dagonet."

"We'll see how well stocked the bar is." Lincoln ushered Grace past the podium, keeping his hand on her back as they wound through the worst of the crowd and to the far side of the lobby.

The wide glass doors that led out to the gardens proper had been propped open too, letting the scent of the flowers waft into the welcome center.

Or maybe it wasn't the actual flowers. Maybe some volunteer had sprayed the room with special perfume before the guests arrived.

Outside, hundreds of candles in little glass lanterns led past the fountain garden and beds of spring blooms all the way to the massive conservatory, the candles' feeble glow trying to create its own kind of magic, even though the sun hadn't set.

Lincoln leaned close to Grace's ear. "Are you okay?"

Grace nodded.

"Just get to your position and keep an eye out," Lincoln whispered. "Everything is going to be fine. There's no reason to panic."

"I'm not panicking." A knot pressed against the front of Grace's throat. "It's just...they're normal people. Real, normal people."

She broke away from Lincoln, striding up the path to the conservatory without looking back.

25

Jerek

The music of the string quartet filled the courtyard outside the conservatory, reminding the guests to appreciate the massive urns of flowers flanking the doors before entering the gala proper. Jerek leaned against one of the high top tables around the perimeter of the space, humming along to the tune. The song was familiar enough he must have heard it several times when he was younger. Probably before his mother died—in the happy days when music filling the halls of Holden House was a regular occurrence.

A server stopped beside Jerek. "Canape?"

"No, thanks." Jerek gave the woman a fleeting smile before turning his attention back to the guests trickling up the candle-lined path.

The server moved on to the next table, offering them hors d'oeuvres, and getting rejected again.

At least I'm not stuck with a tray this time.

A jolt of something between hope and excitement hiccupped in Jerek's chest as Grace appeared on the path. The hem of her blue dress fluttered with each step as she strode toward the conservatory.

She stopped in front of the quartet, standing still as she looked around the courtyard. Her gaze caught on Jerek's.

He looked away, pressing his palms to the table, hoping Grace had the sense to keep looking around even after she'd spotted him.

By the time Jerek dared to glance back toward the musicians, Grace had disappeared.

Another server had approached, offered food, and been rejected before Lincoln walked up the path. He had a subtle bounce to his head as though his earbuds were actually playing music.

Well done, friend.

Lincoln cut straight toward a server and snagged two canapes from their tray, popping them both into his mouth before he'd even gone through the conservatory doors.

Two down, one to go.

Jerek drummed his fingers on the tabletop, fighting the urge to check his phone as the quartet began a new song.

"What kind of party doesn't have any gorgeous girls?" Jerek stared at the musicians, trying to look as though he were commenting on their performance.

The voice in his ear didn't respond.

Jerek peeled his hands off the table, digging his nails into his palms as anxiety mixed with magic in a way that put anything he touched in danger of being turned a violent red.

"If there's no chance of finding *Love* here, maybe I should go home," Jerek said.

The silence from his earpiece stretched on.

"Don't do this to me," he whispered.

"Juliet is within range."

Relief punched into Jerek's chest as Ford's tinny voice filled his right ear.

"She's talking to a man. No idea who, but he's traveling with her," Ford said. "Patching her into your earpiece now."

"—not what I wanted," Ari said, "but this party might be just what I've needed."

26

Ari

"I've just been so wrapped up in different projects, I haven't really taken the time to enjoy anything." Ari tipped her head back, looking up at the fading sky, letting Regi steer her down the candle-lined path as though it wasn't the first time they'd walked arm in arm.

"What sort of projects keep you so busy?" Regi asked.

"The top-secret kind." Ari winked. "I could tell you, but—"

"Then you'd have to kill me?" Regi furrowed his brow in overacted mock concern.

"More like lock you in a dungeon for your own protection."

"A dungeon?" Regi stepped out of the flow of guests, stopping beside the path that led to the fountain garden. "Is it an elevator leading deep underground to a high-tech facility situation, or a dank hole in the ground with chains attached to the wall situation?"

"I have access to both. So I guess it depends on what sort of mood I'm in."

The steady flow of the fountains shifted, fading for a moment before leaping twenty feet into the air. Colored lights shone from the center of each fountain, changing the hue of the columns of water as they began to sway.

Droplets caught on the breeze, flowing toward Ari, surrounding her in a cool mist as though the fountains were kissing her cheeks as they welcomed her to their home.

"From what I hear, the fountain garden is one of the projects this gala is raising money for," Regi said.

"To take the fountains out?"

"I think it's to install new pumps or something like that." Regi led Ari back onto the path, rejoining the flow of guests. "The fountain shows are too big a draw. They time the water to music, treat the whole thing like a fireworks display."

"I think a fountain show sounds better than fireworks," Ari said.

"You should come see it this summer," Regi said. "If your top-secret work allows."

"If my work's not done by then, the world may very well be doomed."

"Well, if society hasn't crumbled, I have two tickets to the 4th of July celebration. I'd be happy to have you as my guest."

"I might not be the best person to ask." Ari slowed her steps as they reached the courtyard, lingering beside the string quartet, letting blond-haired Jerek slip into the conservatory with a gaggle of older women.

"If you're not interested, I completely—"

"Oh, I'd love to go with you." Ari looked up at Regi, grateful for the shield of her glasses as she met his gaze. "I just can't promise I'll be here in July, and I don't want you to hold a ticket for me."

"I don't mind." Regi's eyes lit up, even though his face stayed perfectly calm. "We'll just keep in touch, and you can let me know when you finish your top-secret mission."

Ari bit her bottom lip, allowing two bars of music to pass before speaking. "That sounds great."

"Good." He bowed Ari toward the conservatory doors. "In the meantime, the invitation said there would be a band inside. Will you allow me to impress you with my less-than-mediocre dancing?"

"How could anyone refuse an offer like that?"

27

Eve

The branches of the tightly packed trees tugged at Eve's sleeves as she crept through the woods. She paused every ten steps, pulling out her earbuds and taking a moment to listen for guards or knights lurking in the growing shadows.

She wasn't alone in the trees.

The undergrowth shifted. The leaves rustled.

Nothing as clomping and clumsy as a human moved through the branches.

She tucked one earbud into her pocket and put the other back in place.

"We'll just keep in touch, and you can let me know when you finish your top-secret mission." A man's voice buzzed in Eve's ear.

"That sounds great," Ari said.

"Goes to kidnap someone, ends up with a date," Eve muttered.

"Not a real date." Ford's voice filtered over Ari's. "She's in character."

"Ari could be in character as an entrails-eating, bog monster, and she'd still have people fawning over her." Eve leaned against a tree to untie her boots.

"But would she be fawning over him?" Ford said. "That's the better question."

"This is gorgeous," Ari said. "I can't believe I've never been here."

"I'm honored to be the one to introduce you to the beauties of Greenwood," the man said.

"If you're tempted to rush in there and fight for her, don't." Eve pulled off her boots and tucked them behind a tree.

"Even if I wanted to, it wouldn't do any good. We've been over for a while. I'm just bad at letting go."

"I think acceptance is one of those steps you're supposed to go through. Guess you're progressing."

"I hope so," Ford said. "I don't want to miss something amazing because I'm clinging to something that's never going to happen."

A low laugh bobbled in Eve's throat as she slunk barefoot through the trees.

"—orchid is one of the rarest varieties," the man said.

"How do you know so much about flowers?" Ari asked.

Eve pulled out her earbud. The faint sounds of voices and music didn't fade. She closed her eyes, trying to judge where the nearest people were.

Too far away to spot her. Too near to risk going any closer to the path. She tucked her earbud back in place.

"—have to save the real treasure for later," the man said.

"Do I want to know what he means?" Eve jumped up, grabbing a tree branch and pulling herself up to perch twelve feet above the ground, tucked behind the leaves and out of sight of anyone passing by.

"You did promise me some less-than-mediocre dancing," Ari said.

"The hardest part about getting your heart broken is trying to let yourself care about someone new when you know you could get your heart broken again," Ford said.

"Sounds rough," Eve said.

"Have you ever had your heart broken?" Ford asked.

"I don't date."

"Why not? Is it against your pack's rules?"

"Gran would love for me to find a nice guy, but I'm more interested in vengeance than dating. I'll worry about love after I kill the butcher and tear open the throats of anyone who helped him murder my family."

28

Lincoln

The bartender hadn't even asked to see Lincoln's, or rather, Mr. Dagonet's ID. He'd just passed Lincoln a glass of wine and moved on to the next person desperate for a drink.

Lincoln weaved through the guests, cutting around the curve of the atrium to his planned position near the band that played beside of the southern waterfall.

The cluster of dancers in the center of the atrium hadn't grown beyond a dozen couples, leaving everyone else either at the high top tables near the northern waterfall or wandering the smaller gardens scattered throughout the conservatory.

Lincoln searched the crowd for any hint of fellow Maree trying to blend in with the sombs. The only familiar—or newly familiar—face he found was Grace, who had already taken her position across from him in front of a wall coated in flowers and vines.

She fidgeted with her hair, constantly glancing toward the path that led to the front of the conservatory as though waiting for a chance to run.

Relax, Grace.

He let out a long breath, like she might be able to sense him trying to calm her from across the room.

She started tugging on the front of her hair, like she wanted to stretch it back to the length it had been a few hours before.

"That wallflower is looking a bit antsy." Lincoln raised his wine to his lips. "Wish she had a friend to tell her to calm down."

"Firefly, this is DJ Cricket, you okay?" Ford's voice broke through the constant droning of the man near Ari's mic.

Grace turned away from Lincoln to face the wall of vines.

"Do they always have lights in the trees?" Ari's voice, light and playful, carried over the com. "Or do they only create a fairy land when there are donors around?"

"Dagonet, Firefly says she's fine," Ford said. "She also asked me to tell you to...well, to mind your own business. Firefly didn't use those words, but close enough."

"I didn't think there would be an actual party," Ari said.

The band's music filtering through Lincoln's earbuds muddied the man's reply.

Lincoln glanced toward the entrance of the atrium.

Ari stood at the edge of the path, arm in arm with a man Lincoln had never seen before.

"Does this mean it's time for mediocre dancing?" She looked to the man with a glint of laughter in her eyes.

"And spoil my chances of getting a second date with you?" the man said.

"Is this a date now?" Ari took the man's hand, luring him toward the dance floor.

"I'd like it to be," the man said. "If you're interested."

"Dance with me and I'll let you know."

The man stepped in front of Ari, taking the lead as he chose a position on the edge of the dancers right in front of the band.

She laughed as he twirled her into his arms.

"Don't get excited," the man said. "That's the only move I know."

Ari took his hand, settling it on her hip. "Well, this is step one."

"Any sign of Cinderella?" Ford's voice cut over Ari's.

Lincoln tore his gaze from Ari to scan the space. "Nothing."

"No sightings from anyone yet," Ford said. "Don't worry, she'll show."

Lincoln scanned the space again, searching for any hint of Mariah Chanler and whatever entourage was bound to follow in her wake.

Ari's laugh carried over the music.

Lincoln looked back to her without even meaning to.

She turned her head coyly to the side as she laughed again, leaning close enough to the man her cheek nearly rested on his shoulder.

The man watched her in wonder, like he couldn't quite understand how such an exquisite beauty had ended up in his arms.

An odd ache that bordered on painful twisted in Lincoln's chest.

Ari was the most beautiful and entrancing person in the room. Even with the glasses and wig covering so much of her face, everyone around her kept glancing her way, captivated by a girl they didn't even know.

The song ended, but she didn't break away from the man. She stayed in his arms, like she'd forgotten that dancing was the only reason she'd been so close to him.

"A-one, two, three—" The bandleader counted in a new song.

"I'll have to apologize to my mother," Ari said.

"Why's that?" The man's hand drifted from Ari's hip to the small of her back.

"If I'd have known tonight would be fun, I wouldn't have made her bribe me into coming."

"I'm glad you took the bribe."

"Chameleon has eyes on Cinderella," Ford said. "Entering the atrium now."

Lincoln shifted, angling himself to watch the band and the path beyond, still keeping Ari in his peripheral vision.

Four men wearing plain black suits, too familiar to not have been made by a Maree tailor, entered the atrium. They shifted to the side, flanking the walkway.

Mariah Chanler stepped beyond the shadows of the path, letting the glittering lights hanging from the ceiling catch on the sheen of her floor-length, red gown, ignoring the stares of the middle-aged women as they ogled Louis Chanler, handsome widower and potential mass murderer.

29

Ari

Regi twirled Ari under his arm, catching her even closer to him than she'd been dancing before. Beads of sweat sparkled on his brow, but he kept beaming at her.

She let herself drift closer still.

The musk of his cologne tempered the sweet fragrance of the flowers that filled the conservatory.

The horn player took over the melody.

Regi furrowed his brow, shifting his hold on Ari's hand to twirl her again.

As she spun, a flash of red caught her eye.

She stepped past Regi, positioning herself so he'd have to face away from the path leading into the atrium if he wanted to hold her.

Ari swayed with him for a moment before daring to glance past his shoulder.

Mariah Chanler sauntered to the center of the atrium on

her father's arm. Her gaze swept over the crowd. A little wrinkle formed between her eyebrows in a way that could have been either judgment of the guests or worry that she hadn't spotted one guest in particular.

She let go of her father, abandoning him to promenade in front of the high top tables on the northern side of the atrium. Mariah met the gazes of the people who stopped to watch her, tantalizingly aware of her beauty, graciously accepting the effect it had on the sombs around her.

Ari leaned closer to Regi, hiding her face behind his as Mariah looked their way.

"Is there dancing at the 4th of July party?" Ari let her fake, rice-filled breasts brush against Regi's chest as she spoke close to his ear, making sure he would hear her over the music.

"Not really. But if you're willing to put up with my bad dancing, I know some places in New York we could go."

"New York?" Ari leaned back, catching a glimpse of Mariah as she wound her way to the western side of the atrium.

"Manhattan," Regi said. "I'm a student there."

"Dancing in Manhattan. Sounds like fun."

"I could show you the real New York, hidden away from the tourist crowds." Regi tipped his head. A lock of hair fell across his forehead.

"You had me at dancing." She brushed the hair away from his brow.

"Juliet, I—"

"Cinderella has left the atrium." Ford's voice pounded into Ari's ear.

"What?" Ari froze.

"I'm just"—Regi tucked Ari's wig hair behind her ear, dangerously close to the earpiece that had gone horribly silent—"I've never been so grateful for a late car pickup."

"Me either." Ari leaned away, trying to look shy as she searched for a beauty in a red dress.

"You can tell me you're done with me for the night whenever you want." Regi loosened his hold on her, giving her room to escape. "But if you'd like, maybe we could dance a few more songs, get a drink and talk. Or there's another band by—"

"Cinderella is in the rose garden," Ford shouted.

"Let's go to the rose garden." Ari trailed her fingers across Regi's chest and slid her hand down his arm, locking her fingers through his. "I've heard it's exquisite."

"Like something out of a dream." Regi placed his free hand behind her waist, keeping their fingers laced together. He led her through the dancers, his chest puffed up with grandiose pride, as though he were escorting a princess to her bower.

30

Jerek

Louis Chanler headed straight for the bar, not bothering to stop and speak to the wealthy sombs who could never understand that, rich or not, the Chanlers had no place at the Greenwood Gardens Gala.

The four Maree in matching black suits split off into pairs, two of them following Mariah as she cut across the atrium, the remaining two keeping close enough to Louis that the other guests waiting at the bar cleared a path, allowing Chanler to stroll right up to the bartender.

Jerek cut around the bar to the northern waterfall. He leaned against the rocks at the edge of the pool, peering behind the bar as though trying to see which liquors had been stocked.

Louis Chanler's lips were flattened into one, narrow line. He drummed his fingers on the bar top as he watched the bartender mix his martini.

But there was something in his face that made the cause of

his furrowed brow seem deeper than annoyance at his drink not being instantly placed in his hand. And a sallow hue had tainted his face, marring the well-maintained bronze.

Good.

Though vengeance had never been Jerek's primary aim, Chanler worrying his way through sleepless nights did hold a certain, undeniable appeal.

"Cinderella has left the atrium." Ford's voice crackled in Jerek's ear.

His heart flipped up into his throat. He cut through the growing crowd around the bar, walking in the direction Mariah had been heading.

A shock of red cut through the dim light in the entrance of the rose garden.

"I've got eyes on her." Jerek scratched his nose to cover the movement of his lips. "She's in the rose garden."

"Is Firefly following her?" Ford asked.

Jerek changed his path, heading toward the green wall on the far side of the waterfall that had been Grace's assigned post. It took him a moment to spot her, even though he'd been the one to lighten her hair.

She sat on the edge of the pool at the base of the waterfall, her hands soaking in the water.

"Cinderella is in the rose garden," Ford shouted.

"I found Firefly," Jerek said.

"Is she following Juliet?" Ford asked.

"No," Jerek said.

"Juliet is going after Cinderella," Ford said. "Someone needs to stay with her."

Jerek turned back toward the entrance of the rose garden in time to watch Ari stroll down the path. The golden threads in her dress glittered beneath the lights dripping from the top of the atrium, as though she needed the dress's help to capture the attention of everyone around her so she could prove the inescapable enchantment of her beauty.

The man she'd entered the party with seemed to have realized the gem he'd stumbled upon. He kept his hand behind her back as they walked, guarding her as though the potential theft of his dance partner were the true danger of the evening.

Ari didn't pause or check the shadows for guards before stepping into the rose garden.

"Ari," Jerek murmured.

"What is it?" Ford said. "What's wrong?"

Lincoln weaved through the crowd, not slowing until he reached the entrance of the rose garden.

"Dagonet is with Juliet." Jerek scratched his nose again.

"Okay." Ford's sigh carried over the com. "Okay. What about Firefly?"

"I've got Firefly," Jerek said. "Keep your ears on Juliet."

He cut back to the northern waterfall, stopping beside the green wall to plant himself ten feet away from Grace, right in her line of sight. He pulled a coin from his pocket, tossing it to land in the pool right beside her hands.

She looked up at him.

Tears streamed down her face, leaving smears of makeup below her eyes.

She met Jerek's gaze, staring at him for a moment as though trying to process who he was, before mouthing, "I can't make it stop."

Grace lifted her hands from the water. Sparks danced across her fingertips.

31

Ari

The person who'd designed the rose garden seemed to have had moonlit romance in mind. Benches had been tucked into shadowy corners, shielded by trellises dripping with flowers. The fountain at the center of the garden had a wide rim, perfect for sitting to enjoy the blooms if you didn't mind people watching you.

A series of statues circled the outside of the path. The Red Queen and her card soldiers took up half the niches between trellises, while less recognizable characters filled the rest. Bronze plaques dotted the periphery of the space, explaining each of the statues and giving shy guests an excuse for wandering as they searched for a private nook that had yet to be claimed.

Mariah Chanler stood at the plaque farthest from the atrium, trailing her fingers across the words etched into the bronze. In the dim light, the red of her dress seemed deeper.

Less like an heiress allowing her beauty to entrance all she passed, and more like a warrior queen—her gown dyed with the blood of the fools she'd slain.

"This is one of my favorite gardens in Greenwood." Regi led Ari to the fountain.

Mariah's Maree guards had positioned themselves six feet away from her on either side, flanking their charge in a far from subtle way.

"Look down there." Regi pointed into the basin of the fountain.

Below the water, a tiled mosaic told the story of Romeo and Juliet in eight stages. The images circled the fountain, leaving the start of the romance right beside the lovers' doom.

"I suppose it's only right for a place this beautiful to have a bit of tragedy." Ari let Regi ease closer, so the back of her shoulder pressed against him.

"How do you mean?"

"Even beautiful things end." Ari turned to face him. "It's the tragedy of an inevitable end that makes beauty precious."

"I'd never thought of it that way."

Ari's breath caught in her chest as Regi gazed deep into her eyes.

He dipped his chin, lowering his lips toward hers.

"Are all the plaques about the statues?" Ari turned her face away from his, looking toward the nearest plaque.

"There are a few quotes, too. From love stories, mostly."

Ari took a step toward the plaque.

Regi let go of her hand. "Juliet, if I made you uncomfortable, I'm truly sorry."

Ari reached back for him, not looking his way until he stood beside her. "It's not you."

She guided him to stand in front of her, placing him as close as he'd been before. She trailed her finger along his chin, enjoying the smooth skin of his freshly shaved face.

She leaned in to whisper in his ear. "I don't know who here might be one of my mother's biddies."

Mariah moved on to the next plaque in the circle, stopping right beside the artfully subtle emergency exit.

"If someone sends my mother a picture of me kissing a strange man at a gala, I'll still be locked in my room when July 4th rolls around." Ari stayed close to him for another moment. "I wonder which quotes were romantic enough to deserve plaques."

She led him onto the path that circled the edge of the garden, glancing at the plaques instead of slowing to peer into the shadows beneath each of the trellises.

"What's your favorite quote from Romeo and Juliet?" Ari stopped in front of the last plaque Mariah had been reading.

"*He that is strucken blind cannot forget the precious treasure of his eyesight lost.*" Regi furrowed his brow. "Not very romantic."

"In a grim sort of way, it is."

"What's your favorite?"

Ari crossed in front of Mariah's guard as though she hadn't noticed the hulking Maree. "*Did my heart love till now? Forswear it, sight! For I ne'er saw true beauty till this night.*"

Mariah froze.

"It wasn't my favorite quote until a few days ago," Ari said. "Someone sent it to me as a message. Now I can't get it out of my head."

"He sent you a quote like that but didn't come as your date tonight?" Regi said. "Not that I'm complaining."

"Her father would never allow it," Ari said. "We met at a party that ended badly. She'd have to run away if she wanted to be with me. I'm not sure she's willing to risk that much, even if it would be a breathtaking tale of star-crossed lovers."

"I'm sorry." Regi pressed Ari's hand to his lips. "And very grateful."

Ari took a step back, pulling Regi with her as though ready to lead him into the shadows. She took another step and stumbled, tripping right into Mariah Chanler.

32

Ari

"Sorry. I'm so sorry." Ari let go of Regi and turned toward Mariah.

"Step back." Both Maree moved closer.

"Sorry." Ari took Regi's elbow, pulling him around to the far side of the plaque, using it as a pathetic barrier between them and the Maree.

"It's fine." Mariah leaned against the plaque, like she was afraid to stand on her own. "Just an accident."

"Did I hurt your shoes?" Ari said. "I'd be happy to get them cleaned, or I could replace them."

"It—it's fine." Mariah stared at Ari with a heart-stopping blend of hope and confusion filling her eyes. "I didn't think you'd come."

Ari's heart rocketed up into her throat. She adjusted her glasses and turned her forced laugh into a strained giggle. "There aren't many young people here, are there?"

The Maree inched closer.

"I almost refused when my mother decreed I come tonight." Ari took Regi's hands and wrapped his arms around her waist. "I'm so glad I let her bribe me into it."

"Me too." Regi beamed down at her.

"Right." The hope faded from Mariah's eyes. "I'll leave you two alone."

"You were here first," Regi said.

"This is a spot for romance, and that's not on the menu for me," Mariah said.

"Of course it is." Ari let go of Regi and reached for Mariah's hand. Regi kept his arms around her waist even as Mariah placed her hand in Ari's. "Fate can find you in the strangest places. Maybe you'll meet the one you're meant to love while standing in line for the ladies' room." Ari squeezed Mariah's hand.

"I'll keep that in mind." Mariah slid her hand free. "I should go find my father."

"I hope you enjoy the rest of the party," Ari said.

Mariah nodded. She looked down at the plaque for a moment, then turned to leave.

"Just don't forget," Ari said, "anything is possible. It all depends on whether or not you're willing to take a risk and give Cupid a chance."

Mariah walked away, leaving the rose garden without looking back.

A shadow by the path to the atrium shifted, then froze as Mariah and one of her two Maree guards passed.

The other guard positioned himself by the fountain, keeping Ari and Regi in his line of sight.

"Poor girl," Ari said. "I hope she has some friends here that can keep an eye on her."

"She seemed okay," Regi said.

"Cinderella is watching the band." Ford spoke in Ari's ear.

The Maree shifted his stance, giving up any pretense of not watching Ari as he planted his feet like he'd decided to become one with the rose garden.

Shit.

"Have you two met before?" Regi asked.

"No." Ari turned to him. "Just sympathy for a girl who didn't end up catching a ride with a stranger." She placed her hands on his chest, letting a grin curve her lips as she backed him into the shadows hidden behind a rose trellis.

33

Grace

The sparks leaping from Grace's fingertips didn't seem bothered by the flow of cool water washing over her hands. They burst into being and let themselves be swept away. The glowing proof of the magic she couldn't contain would be sucked down into the pump that powered the waterfall.

I'm going to catch the conservatory on fire.

A whimper broke through the panic clenching Grace's throat.

"Breathe, Grace," Jerek whispered. "Let yourself take control."

She tried to inhale, but her lungs wouldn't expand.

"I'm right here." Jerek sat on the edge of the waterfall beside Grace, placing himself in front of her hands like he could hide the horrible truth from the normal party guests. "There's nothing to worry—"

Jerek straightened up, tipping his head as though listening to a voice in his ear.

"What is it?" Grace whispered. "I can't hear anything."

A crease pinched between Jerek's eyebrows. "I don't like it."

"What?" The sparks brightened, sending their light glittering through the pool below the waterfall. "Shit."

"You're the omniscient one," Jerek said.

Grace tipped her head to her shoulder, trying to push her earpiece farther in without taking her hands out of the water. The uncomfortable pressure of the earpiece was still there, but all the voices had gone silent.

She couldn't remember when she'd stopped being able to hear Ari.

Jerek leaned away from Grace to peer through the crowd. She followed his gaze.

Mariah Chanler strolled across the atrium, one bodyguard trailing behind her.

"No, I've got eyes on her," Jerek said. "I'll follow."

"What?" Grace reached for Jerek's arm. The sparks dancing between her fingers crackled in the open air. She plunged her hand back into the water.

"We can't lose Cinderella." Jerek stood and straightened his suitcoat.

"Don't leave. You can't leave me."

"Someone has to follow her and you're in no fit state," Jerek said. "If she disappears, this whole night was for nothing."

"There are sparks flying out of my hands, Jer—"

"We can't risk being recognized. I've already spent too long near you." Jerek eased away from Grace, still watching Mariah freakin' Chanler. "Shove your hands under your arms to hide the sparks and go find a quiet corner where no one can see you. Try to calm down. Get the sparks to stop, then go back to the car. Lincoln will meet you there when it's over."

"I can't just hide magic in my armpits." Tears burned in Grace's eyes. "I need help. Please."

Jerek glanced down at her. "You'll be fine. I have faith in you."

He strode away, pausing long enough to claim a flute of champagne from a caterer's tray before following Mariah Chanler onto the treelined path leading to the front of the conservatory.

"Shit." Grace forced her lungs to take in as close to a full breath as she could manage before pulling her hands out of the water and shoving them into her armpits.

She gasped as the sparks burned her skin.

"Shit. Shit." She stood, trying to remember the conservatory map well enough to guess where she could find an abandoned corner to hide the magic she couldn't control.

The sparks got hotter, feeding on her panic.

She sat back down, plunging her hands into the water as a sob born of fear and pain tore from her throat.

34

Eve

Even in the dark, the woods beside the over-manicured garden couldn't pass for a real forest. It wasn't just the two kinds of music filtering into the trees, or even the hum of too many voices.

The place felt sterile. The trees too trimmed. The ground too well-cleared. The air smelled of flowers but not the necessary stench of decay, like the gardeners had forgotten that death fed life.

Eve pulled the curl Jerek had changed to silver out from under her hat. The hair still matched the color of the moonlight.

Wolves aren't built for patience.

She shoved the curl back under her hat.

"...not going to be happy if I screw this one up," a voice emerged from the muddied hum of the party.

"You can buy her a present in the morning." A second voice broke out of the chaos. "Just get up early, grab something from the store, and pick up breakfast on your way home. Bam, looks like you planned it."

"How long do you think they're going to keep us here tonight?" the first person asked.

"Who cares? We're getting double pay," the second said. "If some rich twit wants to pay out the ass so we can keep his little princess safe from all the big scary old ladies at the party, I'll walk loops through the gardens until dawn."

Two sets of footfalls passed on the path just beyond the trees.

"Man, I'm not gonna get any sleep tonight."

"Sleep when you're dead. Right now, take the easy money."

"You're right. I know you're right."

The voices faded back into the hum of the party.

"DJ Cricket," Eve whispered, "I think we have a problem."

35

Ari

Of all the people to have their hand sliding toward her breast, Regi wasn't the worst to be stuck in the shadows with. His lips were firm and practiced as he kissed her. His tongue teased her lips instead of ramming into her mouth. He kept one hand on the small of her back, using his strength to support her as he moved on to kissing the side of her neck.

All in all, if Ari hadn't been busy watching the unmoving shadow of the Maree standing guard by the fountain, Regi's lips trailing across her collarbone as his thumb grazed the side of her breast might have been a delightful way to spend an evening.

Regi shifted his hand forward. The pleasant tingle of his touch disappeared as he caressed the rice-packed front of her bra.

Ari grabbed his hand, pulling it to rest below her hip as she reclaimed his lips.

"Juliet." A glorious little moan caught in his throat as he slid his hand down her thigh, his fingers reaching dangerously close to the dagger strapped to her leg.

She laced her fingers through his hair as she pulled just far enough away from him to give a pleased sigh and catch a glimpse of the Maree.

The knight's polished, bald head glinted in the dim light like a voyeuristic beacon. The only move he'd made was shifting three feet to the right to get a clearer view of Ari and Regi tucked behind the trellis.

Guests prowled through the rose garden as well. Some reading the plaques, most moving from niche to niche, searching for a hiding place of their own. More than one couple paused, as though hesitant to pass by the Maree even though they had no way of knowing he was a trained knight who undoubtedly had weapons hidden at his hips.

He probably had some sort of blades strapped to his ankles as well.

How many weapons could I hide if I wore a suit instead of a dress?

Ari shifted her hips, checking the tension of the straps holding the daggers to her thighs.

Regi's passion rose. He pulled Ari closer, nearly lifting her as he backed her toward the pedestal in the corner of the niche.

The edge of the stone pressed against the small of Ari's back.

Regi moved his hand to the nape of her neck.

She looped her arms over his, pressing her rice-filled breasts to his chest, blocking him from feeling the netting in the back of her wig.

He grabbed the tops of her thighs, scooping her up and setting her on top of the podium.

She tipped her head back, daring him not to kiss her neck as she chanced another glance at the Maree.

The knight had moved away from the fountain, coming closer as though wanting to be sure he didn't miss the show.

Creeper.

Regi kissed the side of Ari's neck, claiming the softness of her skin with the lust of a blood-starved vampire. Heat and panic throbbed through Ari as he laid his hand on the bare skin of her leg, starting below her knee, slowing trailing his fingers up as he leaned closer to her, parting her thighs with his hips.

His fingers grazed the lower strap that held the dagger on her thigh.

"Regi." Ari froze, ready for him to flip up the hem of her skirt and flash the magic-wrought dagger to the Maree.

"Juliet." He breathed her name, not seeming to care about the straps on her thigh as he teased her ear with his tongue. He pulled her forward, wrapping her legs around him.

"Cinderella has gone for a potty break." Ford's angelic voice sounded in Ari's ear.

"Thank you," Ari whispered.

"Tell me what you want." Regi locked his hips against hers.

"A minute." Ari took his chin, tipping his face so she could look into his eyes. "I just need a minute."

"I'm sorry." Regi leaned back, granting an inch of air between them. "I thought you were into it."

The Maree came closer still, casting a shadow across the opening of their niche.

Ari tightened her legs around Regi, pressing his hips against her. She kissed him, letting him gasp before she pulled just far enough away to speak. "I didn't say I was done." She brushed her lips against his. "I just need a minute."

"Okay." Regi rested his forehead against hers. His uneven breathing rasped in his throat. "Whatever you need."

"I'll be back." Ari freed Regi from between her legs and slid off the podium. "Don't let anyone steal our spot."

She kissed him one more time before stepping toward the trellis. She stopped to brush out her skirt and give a look over her shoulder to the poor boy clinging to the stone podium as though his legs might give out. Giving Regi a wink, she sauntered past the Maree.

The guests moving through the rose garden glanced Ari's way as she passed, as though they knew exactly what had almost happened in the shadows at their fancy gala.

Ari swallowed her laugh as she tried to suss out if the old woman staring at her with wide eyes and a gaping mouth was appalled or remembering a passionate tryst from her youth.

Ari paused at the end of the path to the atrium, giving one more look behind to make sure the bald Maree hadn't followed, biting her bottom lip as though longing to run back into the shadows and devour Regi.

The Maree had returned to his place beside the fountain, like he was going to wait and see if he could catch any more of the shadowy floorshow.

Sorry, Regi.

Ari cut across the atrium, weaving through the pack of dancers, which had tripled while she'd been giving Regi a night he'd either dream about or curse for years to come.

"Thanks for the rescue, DJ." Ari tipped her head, hiding her face behind the curtain of her wig's hair. "One more minute and actually having sex with Regi might have been the only option."

"I just interrupted the most amazing night of that poor guy's life," Ford said.

"If we weren't trying to save the fcu, I'd feel bad for using him as a prop," Ari said.

"I don't think he minded playing the part."

Ari reached the far side of the atrium. The urge to scan the space, just to make sure she hadn't been abandoned by everyone but Ford, prickled at her lungs.

"You okay?" Ford asked.

"Sure. Just stay with me."

"Of course. It would be wrong to kidnap a fairytale princess without a narrator chirping in your ear."

36

Lincoln

The bench tucked between two stone statues of sword-wielding playing cards didn't provide a clear enough view of the niche across the way to suit Lincoln's Maree training. Even if his fellow knight hadn't been inching closer to the niche like a starved pup who'd scented a bone, and guests hadn't been strolling through the dim light of the rose garden, the shadows behind the trellis were too dark to allow either thorough surveillance or the safe aiming of a weapon.

The view was still too clear.

Lincoln sat with his elbows resting on his knees, trying to look bored. Only interested in the music in his earbuds. Bitter at having been forced to attend the gala.

The ivory of Ari's dress shifted in the shadows. The dark suit of the man blocked more of her from view as he backed her into the corner.

Lincoln's leg began to bounce. He sat up straighter, digging his nails into his knees, trying to dampen the energy that threatened to burst out of him.

Ari's gold shoes left the ground as the man lifted her.

The Maree took a full step toward the niche, abandoning subtlety as he watched the shadowy show.

I should have a weapon. I should have found something to bring as a weapon.

He could leap up onto the rim of the fountain, cut behind the Maree and attack from above. If he could get the Maree to the ground before he could call for help—

The hem of Ari's dress shifted as the man moved his hand up her thigh. Her gasp pounded through Lincoln's earpiece.

A fire alarm.

There had to be a fire alarm he could pull. Have everyone evacuate the conservatory. Grab Mariah in the commotion.

The faint glimmer of the lights caught on Ari's shoes as she wrapped her legs around the man's hips.

There was an emergency exit across the room. That might sound an alarm.

He could run across the rim of the fountain, take down the Maree who was devouring the sight of Ari like he wanted to be sure he could explicitly remember the way her skirt shifted as the man pulled her hips toward his, shove open the emergency exit, and sound the alarm.

Ari would have to let go of the man to evacuate with everyone else. Then they'd grab Mariah and be done.

"Cinderella has gone for a potty break." Ford's voice crackled in Lincoln's ear.

"Thank you," Ari whispered.

Lincoln edged forward on the bench, ready to follow Ari out of the poorly lit rose garden from hell.

A tap on his shoulder sent Lincoln springing to his feet.

"Sorry dear. I didn't mean to scare you." An older woman

on the other side of the bench gave an apologetic smile as she spoke over Ari's voice in his ear. "You looked like you might be leaving."

"I didn't say I was done." The warmth of Ari's voice stabbed ice into Lincoln's spine.

"Are you done?" the woman asked.

"What?" Lincoln fixed his gaze on the woman's wrinkled face, trying to hear both her and Ari.

"Tsch." The woman mimed pulling out earbuds. "Technology complicates everything. Come on then." She mimed pulling out earbuds again as she shuffled around the bench. "You should hear the people you're talking to." She reached for his ears.

Lincoln pulled the earbuds out before she could snatch them. "Can I help you, ma'am?"

"I was wondering if you were done with your seat," the woman said. "There's a shocking lack of seating in the atrium."

"I'm actually waiting for someone," Lincoln said.

"Have they turned eighty?" the woman said. "Because I have. And after eighty, standing for long times—pfft—what disrespectful sort would expect me to stand?"

"Ma'am, I..." A hint of white caught Lincoln's eye.

Ari strode toward the path to the atrium alone, the man she'd been with left behind, cast aside in the shadows.

She looked back. She bit her bottom lip, a smile lighting her eyes as though she could taste the desire of the man who craved her.

"Young man," the woman said.

Still alone, Ari walked down the short path and disappeared into the atrium.

"Young man." The woman swatted Lincoln's arm. "Have you ruined your hearing by shoving those things into your ears? I'm telling you my feet are tired."

"Take the seat, ma'am." Lincoln bowed. "It would be better for everyone at the gala if you pursued solitary enjoyment for the rest of the party."

"What?" The woman's jowls sank as she frowned.

"Good evening." Lincoln shoved his earbuds back in and strode after Ari.

"One more minute and actually having sex with Regi might have been the only option." Ari's words crashed into Lincoln's ears.

37

Ari

The line for the ladies' room stretched down the stairs, cutting past the platform elevator and into the subterranean bathroom. Trying not to feel like she was descending into a cave of doom, Ari took her place with the other women, leaving her standing ten feet away from Mariah's Maree guard.

Ari ran her fingers through her wig, smoothing out the hair in what felt like a natural way.

The line inched forward.

She pulled out her phone, using the camera as a mirror so she could check her lipstick.

The Maree glared at the bathroom line, a hint of confusion wrinkling the corners of his eyes, as though he couldn't understand how getting in and out of a restroom could take so long.

Ari placed the tip of her tongue between her teeth, keeping

her face bland and mouth silent as the line shifted down another step.

"This is what happens when you set the minimum donation too low," a middle-aged woman said.

She walked side-by-side with another biddy near her age, who nodded solemnly at the first woman's words, completely ignoring the people in the bathroom line who had to cram themselves against the wall to let the pair pass.

"There used to be a certain *quality* expected of guests for these events." The woman kept talking. "Now it's just a mass of tax write-off-seeking riff-raff who flock straight to the free booze."

"Appalling." The second woman looked toward Ari as she passed, as though wanting to make sure Ari knew exactly where on the quality vs. riff-raff scale she landed.

If only you knew.

The line shifted forward again, letting Ari reach the bottom of the steps where she could see into the restroom. Fancy soap and real hand towels had been left out for the gala guests in a vague attempt to disguise the bathroom as something other than stalls visited by normal, low-class guests every day. They'd even placed a sign on the door at the far end of the stalls with *Emergency Exit Only* written on it in a swirling font surrounded by watercolor flowers.

A woman exited a stall and held the door open for Ari.

"I'm going to touch up first. Thanks though." Ari flashed the woman a quick smile and headed toward the mirror.

The gardens hadn't gone so far as to replace the fluorescent lights in the bathroom. Their harsh glow gave a distinct tinge to everything, glaring off Ari's glasses, leaving her face bordering on too pale and making the reddened skin around her lips even more obvious.

Ari laughed, drawing the attention of the woman at the

sink beside her. "I finally find a dress with pockets, and they still aren't big enough to fit everything I need." She spoke louder than necessary as she pulled her lipstick from the pocket in her dress that was barely big enough to squeeze her phone into.

"It's the price we pay for a flattering silhouette," the woman said.

"Could someone help me?" Mariah Chanler peeked out of a bathroom stall. She met Ari's gaze in the mirror. "I swear there's something wrong with this zipper. It keeps feeling like my dress might fall off any second."

"I've got you." Ari tucked her lipstick back into her too-small pocket. "I've got a knack for naughty zippers."

"My hero." Mariah backed into the stall, squeezing herself against the wall to let Ari join her.

"Is it one of those hidden side zippers? They really are the worst." Ari pushed the stall door closed behind her and turned the lock.

"It's you." Mariah took Ari's hand before Ari had managed to twist around to look at her. "You're really here."

"Whoever designed your dress needs a lesson in closures." Ari spoke loudly enough for the other women to hear before dropping her voice. "You really were asking me to come?"

"I didn't know how else to find you," Mariah whispered. "They took you up to LeBlanc's office and then everything went to hell. Did he hurt you? Did the Maree hurt you?"

"I got out before they had a chance."

"You got out? How?"

"Does it matter?"

Mariah loosened her grip on Ari's hand. "If you were with the people who murdered Maree at Daddy's party, then yes, it does."

"There was no murder." Ari shifted, easing closer to Mariah

while blocking her path out of the tiny stall. "The Maree attacked us. They nearly killed two of us."

"The Maree wouldn't just attack guests for no reason. Were you there to steal something? Did you just want to sabotage the museum opening?"

"It's not something I can explain in a somb-filled bathroom." Ari took Mariah's shoulders. Mariah didn't try to bat her away. "There is something very wrong in your house and you know it. I don't think you're safe, Mariah."

"That's ridiculous."

"Then why would you try and get me to come here tonight?"

Mariah looked away.

"You weren't shocked when I said I was with the party crashers at the museum opening," Ari said.

"Party crashing doesn't involve pools of blood on the floor."

"You knew I was with the crew who got in and out of the museum, and you still wanted to meet me. Not to turn me in or you wouldn't have crammed into this stall with me."

"I have Maree following—"

"You lured me here so I could get you out." Ari leaned into Mariah's view. "Away from the Maree. Away from LeBlanc."

"There is no getting away from LeBlanc." Mariah met Ari's gaze. "It's been worse since the museum opening. He has Maree watching Daddy and me all the time. He hasn't even bothered hiding how angry he is."

"Did he hurt you?"

"No." Tears pooled in the corners of Mariah's eyes. "But he told Daddy that isolating me is the only way to protect me. Keep me in my room. No phone, no contact with anyone outside the mansion."

"Why?"

"LeBlanc told Daddy he wants to keep me safe from people

like you. I've only managed to hold on to my phone because people might start to ask questions if I suddenly stop posting online right after the museum opening went so badly. We wouldn't have been allowed to come tonight, but Daddy and I have been attending the gala for years. I told LeBlanc my friends would worry if I didn't show up. He doesn't want anyone wondering why I've disappeared."

"Shit."

"You girls okay in there?" Someone tapped on the stall door.

Fear filled Mariah's eyes.

"The zipper caught on her bra," Ari said. "I think I've almost got it."

"Alright then," the woman said.

"I can get you out," Ari whispered. "Now. Tonight."

"What?"

"I have people to help us and a car waiting."

"I can't just run." Mariah looked past Ari to the stall door. "The idea is ridiculous."

"The idea is yours." Ari took Mariah's face in her hands. "You didn't try to get me here to check on me or hand me to the Maree. You want me to rescue you. And that's exactly what I came here to do."

"I..." Mariah started to tremble. "It's not even possible. LeBlanc hired extra somb guards. They're everywhere on the property."

"I'm not worried about it." Ari brushed Mariah's hair away from her cheek. "Tell me you want to come with me and let me handle the rest."

Mariah leaned her cheek against Ari's hand even as her trembling got worse.

"If you don't want to come with me, that's fine," Ari said. "But it's now or never."

"Give the code word if we're switching to plan b," Ford

whispered in Ari's ear. "I'll need two minutes to move the crew into their new positions."

"Goodbye, Mariah." Ari leaned in, giving Mariah one gentle kiss. "Be careful."

"I'll come with you." Mariah gripped Ari's hand. "Please don't leave me behind."

"Good." True relief melted through Ari's chest. "Just one question. How well can you run in heels?"

38

Jerek

He let his brow furrow as he headed toward the main doors of the conservatory, allowing the bit of his mind he'd been using to maintain a calm façade move on to more useful matters.

Near the doors, a cluster of middle-aged guests had gathered, standing too close to be a random grouping and too far apart to be a gaggle of chatting friends.

They're not Maree. You can't tell Grace to breathe if you're going to panic.

Jerek pulled his phone from his pocket, giving the screen a few taps before holding it to his ear.

"I'm telling you it's an oak tree." One of the men in the cluster pointed to a tree with wide, deep green leaves.

"And I'm telling you"—a woman pointed to the man—"you have the brain of a kakapo!"

The onlookers gasped.

"Hi DJ, I was hoping you'd keep a close eye on Firefly for me." Jerek cut a wide path around the group. "I'd like an update."

"I have been a patron of Greenwood Gardens for over a decade," the man said.

"Clearly, you haven't been utilizing their educational programming," the woman said.

"My name is on four different plaques. There is a bench—"

Jerek was out the door before the man could finish listing his philanthropic accomplishments.

"Can you hear me, DJ?" Jerek glanced at his phone as though checking for reception as he weaved through the guests enjoying the string quartet.

"Nothing coming from Firefly but sniffles," Ford said.

"Damn." Jerek cut around to the long southern side of the conservatory.

"What do you want me to do?" Ford asked.

"Keep an ear out. If the crying gets worse, try to keep her calm."

A moment passed before Ford spoke again. "There's no way Dagonet can get her out?"

"Not until Cinderella and Juliet are clear," Jerek said. "Firefly is on her own."

39

Ari

A tinge of guilt squirmed in Ari's stomach as she slipped Mariah's cell phone into the massive purse one of the women had left open on the bathroom counter. The woman was so focused on wrapping meringues in hand towels, she didn't even glance Ari's way as Ari tucked the phone beneath the layers of hoarded sweets.

Mariah took her time, staring at herself in the mirror as she washed her hands, fixed her hair, and checked her makeup.

"I need some fresh air." Ari reached for Mariah's hand. "Buddy system?"

Mariah held her own gaze in the mirror as she straightened the straps of her dress.

Take my hand. Don't make this hard, just take my hand.

"Sure." Mariah slipped her hand into Ari's. "I've put in enough face time to keep Daddy happy."

"Perfect," Ari said. "It's amazing that a glass building with so many trees can seem so stuffy."

Mariah's eyes widened as Ari led her toward the door with the handwritten *Emergency Exit Only* sign.

Ari winked as she pushed the door open, giving Mariah a moment to realize alarms hadn't begun to wail before dragging her out into the stairwell beyond.

The short set of stone steps cut up to the path that ran along the southern side of the conservatory, taking advantage of the slope the glass structure had been built upon.

Mariah jolted as the door closed behind them.

"I need you to trust me." Ari led Mariah up onto the path.

"I'm out here with you, aren't I?"

"And that's step one. Step two takes a bit more faith."

Ari stopped twenty feet away from the staircase, along the flat side of the wall that offered no niche to hide in, only thick shadows that somehow felt more dangerous than trying to escape in broad daylight.

A figure strolled toward them, phone pressed to his ear, walking as though oblivious to the world around him.

The details of Jerek's altered face weren't visible until he was ten feet from them. Even then, Mariah just stayed silently beside Ari, gripping her hand.

"This is perfectly safe," Ari whispered.

Jerek brushed his fingers against Ari's dress as he passed. Black devoured the ivory fabric, erasing the ingénue, leaving a darker, more dangerous heroine in her place.

"Who is he?" Mariah whispered.

"A friend," Ari said. "He needs to change your dress and your hair."

"My hair?" Mariah tightened her grip on Ari's hand.

"He can put it back later. But the less you look like you, the better off we'll be."

"Okay." Mariah gave a tremble that might have been an attempt at a nod. "Okay."

Jerek turned around, looping his path back toward the front of the conservatory. He slowed as he neared them, his phone still held to his ear. He reached out, brushing his fingers against the strap of Mariah's dress before grazing them against her hair.

Her hair darkened to a rich chestnut brown as her red dress became midnight blue.

"Chameleon's work is done." Jerek kept walking toward the front of the conservatory, not looking back to check his work.

40

Ford

The air beneath the thick, black blanket had turned from pleasant to stifling faster than Ford would be willing to admit to anyone. Sitting in the woods in a poorly built blanket fort was bad enough. Complaining about the arrangement might cause insurmountable humiliation or steal what little faith the rest of the crew had begun to grant him.

The light from the tablet had to be hidden. So, holing up under the blanket was necessary. And running tech for Operation Snatch Cinderella would help the crew and might even save the feu.

Really, the whole thing was a perfectly reasonable plan and well worth the itching from whatever had been biting the backs of his legs.

He held the tablet in one hand, swiping his other down the

backs of his legs in a vain attempt to avoid being unnecessarily feasted upon.

The six vertical bars on the tablet's screen had been labeled with everyone's code names. All the sound levels kept to a predictable pattern, except Grace's. The feed from her mic kept shooting up in odd spikes.

Ford dragged his finger up her bar, raising the volume on her feed. She gave a sob that turned into a cough. The cough turned into shaky breaths.

"Good enough, I guess." Ford lowered her volume to focus on the only channel with the constant rolling up and down of conversation.

"He can put it back later. But the less you look like you, the better off we'll be," Ari said.

"Let him do it," Ford whispered. "Just go along with it."

Ford held his breath, listening past the faint hum of music through Lincoln's mic and the painfully panicked breathing from Grace's.

"Chameleon's work is done," Jerek said.

"Yes, yes, yes!" Ford punched the roof of his blanket fort. "Sorry." He checked the corners of his shelter. "Sorry."

He shook out his shoulders and sat up straight. "And here we go." He cleared his throat and brought his own voice up on all channels. "Ladies and Gentlemen, stage one is complete. Cinderella is cleared for takeoff."

He pulled his voice back down. "God, I love my life."

41

Grace

"Cinderella is cleared for takeoff." Ford's voice sliced into Grace's ears.

She'd actually agreed to it. Mariah Chanler was going to walk away from her life and join the death-defying chaos of seven teens crammed into a VW van trying to save the world.

"All units, we are moving to phase two," Ford said. "It's glass slipper time, people."

Phase two.

Easy.

Her job was easy. Accomplishable. Just move one step at a time.

Grace's throat tightened as fresh tears welled in her eyes.

The flashes of light sparking through the water grew brighter.

The panic in Grace's chest rose, pressing on her throat, stifling her supply of air.

"I can do this," Grace whispered. "I can do this."

"What on earth are you doing?" An elderly man loomed over Grace, glaring at her in furious disgust as though he understood what a weak waste of magic she was. "If you aren't allowed to touch the plants, you most definitely aren't allowed to contaminate the waterfall. What kind of chemical are you using? Waterproof sparks may seem like a fun party trick, but tainting—"

"Don't lecture me." Grace stood, pulling her hands from the water and shoving them back under her arms to hide the sparks still flying from her fingers.

"Vandalism *and* attitude," the old man said. "Where are your parents, young lady? I hope they'll be mortified by your actions."

Grace met the man's gaze, refusing to look away even as he shrank into himself, cowering like he could see the danger of the magic she fought to control blazing in her eyes.

She opened her mouth, ready to say something witty and confident before striding away. She couldn't find any words. Panic and pain had stolen them all.

Ducking her chin to hide the tears sliding down her cheeks, Grace swallowed her sobs and cut through the high top tables toward the path that led out of the atrium.

Lincoln stood near the path, glass in hand as he nodded in time to the music like he was enjoying the band instead of watching Louis Chanler, making sure Chanler didn't notice his daughter was running away until it was too late to stop her.

Lincoln glanced toward Grace as she passed. A wrinkle pinched between his eyebrows.

Grace fixed her gaze on the floor, pretending she hadn't seen Lincoln mutter something to Ford.

Useless. Weak. A danger to the mission.

A hopeless wreck Jerek should have left in Florida. The last person in the world who should have access to the power the Fracture had stolen from magicians.

Lincoln could be muttering any of those things to Ford and all of them would be true.

The sparks pouring from Grace's fingers strengthened, searing the skin under her arms. A sob hitched in her throat as she started to run, heading toward the front of the conservatory.

"Firefly." Ford spoke in her ear. "What's going on? Are you okay?"

She yanked her earpiece out. The stench of burning hair surrounded her as she threw the tiny connection to Ford and the rest of the crew into the trees beside the path.

"What was that?" A woman spoke from behind Grace.

Grace kept running, hiding her hands as she bolted through the doors at the front of the conservatory and out into the night, fleeing as though it were her turn to be Cinderella.

42

Lincoln

The wine in Lincoln's hand smelled like a sad replica of home. Maybe not home, but the compound where he'd lived for most of his life.

If Jerek Holden hadn't plotted to lure Lincoln across an ocean and drag him into this mess, Lincoln would have spent the evening in the compound commons. The full-fledged Maree who weren't on duty would bring out carafes of wine. The ones who'd been training all day would feast from tables laden with food. A herd of children would be running around, terrifying their parents when they got too near the massive firepit that crackled at the center of it all, casting a flickering light that somehow made the scene feel separate enough from the somb world that pledging your life to a secret order of knights seemed like a normal thing to do.

A woman on the dance floor tripped over nothing, somehow

not spilling a drop of her martini as she stumbled to a stop right beside Louis Chanler.

The Maree guarding Chanler stepped toward the woman, ready to defend their charge, but Chanler shook his head, offering the woman a hand so she could steady herself.

She batted her eyes as she apologized to Chanler, laying her hand on his jacket-covered bicep in a way even a drunken squirrel would have recognized as her wanting to stumble all the way into Chanler's bed.

Grace cut through the crowd, heading toward the front of the conservatory, her hands tucked under her arms as though she were either pouting or freezing.

Lincoln dipped his chin toward his wine. "DJ Cricket, Firefly is on the move. Has the plan changed? Is Juliet—"

"Firefly is out of play, but the plan hasn't changed," Ford said. "Stay on Kahn."

"Was Firefly recognized?" Lincoln asked.

"More like a technical malfunction," Ford said. "Firefly is handled, focus on Kahn."

"Got it." Lincoln let his drink touch his lips, trying not to grimace at the overly sweet wine.

Chanler spent a few minutes chatting to the woman who'd *stumbled* into him. He made grand gestures toward the waterfalls on either side of the space, as though he himself had paid for their installation.

He might have. Their research for the mission hadn't covered why Mr. Chanler had chosen to grace Greenwood Gardens with his presence.

Chanler bowed away from the woman, gaining himself less than a minute of peace before another woman placed herself in his path.

The two Maree hovering nearby seemed to add to Chanler's appeal.

You're not a victim or a hero. Maree protection can't cleanse your sins.

The need to run forward and scream at his brethren scraped down Lincoln's spine. They had the right to know their charge might very well have caused the deaths of hundreds of Knights Maree. Even if Chanler hadn't been the one to cast the curse that caused the Fracture, he was too close to the center of it all to be completely innocent.

Whether the pawn of a monster or a murderer himself, the difference hardly left his hands any cleaner. Complacency, living in luxury while the world crumbled, was still an offense too grave to leave a man worthy enough to deserve the honor of Maree risking their lives for his protection.

They have a right to know.

Lincoln took two steps toward Chanler before sense squashed instinct.

Both of Chanler's knights froze, an almost identical furrow pinching their brows.

Lincoln raised his glass to his lips, maintaining his calm façade, resisting the temptation to glance toward the path to the front of the conservatory to gauge his best chance for escape.

The knights didn't surge toward Lincoln. Instead, they looked at each other. The one on the right raised his wrist to speak into his watch.

The Maree didn't send anyone to run the show. DJ Cricket could have kept them out of trouble.

Lincoln's swelling pride in Ari's plan snapped as the right-hand Maree stepped closer to Chanler. The knight said something that drained the color from Chanler's face.

Chanler turned his back on the latest lusting woman to corner him. He gestured toward the path that led to the front of the conservatory.

The knight shook his head as he replied to Chanler.

"DJ Cricket"—Lincoln didn't bother hiding his speaking with his glass—"are the others okay?"

"All systems are go," Ford said.

Chanler backed away from the knights, dodged around the woman who was still trying to talk to him, and bolted down the path.

"Ari. Where's Ari?" Lincoln's heart surged into his throat, begging him to run after Chanler and the Maree storming behind him rather than calmly follow with his wine still in hand.

"Juliet and Cinderella are making their way to Little Red," Ford said. "What's going on?"

Lincoln's heart froze, crashed down into his stomach, and shattered as he stepped onto the path.

Even the shadows coating the path couldn't hide Chanler's panic as he shoved his way through a cluster of ladies and into the women's bathroom.

Ari

The music from the string quartet in the square at the front of the conservatory hadn't fully faded before the rhythm of an instrumental piece made for dancing filled the night. Mariah gripped Ari's hand as they passed through the rows of hedges to reach the terrace.

Streetlights had been set up around the clearing, giving the place the feel of a secret hideaway in some glamourous and romantic city. The moonlight cast shadows across the forest to the north and glimmered on the smooth surface of the pond that stretched across the southeastern corner of Greenwood Gardens.

The three people in the terrace's band didn't have any music in front of them. They played with the comfortable confidence of those lucky enough to be certain of their success.

You'll get there. It's natural to be nervous the first time you're helping a girl run away from her potentially murderous father and probable serial killer estate manager.

Dammit.

You got yourself into this, Ariel Love.

Mariah's breath tickled Ari's neck as she whispered in her ear. "It's too open here. We've already been spotted, I know it. We'll never get away."

"Of course we will. New dress, new hair, walk calmly and no one will look too closely." Ari cut around the dancers, heading toward the far side of the terrace where a dark pathway had been blocked off by a sapphire rope. "They might not even know you've left the bathroom."

"This is insane," Mariah whispered. "They'll catch us. LeBlanc will be so angry. He'll lock me in my room and never let me out."

"I'm not going to let that happen."

"He'll come after you."

"Perfect." An unintentional smile curved Ari's lips. "I'd love to get my hands on that monster."

"You don't underst—"

"Juliet." Ford's voice crackled in her ear. "Kahn knows Cinderella's gone. Chameleon's spotted guards heading into the gardens."

"Damn." Ari stopped and turned to face Mariah, placing Mariah's back toward the center of the terrace, giving herself a clear view of the path that led to the conservatory.

"What is it?" The last bit of color drained from Mariah's face.

Two guards stalked up the path, pausing to glare at every woman they passed. The men wore normal somb uniforms, not the sleek suits of the Maree.

"What's wrong?" Mariah's hand started to shake.

"Nothing." Ari brushed away the hair that had tumbled

across Mariah's forehead. "I'm going to get you out of here. You're so much closer to freedom than you know, you've just got to trust me a little while longer."

Mariah bit her lips together, giving the tiniest nod.

"Good." Ari took Mariah's other hand. "When I tell you to, you're going to duck under the fancy blue rope right behind me and run down the path as fast as you can. One of my people will meet you at the bend in the trail. She's probably going to toss you over her shoulder and bolt into the forest before introducing herself, but just go with it. She'll keep you safe."

"No." Mariah shook her head, sending her hair tumbling over her forehead again. "We have to stay together. You say when, and we'll both run."

Ari leaned in, grazing a kiss on Mariah's cheek. "I'll see you on the other side."

The guards stopped to stare at a middle-aged woman in a red dress.

"Run." Ari cut behind Mariah, clearing her path to the sapphire rope. "Now."

She gave Mariah a little push toward freedom but couldn't risk turning to see if the feu heiress had actually managed to run as two Maree stepped out of the shadows on the northern edge of the terrace.

Ari shut her eyes, listening for the crunch of footsteps on gravel over the music.

The faltering rhythm of someone running in heels faded away.

"Cinderella's on the move." Ari opened her eyes, savoring the feel of a terrible weight sliding off her shoulders. A better feeling, powerful and reckless, grew in its place. "Tell me when she's clear."

The knights moved closer, weaving through the crowd as

though hoping they'd find a beautiful girl in a full-length red dress they somehow hadn't spotted at first glance.

One of the guards stopped to stare at Ari. The same one who'd spent so much time indulging his voyeuristic lust as he'd watched her with Regi. His polished bald scalp glinted in the glow of the faux streetlights as he tipped his head as though trying to figure out why Ari looked familiar and wrong all at once.

"Cinderella's been spotted," Ford said. "We're going to need a redirect."

"With pleasure." Ari took two steps forward and punched the creepy Maree in the face, breaking his nose with a satisfying crack.

44

Eve

"Little Red, Cinderella is heading your way." Ford's voice banged into Eve's ears, painfully loud compared to the footsteps and heartbeats she'd been listening to a moment before.

"Tell Juliet to hold," Eve whispered.

"Why? What's wrong?"

"The security stooges are making another pass. I'll tell you when it's clear." Eve leaned forward on her perch, gripping the branch with both hands.

"It's too late," Ford said. "Cinderella's fled the palace."

"Damn." Eve turned, dropping out of the tree, landing silently on the ground.

"Juliet's still on the terrace," Ford said.

"Does she need me?" Eve crept toward the edge of the trees.

"Negative. Take Cinderella and get out."

The crunch of running footsteps fumbling down the path neared. The one running breathed in panicked gasps.

"This path is closed." A male voice cut through the darkness.

The running didn't slow.

"Stop. Now," a second man said.

Eve leapt out onto the path, barreling toward the guards.

Both men had their backs to her.

Eve caught the first somb guard between the shoulders with the heel of her hand, knocking him face-first into a shrub.

The second stooge whipped around.

Eve punched him in the chin as he turned, sending him spinning back in the other direction.

"Help," the stooge in the bush said. "We need backup!" Feet still in the air, the man had managed to grab his walkie-talkie.

"Shit." Eve dove forward and grabbed the man's ankle, yanking him out of the bush far enough to snatch the walkie-talkie from his hand. She threw it into the woods, smashing it against a tree. "Buy me some time, Cricket."

"Put it down," a female voice said as the second stooge yelped.

Eve shoved the shrub stooge back into place as she turned toward the sound.

Mariah Chanler stood over the second guard, one foot pinning down his wrist as she beat his walkie-talkie out of his hand with a broken stiletto.

"Get off me!" The man twisted toward Mariah, shoving her to the ground.

Eve grabbed the man by the back of his pants, skidding him face-first down the gravel path as he howled his rage.

Mariah pushed herself up to her knees.

Eve didn't give her time to move any farther. Bending low,

she scooped Mariah over her shoulder, carrying her like an overpriced sack of potatoes.

"Put me down," Mariah squeaked as Eve charged back into the forest. "Put me down, I can run on my own."

"Not as fast as I can." Eve tightened her grip on Mariah as the heiress began to wiggle, kicking her feet into Eve's stomach.

"Keep moving, Little Red," Ford said. "The Maree have eyes on Cinderella's escape route."

"Too bad. I was going to sit and have a nice nap," Eve said.

"Then put me down." Mariah twisted sideways, tipping herself away from Eve's shoulder.

"I wasn't talking to you." Eve bounced Mariah, bumping her back into place with a satisfying squeak from the potato-sack heiress. "Here's the deal. You don't kick me, and I won't drop you. You wiggle, you scream, you act anything less than grateful for my carrying you, I knock you out and haul your unconscious ass through the woods. Got it?"

Eve dodged around a thick stand of trees, changing her path to head due north.

"I said *got it*?" Eve gave Mariah another bounce.

"Got it." Mariah crossed her ankles and braced her hands against Eve's back. "Is Ari going to be okay?"

"She's fine," Eve said.

"I don't want her to get hurt because of me. I left her, and there are Maree here. What if she needs my help?"

A laugh rumbled in Eve's chest. "You're in for a really rough night, princess."

45

Lincoln

The violin screeched as screams cut through the dark, crashing into the calming lilt of the string quartet. The other players only had a moment to glance toward the violinist before another round of screams yanked their attention to the shadowed path that led to the terrace.

"What's going on?" Lincoln kept his pace steady as he followed the screams, trying to look like a curious spectator rather than a frightened boy drowning in the terrifying possibility that he might be about to watch someone he cared for die.

A surge of guests hurried up the path, fleeing the terrace. A man cradling a trumpet in his arms banged into Lincoln's shoulder as he sprinted past.

Bellows of pain came before a third round of screams.

Giving in to fear, Lincoln broke into a run, skidding on the gravel, stumbling onto the bricked-over terrace.

Drops of red stained the carefully swept brick.

Two somb guards lay motionless on the ground.

The guests who hadn't fled clustered against the hedges along the sides of the terrace, watching the three people in the center of it all with glee and horror.

Ari stood barefoot between two of Chanler's Maree guards. She held a magic-made dagger in each hand, but no light burst from the blades. Even as she flipped the hilts in her hands, the daggers looked like ornately made somb weapons.

One of the knights lunged toward Ari, raising his black billy club, swinging for her shoulder. She countered, kicking out, catching him in the knee and slashing a blade across his ribs. The knight pulled back, joining his partner in prowling around Ari.

"Careful there," Ari said. "We wouldn't want to give these people too good a show."

The second knight swung his club for Ari's head. She ducked the blow and elbowed him in the stomach.

A gleam not born of the streetlights began to sparkle on the blades in her hands.

"Must be hard." Ari grinned, tossing a wink toward a younger man who knelt beside the path, recording the fight on his phone. "Do you risk me deciding to play dirty and destroying the very thing you've sworn to protect, or do you back the hell off and let me leave? What are you more afraid of—a hit viral video, or a temper tantrum from Chanler?"

The knights stopped prowling and held each other's gaze.

Lincoln crept sideways, keeping in front of the terrified bystanders as he edged closer to Ari.

"You're really thinking about it, aren't you?" The touch of fear in Ari's voice sent shocks of panic through Lincoln's chest, quickening his heartbeat. "You would betray your vow to keep on Chanler's good side. What the hell happened to get you so twisted up?"

"Put down the weapons," the bald knight said. "You're the one who can end this."

"Fat chance, creeper," Ari said.

There was a faint smile on the bald knight's face, as though he relished the thought of attacking Ari even if that fight could expose magic and endanger the feu.

Let her go. You have no idea how bad things could get.

"The only way this ends is with your surrender," the second knight said.

"Cinderella's clear," Ford shouted in Lincoln's ear. "Get out of there, people. It's time to exit stage left."

"Finally." Ari ran two steps forward, dodging to the left of the Maree nearest Lincoln.

The knight swung his billy club for Ari's face.

"No!" Lincoln leapt toward the Maree as another shout covered his own.

"Juliet!" The man from the rose garden niche stood in the center of the path, fear marring his face as Ari ducked.

The club cracked against her head, but the sound of the blow was covered by the knight's scream as she sliced through his hip.

Lincoln reached for her as she stumbled sideways, but she didn't stop long enough for Lincoln or the knights to grab her.

Dodging around the man from the rose garden, she ran down the path.

The unwounded Maree chased after her.

Lincoln rounded on the knight, placing himself in the Maree's path at the last moment, crashing his shoulder into the knight's.

The knight tripped but kept his momentum going forward, barely slowing as he sprinted after Ari.

"We've got a girl on the run." The wounded knight spoke into his wrist. "She's heading west on the—"

Lincoln didn't hear the rest of the knight's words as he raced down the path, following Ari and the Maree.

"Juliet!" The boy from the rose garden kept pace beside Lincoln, both of them gaining on the bald knight chasing Ari.

Four figures sprinted up the path from the conservatory.

Ari dodged through a break in the hedges, cutting south through the flower gardens, away from the car that should have been her escape.

"Juliet!"

Lincoln cut through the narrow gap in the hedges before the rose garden man, ready to tackle the Maree, but the bald knight was still too far ahead of him.

Faint moonlight glinted off the ground in front of Ari. The ground was smooth, flat.

They'd reached the pond on the southeastern corner of the gardens.

But Ari didn't try to cut around the water. She sprinted straight toward it and kept running, her pace not slowing as she crossed from ground to pond.

Her feet barely seemed to touch the surface, leaving only faint ripples in the water.

The Maree charged after her, slogging into the pond, the water reaching up to his knees before he'd made it three steps.

But the water never even splashed Ari's skirt as she reached the far side of the pond and raced into the woods.

Lincoln skidded to a stop beside the water, letting the Maree keep trudging through the waist-deep pond as he tried to maintain pursuit.

"What the hell?" The rose garden man stood beside Lincoln, swaying as he stared at the place in the trees where Ari had disappeared. "Did she ju—Did she walk on water?"

"No. She ran." Lincoln shoved his hands into his pockets to hide their shaking.

"How?" He looked to Lincoln, wonder and confusion filling his eyes.

The somb guards swarmed the edge of the pond, all of them shouting about finding the girl, the noise of it saving Lincoln from having to answer a question that could destroy the secret centuries of knights had fought to protect.

46

Ari

The trees swayed as Ari ran. The water beneath her feet promised salvation. But a predator kept right behind her, waiting for a chance to strike, and solace could not outweigh survival.

The pond gave way to the forest. Ari gritted her teeth as her feet met solid ground, not needing the throbbing in her head or blurring of the trees to know why instinct begged her to turn around and dive into the shallow water.

Hide in the darkness. Let the troubles above the surface tend to themselves.

Keep running.

"Juliet, are you clear?" Ford's voice sounded muddy, too far away. "Juliet, I need a location."

"I'm—" Her foot snagged on a root. She tripped forward.

The daggers fell from her hands as she caught onto a branch to keep upright. She grabbed both daggers in one hand and pushed away from the tree, forcing herself to keep moving. "I'm south of the pond. I'm going to cut east and around to the road. Tell Dagonet to leave with the others. He tried to come after me. Don't let him. Make sure he gets out."

"I'll worry about Dagonet," Ford said. "Just keep moving. I'm not going to lose you."

"Couldn't if you tried."

"I'm counting on it."

The ground shifted, rising in a steep slope. Ari reached forward, ready to drag herself up the hill. Her hands met only air. She tipped forward, landing on the flat forest floor. A rock pierced her palm as she pushed herself back to her feet.

"Juliet?" Ford said.

"I'm fine." Ari gripped a tree branch, making herself move forward another step. "Con—concussions can do weird things to the ground, right?"

"Juliet, there are guards searching the woods. If you can't run, can you climb? Get up above eye level? You just have to hang on a little longer."

"I can keep going." She reached for the next tree, using the branches to stay upright for another few feet.

A thumping pounded in Ari's head. Something not quite a heartbeat and too fast for running.

She braced her back against a tree, switching her grip on the daggers to hold one in each hand.

"If they get me, don't let anyone come after me," Ari said.

"Ari."

"Promise me, Ford. No one tries to help me until after this thing is done."

The pounding came closer. A shadow cut through the woods.

"I'm not worth it." She tried to steady her stance, but the trees wouldn't stop tipping.

"Like hell you aren't." Cold hands gripped Ari's wrists. "Please don't stab me while I rescue you."

"Jack?" Ari's arms sagged, giving in to fatigue as Jack lifted her, cradling her to his chest.

"I've got you." Jack took off, sprinting through the woods at a pace no human could hope to match. "You're going to be fine. But once your head stops bleeding, we're going to have a serious chat about you thinking any of us would abandon you."

47

Jerek

The lights of the welcome center bled out into the gardens, giving a garish look to what should have been a serene scene.

Jerek lingered at the crossing of the two main garden paths, watching the people passing by.

Two drunk men stumbled toward the welcome center. A gaggle of women made a beeline for the terrace, heading straight toward Ari's escape route.

Jerek forced himself to maintain a relaxed demeanor.

Better to have a crowd. Let the sombs disguise the plan.

A woman in a sparkling pantsuit left the fountain garden and sauntered toward the conservatory entrance.

"Cinderella's clear," Ford shouted. "Get out of there, people. It's time to exit stage left."

The pantsuit woman leapt aside as Chanler himself

stormed out of the conservatory, followed by his two Maree guards. They cut right down the path to the terrace.

"Not yet. I've got Kahn and his guards heading toward the terrace." Jerek kept his voice low. "Is Juliet out?"

"She's clearing herself a path," Ford said. "Keep watching."

"Of course."

I'm the lookout.

It should be him trying to get Mariah off the property. It should be him Chanler was after.

I'm the one who dragged them all into this.

Jerek shifted his stance, fighting against the burning in his body that begged him to scream for all the world to hear, *I am to blame!*

Shouts traveled up the path from the terrace. A flock of guests surged into the square.

"I've got a pack of sombs running from something," Jerek said.

Some of the guests fled to the conservatory. More of them headed toward the welcome center, ready to leave the grounds entirely.

Before all of them could funnel through the doors, seven somb guards shoved their way through the pack, charging out of the welcome center, heading for the terrace.

"We've got somb guards heading Juliet's way," Jerek said. "Do I engage?

The silence from his earpiece sent more panic through Jerek's chest than the screaming sombs had managed.

"Cricket, do I engage?"

More silence.

The guards passed Jerek.

He bolted after them, pulling the pen-sized hilt of his magic-made sword from his breast pocket.

"Last chance, Ford," Jerek said.

"She's out!" Ford said. "She's in the woods."

Jerek skidded to a stop, letting the guards run out of sight.

"You're sure she's safe?" Jerek asked.

"I've got her from here," Ford said. "You grab your ride and come on home."

Jerek dragged his hand over his face, trying to ignore the unfamiliar shape of his nose.

"Do you know where Firefly is?" Jerek turned around, heading back toward the welcome center.

"Still silent," Ford said. "I'm tracking Juliet. Can't do anything about Firefly."

"Got it." Jerek tucked the sword hilt back into his breast pocket. No amount of forced calm could stop his hand from shaking.

He turned around, strolling back toward the conservatory, listening for the piercing screech of fire alarms.

The excited chatter of the people in the square drowned out the string quartet, but all the sombs seemed to be looking toward the terrace, as though hoping for another dose of excitement.

Jerek rounded the end of the path and headed toward the fountain gardens. Couples strolled through the shadows, enjoying the smoke-free evening air.

Where did you go, Grace?

Not being able to locate her by the presence of unexplainable fires or sombs running from a super-human spark show was the best that could be hoped for. Unfortunately, it also made finding Grace significantly more difficult.

Lincoln's bright red hair shone like a beacon of hope as Jerek caught sight of him heading toward the welcome center, reaching the doors before Jerek.

Jerek opened his mouth to speak to Lincoln, then swallowed his words. He hadn't arrived with Lincoln and Grace. Being seen with Grace in the atrium was bad enough. Being linked with Lincoln allowed too many connections that might be made when Chanler inevitably ordered the poor somb guards of Greenwood Gardens to pore through every second of security footage they could patch together.

Lincoln headed straight toward the row of volunteers still manning the lobby, stopping in front of the oldest women in the group.

"Sorry to bother you," Lincoln said. "But did you happen to see a crying girl pass through here? She's got brown hair, about this tall." He held up his hand.

"That one ran out the door." A man in the group pointed to the front door of the welcome center. "Bolted right through here. Then a whole bunch more people left early. The gala isn't supposed to be done until eleven."

"Thanks."

"Don't complain about people leaving, Harold," the oldest woman said. "We get to have the leftover finger food. The sooner the guests leave, the more snacks for us during cleanup."

"Right." Lincoln nodded. "I hope there's plenty to go around."

"All parties confirm when you've cleared property," Ford said. "I love my blanket fort, but I'm ready to head home."

Jerek reached the outer doors of the welcome center first. He stopped right beside the valet booth and pulled his phone from his pocket. "Guess this gala is a bust," he said loudly to no one in particular. "I couldn't even find a girl to party with."

"Bad luck, brother," Lincoln said. "I'm going to find my date and get the hell out. You have a good night."

Lincoln passed the valet his ticket.

"You, too." Jerek pulled up the rideshare app, requesting a car back to the hotel that would be his first stop on the round-about trip leading to the rental that was the closest thing to a home their path would allow.

48

Lincoln

The valet took his time pulling Lincoln's key from the rack, doublechecking the tag read #127 before looking up at Lincoln.

"Did you—" The valet inched closer to Lincoln. "Did you say you were looking for your date?"

"Yep." Lincoln rocked back on his heels. "I was told she ran this way sobbing."

"Yeah." The valet dragged out the word. "She asked where the one-twenties were parked and bolted in that general direction." The valet narrowed his lips into one tense line and looked down at the key in his hand. "So, I guess I'll just go get your car for you. I'll let you know if I see her over there. And if she's still just...sobbing. Hysterically. With, you know, tears."

It was Lincoln's turn to narrow his lips into a tight line.

You're a Maree. You're not allowed to be a coward. An upset Grace is too dangerous for somb interaction.

"If it's okay, I'd like to go get the car myself," Lincoln said.

"That's great." The valet thrust the key into Lincoln's hand. "Toward the left end of the third row. You have a good night."

"You, too." Lincoln headed toward the rows of cars.

"Good luck!" The valet called after him.

Lincoln scanned the shadows the parking lot lights cast between the cars as he headed down the third row. His nerves zinged and muscles tensed as though he were hunting a dangerous enemy.

She's more dangerous than most of the feu I've trained to face.

He hated himself for thinking it.

Hated himself more for not being able to argue that it wasn't true.

As he neared the car, he began to hear a faint, coughing sniffle.

He let out a long breath, releasing the tension in his neck, not allowing his voice to sound anything but soothing. "Grace, is that you?"

The sniffling stopped.

"We're ready to head out," Lincoln said. "Can you get in the car?"

"My fingers have stopped sparking if you're worried about the upholstery."

"I don't care about the upholstery." Lincoln slowly approached the front of the car.

Grace sat huddled against the front tire, her blue dress pooled around her on the concrete.

"If you need to sit for a bit before we dive into everything that comes next, that's okay," Lincoln said.

"What does come next?" Grace looked up at Lincoln. Her eyelids had gotten puffy from crying, making her face even more unrecognizable than Jerek's magic had managed. "We kidnapped someone. Now what?"

"We didn't kidnap anyone." He knelt beside her. "Mariah wanted to be rescued."

"What if that makes it worse? If she wanted to leave her home so badly, what the hell was going on there?"

"We'll find out when we get back to the house."

"And then?" Grace wiped the tears from her cheeks with the hem of her dress.

"We take whatever information she has and come up with a new plan."

"Great, a new plan. And when that goes to hell, we'll need a new plan. And another new plan. And another new plan. And on and on and it'll never be done."

"That's not true."

"You don't know that."

"I…" Lincoln looked down at his hands, trying to remember the calm he had felt when his path in life had been simple and hitting things meant another day in training, not an unsanctioned mission to save the feu. "You're right, Grace, I don't know what comes next. I don't even know where we'll be in the morning. But I know what we're fighting for. And I know that whatever we have to do, it'll be worth it.

"The feu need us to keep pushing forward, even if they don't know it. We're saving the magical world—hell, maybe even the whole world—and that was never going to be easy, but it's worth more than anything else we could ever fight for. That much I can promise you."

"Don't make promises that aren't real." Grace pushed herself to her feet. An odd stillness had replaced her tears.

"It is real."

"Not to me." Grace pulled open the door and climbed into the car.

49

Eve

J ack had parked the jeep right where they'd planned. He'd even left the doors unlocked so Eve didn't have to smash any of the windows. Not that she would've minded smashing through glass, but avoiding extra noise was for the best, since the wriggling heiress refused to stop talking.

"Where are you taking me?" Mariah asked for the twelfth time.

Eve didn't bother answering as she opened the hatch of the jeep.

"How do you know Ari?" Mariah squeaked as Eve flopped her down in the back of the jeep. "Is your whole pack here?"

Eve pulled a zip tie from her pocket.

"What's that for?" Mariah sat up, trying to scramble away but penned in by the back seats of the jeep.

Eve grabbed Mariah's arm, flipping her onto her stomach and pinning both her wrists together above her head.

"What are you doing?" Mariah tried to twist free.

Eve squeezed Mariah's wrists together just hard enough to make her gasp before pulling the zip tie tight.

"Why are you doing this?" Mariah kicked for Eve's stomach.

Eve hopped up into the trunk, sitting on Mariah's thighs as she bound her ankles together.

"I'm not going to try and run," Mariah said. "I want to be here. I want to be with her."

"Since you were dumb enough to run away with a girl you don't really know, I have to assume you'd be dumb enough to try and run away from a werewolf who would really enjoy eviscerating a Chanler." Eve flipped Mariah back over, shoving her to sit in the corner of the trunk. "Leaving your intestines hanging from the gate of your Daddy's grand estate would bring me endless amounts of joy, so sit still and be quiet or I'll make my daydreams come true."

"No." Mariah leaned toward Eve, a flare of hatred burning in her eyes. "Ari would never let you hurt me. She came to get me."

"You're right." Eve sneered. "I am the only one in our motley crew who would prefer to kill you and get it over with, but I'm also the strongest and the fastest. So play nice with my friends, or I'll rip your throat out before Ari can scream. Is that clear enough for you, or do I have to explain how I would end your useless, unworthy life in more graphic detail?"

The cracking of branches sounded from far off in the woods.

"Should I start with the satisfaction of tearing through your flesh with my teeth, or do you understand?" Eve leaned closer to Mariah, letting her hatred glint in her eyes.

"Yes."

Eve slammed the hatch shut before Mariah could say anything else. She planted her palms on the cool metal of the jeep and closed her eyes.

I know we need her alive. I know that, Gran. But stay on my shoulder.

Killing her would be such an easy way to hurt Chanler.

He should suffer like we suffered.

We're better than that, Evelyn, Gran whispered.

Eve rolled her shoulders back, making sure her anger was tamped down, and headed toward the driver's door.

Before she'd gotten her seatbelt on, a dark figure sprinted out of the woods two-hundred yards west of the jeep.

Jack stopped for a moment, looking both ways before running toward the jeep.

He held Ari tightly in his arms, cradling her to his chest in a much gentler way than Eve had hauled Mariah through the forest.

Jack didn't set Ari on her feet as he reached the jeep. He opened the back passenger door and placed her gently in her seat, buckling her in before closing the door and climbing into his own seat.

"You okay?" Eve looked at Ari through the rearview mirror as she started the engine.

"Just a little concussion," Ari said. "Nothing to worry about."

Eve made a careful U-turn—not for Mariah, for Ari.

"You're here," Mariah said from the trunk. "The wolf tied me up. She—"

"Brain injuries are serious," Jack said. "I wish we could just take you to a doctor."

"How bad is it?" Mariah asked. "My father can—"

"No, he can't." Ari pulled off her wig, tossing it onto the seat beside her.

"Asking Daddy for help is no longer an option," Jack said. "Welcome to the bitter realities of the real world."

50

Lincoln

T he living room of their new rental house didn't have enough space for pacing. Neither did the kitchen that took up the wall by the front door. The place didn't have a dining room.

Four bedrooms, two baths, a windowless pantry big enough to protect Jack during the daylight, a patio with a view of a gently flowing creek—the rental had all those features, but not enough space to pace.

"They'll be here soon." Ford knelt beside the coffee table that took up too much space, carefully packing away the devices he'd used to orchestrate the evening.

Lincoln sat in one of the oversized armchairs. He made it less than a minute before his leg started to shake. He jumped back to his feet and returned to his sad mockery of pacing.

Four steps forward. Turn. Four steps back.

Grace had curled up in the chair nearest the door. She

didn't move or pace. Just stared at the door. No tears. No trembling. Just blank.

"They had to get through the woods," Ford said.

"They should have been ahead of us," Lincoln said.

"We've only been here for"—Ford checked his watch—"less than five minutes."

"They still should have been here."

He'd seen Ari reach the woods. Ford had gotten the all clear from Jack and Eve.

That didn't mean they hadn't been stopped on the road.

Or Mariah could have tried to escape.

If she had a weapon hidden on her. Or a tracker.

I should've gone after Ari.

Headlights flashed through the front window as a car pulled into the drive.

"I told you they'd be here soon," Ford said.

Lincoln grabbed a knife from the kitchen and was by the door before the car's engine had turned off.

"What are you doing?" Ford asked.

"Just because someone's here doesn't mean it's them," Lincoln said.

"Don't stab anyone we like." Ford shrugged.

Lincoln's heart shot into his throat as the doorknob turned.

"At least let me put some ice on it." Jack sidled into the house, his arm locked around Ari's waist as she leaned against him.

"I'm really fine," Ari said.

Lincoln dropped the knife on the counter and reached out, ready to catch Ari as soon as she'd crossed the threshold. "What happened?"

"Head bashing." Ari blinked at the living room, as though trying clear her vision. "Don't worry, I'll be fine."

"Let's just sit you down." Jack tried to steer her toward the couch.

"I promise I'll sit. You go make sure Mariah behaves on her way in," Ari said.

Jack eased away from her, waiting for Lincoln to take hold of Ari's arm before dashing back out the door.

"It didn't sound that bad over the coms." Ford stood as Lincoln lowered Ari onto the couch.

"I'm fine," Ari said.

"You have blood on your face. That's not fine." Lincoln knelt in front of Ari.

A streak of still-drying blood reached from the gash just above her hair line all the way down to her chin. Dots of red stained the pale skin of her chest.

"Get some ice and the first aid kit," Lincoln said.

Ford hurried toward Ari's bedroom.

"It's in the van," Ari said. "But I don't need—"

Ford was out the door before she'd finished speaking.

"If you would cut my ankles free, I could walk." Mariah Chanler's voice came from the doorway.

"Not gonna happen," Eve said.

Lincoln watched the door as Eve stormed in with Mariah Chanler over her shoulder. He didn't look away until Eve had tossed Mariah into the chair farthest from the front door, out of reach of the knife Lincoln had so foolishly tossed onto the counter.

"Untie me." Mariah struggled to her feet.

Eve pushed her back down. "Nope."

"Please"—Mariah fixed her fear-filled eyes on Ari—"tell them I wanted to come with you."

Ari looked toward Mariah.

Lincoln took Ari's shoulders as she swayed.

"They know you wanted to come with me," Ari said.

clear view of where the gash on her head should have been. The skin was perfect, without even a trace of a scar.

"Still think I'm not an abomination?" Ari whispered.

She didn't back away as Lincoln stepped toward her.

"Is the concussion gone?" Lincoln brushed his fingers against the place where the wound had been only minutes before.

"Everything's healed. My feet aren't even sore from spending the night in three-inch heels." Ari met his gaze. "Freaky little trick, huh?"

"Closer to a miracle if you ask me."

"We live in the world of the feu. We deal in magic, not miracles."

"I don't care what you call it as long as you're okay." Lincoln took Ari's hand.

Ari shifted her hand.

Lincoln held his breath, afraid he'd pushed too far, but she laced her fingers through his, pressing their palms together as she led him out of the creek.

She stopped just beyond the water and looked at Lincoln with a hint of mischief in her eyes. Lincoln held her gaze, tumbling into chaos, not having the sense to wonder what torment waited for him when he landed.

Ari tipped her head, letting her perfectly dry hair cascade over her shoulder. Her dress had dried, too. She laid her free hand on the side of Lincoln's thigh.

The cold of his soaked pants drained away, starting from the top and pulling down, as though the ground were helping the creek reclaim its water.

In two breaths, even his socks were dry.

"Still not a freak?" A tiny wrinkle pinched between Ari's eyebrows.

"Never." Nerves fluttered in Lincoln's chest as he dared to tuck her hair behind her ear.

His gaze drifted down to her lips.

She tipped her chin up, welcoming him.

He threaded his fingers through the silken strands of her hair as he leaned down to kiss her.

A gentle knock came from the side door of the house.

"I sincerely hate to interrupt this moment," Jack said, "but Jerek's back."

"Took him long enough." Ari stepped away from Lincoln but kept her hand locked with his as she headed back toward the house.

"I would've given you another minute, but with how well things were going...I thought that might actually be more cruel." Jack held the door open for them.

"Your timing and wingman skills are utterly undeniable." Ari finally slipped her hand away from Lincoln as she stepped back into the house.

Jack

The blush that grew up Lincoln's face was nowhere near as satisfying as the lack of attention Ford paid to Lincoln and Ari's reentrance into the house.

Ari went straight to the tiny kitchen where Jerek stood beside the sink, gulping down his second glass of water.

Lincoln stayed by the side door. He tucked his hands behind his back and kept his gaze front, as though performing the role of a perfectly unperturbed knight would somehow stop everyone from wondering exactly what had been whispered beside the cute little creek out back.

Sultry or tender, either way could be entertaining.

Ari waited for Jerek to set his glass down before giving him a hug. "Any longer, and I might've started to worry, Jer Bear."

"The second car I called went to the wrong hotel to pick me up," Jerek said. "Then I had to make sure no one was following me before I jogged the mile-and-a-half from the gas station."

"Jogged?" Eve asked from her spot in front of the door to Jack's pantry that was currently Mariah's prison.

"I'm afraid running is not one of my talents." Jerek bowed to Eve.

"But changing faces is." Grace looked up from the tiny red wine stain on the carpet she'd been staring at since Jerek had finally arrived.

"Very true," Jerek said. "And it's a talent I hope made tonight's mission a success."

"If you call a Chanler being tied up in the pantry a success" —Eve thumped the door behind her with her heel—"then your creepy face changes definitely helped."

Jerek let out a long breath and squared his shoulders. "Shall we see if Mariah will be worth the trouble?"

"Fix my face first." Grace stood, blocking Jerek's path.

"Your face can wait," Eve said.

"Fix it, Jerek," Grace said.

"We need to talk to Mariah and find out how many Maree are in town guarding Chanler," Ari said. "Once we know we're safe, Jerek can play makeover."

"Happily." Jerek moved to step around Grace.

Grace planted her hand on his chest, shoving him back while keeping her glare fixed on Ari. "So you get to go outside and take the time to make out with Lincoln—"

"That's not what happened," Lincoln said.

"—but my face isn't important?" Grace pressed on. "You were all over the guy at the gala, probably hooked up with Mariah, too. Does the fate of the world depend on your completing the tramp triathlon?"

"That's out of line." Jack's fangs pierced his bottom lip.

"We're trying to save the feu, but please take the time to embrace the patriarchal view of the pure feminine," Ari said. "I let that stranger grope me because using him as arm candy gave

"Then can't—"

"What none of us know is if we can trust you." Ari spoke over Mariah. "There are a lot of people looking for us, several of whom would like us dead."

"I would never hurt you." Tears sparkled in Mariah's eyes.

"Maybe that's true." Jack stepped aside as Ford hurried back into the house. "But what about LeBlanc? What about your father?"

"My father would never hurt anyone," Mariah said.

A growl rattled in Eve's throat.

"You can't be sure of that, and we can't afford to take any chances." Ari lifted Lincoln's hands from her shoulders. "Ford, make sure there's no way her father could be tracking her."

"Easy-peasy." Ford set the first aid kit on the coffee table.

"Jack, do you mind if we keep her in your pantry until Jerek gets back?" Ari asked.

"Happy to have a house guest," Jack said.

"You can't put me in a pantry." Mariah tried to stand again.

Eve pushed her back down before she'd made it halfway.

"It's only for a little while." Ari gripped the arm of the couch as she got to her feet. "I'm not in the mood to recap questioning you for Jerek, so we're waiting for him. And you're better off locked in Jack's pantry than being growled at by Eve."

Eve spun around, nailing her glare on Ari.

Ari didn't seem to notice as she shooed away Lincoln's offer of help and walked toward the side door that led out to the patio and the creek beyond. She took each step deliberately, as though constantly making sure she knew how far away the floor was.

"Let's put you in the pantry." Jack stepped around Eve and scooped Mariah into his arms. "Before I lock you in, would you like a few words of advice on how not to piss anyone off around here?"

Ari stepped through the side door and out of view.

Lincoln clenched his jaw, giving himself a second to rethink before grabbing the first aid kit and following Ari out the door.

The chill of the night filled the quiet forest, offering peace and hiding enemies all at once.

Lincoln glanced back through the door. He could grab the knife from the counter and then follow her.

A faint splashing came from the creek as Ari waded into the water.

He closed the door to the house and jogged to the creek.

"You didn't have to follow me." Ari turned toward him.

"You have a headwound." Lincoln set the first aid kit down. "You probably have a concussion, too."

"Sounds awful." Ari began pulling the hairpins from her pin curls, letting her blond hair cascade over her shoulders.

"Let's get the blood cleaned up so we can see what we're dealing with." Lincoln opened the first aid kit and pulled out two alcohol wipes.

"Do they teach first aid in Maree training?" Ari tucked the hairpins into the top of her dress.

"I wish they taught more." Lincoln stepped into the creek, ignoring the cold of the water as he slogged toward Ari.

"Did they teach you first aid for feu?"

"A bit." Lincoln opened the first alcohol wipe. "I'm sorry if this hurts."

His fingers trembled as he reached up, gently cleaning away the blood just below the wound.

Ari took a sharp breath through her teeth.

"Sorry." Lincoln wrapped his arm around her waist, bracing her weight against him as he dabbed at the wound.

She laid her hands on Lincoln's chest, not as though she wanted to break away as he caused her more pain, more like when they'd stood in the water before, when she'd found comfort in his embrace. "Did they teach you anything about treating div wounds?"

"No. They didn't."

"Do you wish they had?"

"Yes." Pain pinched in Lincoln's chest.

"Why?" Ari looked up at him, tipping the wound away from him.

"Because you need help. You're hurt, and I'm not even sure if rubbing alcohol is safe for a half-mer."

"A little late to worry about that now." Ari took the alcohol wipe from him. "You already put it on my skin."

"And what if it hurts you? What if my trying to help makes it worse? What if one of those Maree had had a sword? I saw you fight, and you're good, but that doesn't mean you can't get hurt." His words tumbled out as his panic rose. "What if they'd stabbed you? I don't even know where your lungs are!"

"They're in the normal place." Ari took his hand and laid it on her chest. Her heartbeat thumped against his palm. "My heart is in the normal place, too. It just beats a little bit slower."

She let go of his hand and reached up, trailing her fingers from the worried wrinkles at the corner of his eye down to his cheek.

He leaned into her touch without even a flickering thought of the danger.

She rose up on her toes, letting her body press against him as she brought her lips only a breath from his. "Can I kiss you?"

"Ari." All his breath left his lungs as he whispered her name.

"Say yes."

"Yes."

His heart stopped then surged as her lips brushed against his. Gently. Too gently, giving him barely a taste of bliss. She kissed him again, sending him tumbling into a glorious wonderment he'd been too cowardly to seek.

She slid her hand down his chest as she backed away from him.

"Ari." The word promised paradise and pain all at once, a promise that was sure to break him.

She lifted his hand and kissed his palm. "Promise you'll remember I'm not an abomination."

"You're not an abomination."

"Just promise." She backed out of reach.

"I promise." Lincoln hated the chill wind for whisking away the beautiful warmth of her body pressed against his.

She knelt in the creek and lay back, letting the water consume her. Her hair caught in the gentle current, becoming a golden crown as she sank to the very bottom of the creek bed.

She stayed still, not bobbing or drifting, as though the water had wrapped her in a more tender embrace than Lincoln could ever hope to manage.

Time ticked past, longer than a normal somb could hold their breath, but she still didn't move.

"Ari?" Lincoln inched closer to her as fear joined the cold filling his bones. "Ari?" He leaned forward, looking straight down at her.

In the faint moonlight, her pale skin seemed to gleam beneath the water.

She opened her eyes, gave him a little smile, and winked.

Lincoln's fear melted away as a more dangerous warmth filled his chest.

Another minute passed before Ari sat up. Her hair lay perfectly down her back, as though the water had smoothed the shimmering strands in a show of devout affection.

As she stood, she tipped her chin down, giving Lincoln a

clear view of where the gash on her head should have been. The skin was perfect, without even a trace of a scar.

"Still think I'm not an abomination?" Ari whispered.

She didn't back away as Lincoln stepped toward her.

"Is the concussion gone?" Lincoln brushed his fingers against the place where the wound had been only minutes before.

"Everything's healed. My feet aren't even sore from spending the night in three-inch heels." Ari met his gaze. "Freaky little trick, huh?"

"Closer to a miracle if you ask me."

"We live in the world of the feu. We deal in magic, not miracles."

"I don't care what you call it as long as you're okay." Lincoln took Ari's hand.

Ari shifted her hand.

Lincoln held his breath, afraid he'd pushed too far, but she laced her fingers through his, pressing their palms together as she led him out of the creek.

She stopped just beyond the water and looked at Lincoln with a hint of mischief in her eyes. Lincoln held her gaze, tumbling into chaos, not having the sense to wonder what torment waited for him when he landed.

Ari tipped her head, letting her perfectly dry hair cascade over her shoulder. Her dress had dried, too. She laid her free hand on the side of Lincoln's thigh.

The cold of his soaked pants drained away, starting from the top and pulling down, as though the ground were helping the creek reclaim its water.

In two breaths, even his socks were dry.

"Still not a freak?" A tiny wrinkle pinched between Ari's eyebrows.

"Never." Nerves fluttered in Lincoln's chest as he dared to tuck her hair behind her ear.

His gaze drifted down to her lips.

She tipped her chin up, welcoming him.

He threaded his fingers through the silken strands of her hair as he leaned down to kiss her.

A gentle knock came from the side door of the house.

"I sincerely hate to interrupt this moment," Jack said, "but Jerek's back."

"Took him long enough." Ari stepped away from Lincoln but kept her hand locked with his as she headed back toward the house.

"I would've given you another minute, but with how well things were going...I thought that might actually be more cruel." Jack held the door open for them.

"Your timing and wingman skills are utterly undeniable." Ari finally slipped her hand away from Lincoln as she stepped back into the house.

Jack

The blush that grew up Lincoln's face was nowhere near as satisfying as the lack of attention Ford paid to Lincoln and Ari's reentrance into the house.

Ari went straight to the tiny kitchen where Jerek stood beside the sink, gulping down his second glass of water.

Lincoln stayed by the side door. He tucked his hands behind his back and kept his gaze front, as though performing the role of a perfectly unperturbed knight would somehow stop everyone from wondering exactly what had been whispered beside the cute little creek out back.

Sultry or tender, either way could be entertaining.

Ari waited for Jerek to set his glass down before giving him a hug. "Any longer, and I might've started to worry, Jer Bear."

"The second car I called went to the wrong hotel to pick me up," Jerek said. "Then I had to make sure no one was following me before I jogged the mile-and-a-half from the gas station."

"Jogged?" Eve asked from her spot in front of the door to Jack's pantry that was currently Mariah's prison.

"I'm afraid running is not one of my talents." Jerek bowed to Eve.

"But changing faces is." Grace looked up from the tiny red wine stain on the carpet she'd been staring at since Jerek had finally arrived.

"Very true," Jerek said. "And it's a talent I hope made tonight's mission a success."

"If you call a Chanler being tied up in the pantry a success" —Eve thumped the door behind her with her heel—"then your creepy face changes definitely helped."

Jerek let out a long breath and squared his shoulders. "Shall we see if Mariah will be worth the trouble?"

"Fix my face first." Grace stood, blocking Jerek's path.

"Your face can wait," Eve said.

"Fix it, Jerek," Grace said.

"We need to talk to Mariah and find out how many Maree are in town guarding Chanler," Ari said. "Once we know we're safe, Jerek can play makeover."

"Happily." Jerek moved to step around Grace.

Grace planted her hand on his chest, shoving him back while keeping her glare fixed on Ari. "So you get to go outside and take the time to make out with Lincoln—"

"That's not what happened," Lincoln said.

"—but my face isn't important?" Grace pressed on. "You were all over the guy at the gala, probably hooked up with Mariah, too. Does the fate of the world depend on your completing the tramp triathlon?"

"That's out of line." Jack's fangs pierced his bottom lip.

"We're trying to save the feu, but please take the time to embrace the patriarchal view of the pure feminine," Ari said. "I let that stranger grope me because using him as arm candy gave me a better chance of blending in, which protected us all, including you. So get off your delusionally high horse and thank me for letting poor Regi shove his tongue down my throat while a creepy Maree got his jollies watching us."

"That Maree should be stripped of his knighthood," Lincoln said.

"Too bad we can't report him," Eve said. "Can we please get to questioning Chanler's little princess?"

"Yes," Ari said at the same moment Grace shouted, "No!"

Sparks dripped from the tips of her fingers, crackling as they fell to burn tiny holes in the carpet.

"Grace," Jerek said, "take a breath."

"Fix my face." Grace spoke through clenched teeth.

"Alright, but if you catch the house on fire, I won't be able to finish my work," Jerek said.

"Now." The sparks brightened.

Jerek reached up and ran his fingers along either side of Grace's jaw.

"We don't need to watch Jerek work," Eve said. "Jack, can you move the coffee table?"

"Sure." Jack's fangs retracted as he grabbed the edge of the coffee table and tipped it up onto its side, grateful for a reason not to watch Jerek and Grace. He lifted the table up and over an armchair to lean it against the wall.

"Would you like your hair returned to black?" Jerek asked. "I can't fix the length—"

"Make it black," Grace said.

"Great," Ari said, "now that they're done playing beauty parlor, let's get Mariah out here."

"Grab a chair to tie her to," Eve said.

"You can't tie her to a chair." Grace rounded on Eve, her face back to normal as she dared to glare at a werewolf.

"Can and will."

Jack grabbed one of the cane back chairs from the corner and set it where the coffee table had been.

"If you're keeping her tied up, you're admitting we kidnapped her," Grace said.

"She ran willingly into my arms," Eve said.

"And what lies did Ari tell her to make her want to run?" Grace said.

"Both of you stop," Jerek said in a quieter than normal tone. "We have successfully obtained a resource who may be able to give us information that could lead us toward another path to ending the Fracture."

"*May be*," Grace said, "*could?*"

"Any arguments about how we got Mariah here and what our next move needs to be can happen after we know if we're safe to stay in this house," Ari said. "Agreed?"

"Agreed." Eve opened the pantry door.

"No," Grace said. "I'm done."

"Done?" Ari said.

"I'm not doing this anymore." Grace backed away, inching toward the front door.

"Grace, what do you mean?" Jerek's tone still stayed calm.

Eve came out of the pantry, Mariah draped over her shoulder like a compliant corpse.

"This is too much," Grace said.

"Mariah is fine. No bruises or scratches." Ford handed Eve a rope. "Some people would think this is fun."

"And if she won't answer your questions?" Grace said. "Will she still have no bruises or scratches, or is Eve finally going to eviscerate a Chanler?"

"We're not going to torture her," Ari said.

"Should you have let her know that?" Ford nodded to Mariah as Eve tied her to the chair.

"How am I supposed to know how far you're willing to go?" Grace said.

"Because we're the good guys," Jerek said.

"Good guys don't hurt people. I almost killed you, Jerek!" Grace shouted. "You. A person. A living, breathing person. I have blood on my hands now."

"Don't say that like we're supposed to feel sorry for you." Ari stepped past Jerek before he could begin to apologize. "I killed people. Eve killed people. Jack killed people. *Almost* killing someone isn't going to win you sympathy in this crowd."

"I don't want sympathy, I want out!"

Even Mariah froze as Grace's words clanged around the room.

"I'm going home," Grace said. "I'm done."

"How can you say you're done?" Eve said. "Our mission isn't over."

"It is for me." Grace gripped the doorknob, like that somehow made her words less traitorous. "This is your fight, not mine. I belong in the somb world with my family."

"And when you light your family on fire because you don't know how to control your magic?" Ari said. "That will be real blood on your hands."

"I have better control now," Grace said.

"The carpet doesn't agree," Ari said.

"I can handle it."

"And you'll just hope the rest of us can mend the Fracture without you?" Ari said. "After everything we've been through together, you're really just going to abandon us because you've finally realized saving the world isn't all triumph and parades?"

"Everything we've been through?" Grace said. "I don't even know any of you."

"You do know us," Jerek said. "We're a team."

"I've been to summer camps longer than this shit show!" A fresh round of sparks poured from Grace's fingers, leaving a spray of black singes on the wall and door. "We aren't a team. We aren't friends. We're a bunch of teens who have no place pretending they can save anything, let alone magic!"

"There is no one—" Jerek began.

"If you want to keep risking your lives and kidnapping and killing people, fine. But I'm going home." Grace wrenched the door open.

"We won't come after you," Ari said.

"I don't want you to."

"I mean when someone way worse than we could ever be finds you." Ari stepped closer to Grace. "You showed your face at the Museum of Magic. Chanler, LeBlanc, the Maree—do you really think none of them will track you down?"

Grace stayed silent.

"When someone shows up and snatches you, we're not going to rescue you," Ari said.

"Ari," Jerek whispered as the sparks flying from Grace's fingertips brightened again.

"We don't have the resources to track you," Ari said, "not while we're fighting to fix the Fracture. We won't know you've been taken, and we won't be able to come after you. If you leave now, you're on your own."

Grace let go of the door and stepped out into the night.

"Wait!" Jerek pushed past Ari.

Grace froze, her sparks dwindling away.

"The gas station is down the road to the right." Jerek dug into his pocket as he looped in front of her. "They should be able to call you a cab." He pulled out a money clip. He peeled bills free and held them out to Grace. "This will be enough to get you a hotel and a bus ticket home."

Silently, Grace took the money.

"Be careful, Grace," Jerek said. "There are real villains in this world, and you're special enough to be a target for all of them."

He gave her a nod and walked back into the house, closing the door behind him.

52

Ari

An odd silence filled the room. Jerek stood with his hand pressed to the door, like he was afraid moving might signal some finality that could doom them all.

This is not the time to fall apart, Ariel Love.

"Everyone pack up," Ari said. "We're leaving in ten minutes."

"Leaving?" Eve said.

"Grace knows where this house is," Ari said. "That places all of us in danger."

"In danger?" Jack said. "You don't think Grace would tell anyone where we are?"

"Could she even find anyone to tell?" Ford closed his box of earpieces and slid it into his backpack.

"They'll find her." Ari pulled the sacks of rice from her bra and dropped them into the kitchen trash.

"You really think she'd betray us?" A painfully naïve wrinkle pinched between Ford's eyebrows.

"She walked out." Ari turned her back to Jerek and lifted her hair away from her zipper. "Can any of you honestly say you don't think she'd crack if a Maree questioned her?"

Jerek let go of the door to unzip Ari's dress.

"Grace would crack if a turnip questioned her," Eve said. "Which is why you can't let her walk away."

"We don't have a choice," Jerek said.

"Yes, we do," Eve said. "I'll go after her, drag her pouting ass back here, and we'll tie her up until she gets her head on straight."

"And when she lights us all on fire?" Jack carried Mariah to the side of the room, chair and all.

"We'll keep a fire extinguisher handy," Eve said. "Grace knows what the mission is. What happens if Chanler grabs her?"

"What mission are you on and what does it have to do with my family?" Mariah tried to stand.

Eve shoved her back into her seat. "Don't talk. Don't move. Don't breathe in a distracting way. I'm in a bad mood, and I would love to take it out on you."

"Our mission doesn't change," Jerek said. "We'll plan our next step once we're well away from here."

"We leave in nine minutes." Ari strode toward the bedroom she'd been looking forward to sleeping in, clutching the top of her dress to keep it from falling off.

"Ari." Eve chased after her.

"Are you really going to let Mariah out of your sight?" Ari dropped her dress as she stepped into her bedroom.

"Jack's watching her," Eve said. "And I need to go after Grace."

"Grace chose to leave." Ari unbuckled the leather straps from her thighs.

"She doesn't get to just walk away from this," Eve whispered. "Has everyone forgotten that we need her to mend the Fracture? Grace is the only non-broken magician we have."

"It doesn't matter." Jerek slipped into Ari's room, closing the door behind him. "As long as Grace doesn't want to help us, we're better off without her."

"That's a bunch of shit and you know it," Eve said.

"It's not." Ari grabbed a shirt from her bag. "We can't force Grace to perform a spell for us. If we were dumb enough to try it, I'd give it a 95% chance of ending with all of us dead."

"Then what the hell are we supposed to do?" Eve's words rumbled out in a gravelly tone that was barely better than a growl.

"Question Mariah. Hope we get some decently useful information from her." Ari pulled on a pair of leggings, grateful for the soft fabric that somehow made her feel more competent, ready for whatever hell losing Grace would drive them toward.

Most of the team is here. We're not all the way back at the beginning.

"We can't just drive around in a van forever," Eve said.

You are not allowed to panic, Ariel Love.

"I was promised vengeance," Eve said. "You can only ask a werewolf to wait for so long."

"We're already exposed," Jerek said. "Between the museum and taking Mariah, we can't hold out much hope for the butcher not realizing we're circling the Chanlers and their associates. If we play things right, vengeance may be able to come before victory. I don't think you'll have to wait much longer."

"Good." Eve reached for the doorknob.

"Will you leave?" Ari asked. "Once you've gotten what you want, are you going to abandon ship, too?"

"I'm not a traitorous coward," Eve said. "I don't abandon people."

"Thanks." Ari managed a quick smile. She sat on her bed and flipped open her laptop.

The door clicked closed behind Eve.

"We are going to be all right, Ari," Jerek said.

"I know." Ari opened the internet and pulled up a thread of local police reports.

"Then why are you typing like you're trying to stop the world from exploding?"

"We have two stolen cars we need to ditch," Ari said. "Stealing cars is a somb crime. Sombs like to use fingerprints to track criminals, and our fingerprints are all over those cars."

"I assume you have brilliant plan to deal with the issue."

"We're handing the cars over to a chop shop." Ari glanced up to find Jerek leaning against the doorframe, his shoulders relaxed, his face calm. "We'll find a way to fix the Fracture without her."

"Of course we will. We have you."

53

Lincoln

The flashes of light from passing cars had gotten less and less frequent during their second hour on the road. The route Ari had chosen for them crossed state lines, changed between three different highways, took a backroad through the mountains, then hopped onto another highway.

There was no chance of Chanler or the Maree having followed them without being spotted, but there was still an urgent worry burning on the back of Lincoln's neck, as though something worse than sombs or feu might be chasing them.

"How much longer?" Lincoln asked from the back, where he and Eve sat flanking the still-bound Mariah.

"I didn't think I'd get an *are we there yet* from you." Ari twisted in the front passenger seat to face him. "Is patience not part of your Maree training?"

"Maree?" Mariah leaned forward to stare at Lincoln. "He can't be a Maree."

"Why not?" Ford asked.

"Start with the neck tattoo and go from there," Mariah said.

Eve huffed a laugh.

"Ah, dress code," Ford chuckled. "I get it."

"I learned patience from having five younger siblings," Lincoln said. "I'm more worried about getting a non-compliant magician into a somb-run hotel."

"I think I've been more compliant than you have a right to expect," Mariah said.

"I seem to remember you kicking me," Eve said.

"And you didn't whack her against a tree?" Jack asked. "I'm impressed."

"I'm glad someone gets it," Eve said.

"Kicking aside," Lincoln said, "we can't risk drawing attention to ourselves or worse, exposing the feu."

"Do you want me to pinky promise? It'll be easier if you untie my hands," Mariah said.

"What's your trace?" Lincoln shifted to sit on one of the benches that ran along the sides of the van, giving himself a better view of Mariah's face.

"None of your business." Mariah flashed him a cold smile.

"It is absolutely my business," Lincoln said. "We can't risk taking you inside if you could place us, or the sombs in the hotel, in danger."

"So..." Mariah furrowed her brow in mock confusion. "If I don't tell you what my trace is, you'll leave me on the side of the road? You went through a bit too much trouble *rescuing* me to just abandon me like that."

"We wouldn't leave you on the side of the road," Eve said. "We'd tie you up even tighter and shove you under one of the van seats until we're ready to move on. Jack can watch you at night, I'll take the day, and you can learn to love staring at the underside of a van seat."

"It's not an experience I recommend," Jack said.

"Mariah, please just tell them," Ari said.

"No, thank you. I don't think sharing information with people who are keeping you tied up is necessarily the best idea," Mariah said.

Ari knelt between her seat and Jerek's. "Look, I know this is hard. You've been through a lot tonight. Running away is scary, even when you know you've got to get out."

"Preach," Jack said.

"Are you really trying to call this running away?" Mariah held out her bound hands.

"You wanted me to find you," Ari said. "You wanted to come with me."

"I didn't know I was going to end up a prisoner," Mariah said.

"And I don't want you to have to stay tied up," Ari said. "But we have to protect ourselves, and right now, none of us can trust you."

"*You* can't trust *me*?" Mariah tried to scoot forward in her seat. Eve shoved her back. "I haven't tied any of you up. I haven't lied to any of you."

"But you grew up in your father's house," Ari said.

"Your low opinions of my father—"

"Aren't opinions," Lincoln cut in before Eve could speak. "Horrible things have happened to the feu, and the tragedy emanates from your family."

"What the hell are you talking about?" Mariah said.

"Careful," Jerek said.

"Your father, LeBlanc," Ari said, "there is a strong possibility that one or both of them are very, very evil men."

"Murderers," Eve growled.

"My father has never hurt anyone. Never. You're all

completely insane." Mariah laughed. "I'm trapped in a decrepit van with a band of deranged idiots."

"Don't insult the van," Jerek said.

"For your sake, I really wish we were wrong, but it all makes too much sense." Ari ducked her head as she made her way to the back of the van to sit on the floor in front of Mariah. Her shoulder brushed against Lincoln's knee as the van bounced. "Knowing you were raised in that house, influenced by those men, we don't know how much danger you could put us in."

"I'm not the dangerous one." Mariah shot a glare at Eve.

"Glad you noticed," Eve said.

"If you really think your dad has never hurt anyone, then help us prove it," Ari said. "Help us figure out what really happened."

"With what?" Mariah said. "The party where you killed people?"

"Enough," Jerek said. "Tell us your trace now, or Eve will shove you under the seat to sleep while the rest of us get hot showers and warm beds."

"Tell me what you think my father did first," Mariah said.

"This isn't a negotiation," Jerek said. "Talk now, or watch your head while Eve shoves you under the seat."

"Not my seat," Jack said. "I don't want her in my cubby, put her on the other side."

"With pleasure." Eve scooped Mariah into her arms as Ari hopped onto the seat beside Lincoln, pulling her feet up to give Eve access to the space beneath.

"I can hear things," Mariah squeaked.

"What?" Eve lowered her toward the floor.

"I can eavesdrop!" Mariah shouted. "Listen through walls and across big spaces. It's all hearing. I'm not your friend who walked out. I can't light sombs on fire!"

"That's refreshing," Jack said.

"And not very combat-worthy." Eve dropped Mariah back on the seat.

"How well can you hear?" Jerek asked.

"It depends on the space." Mariah scooted back to sit upright.

Ari leaned across Lincoln to straighten the skirt of Mariah's dress.

"Outside, I can hear a whisper at a hundred paces," Mariah said. "Inside, through doors and walls. It's better if I can touch the barrier I'm listening through."

"That's fascinating." Ford's eyes lit up.

"What about in crowds?" Jerek asked.

"It's hard to pick one voice out of the rest of the noise," Mariah said, "but if I'm familiar enough with the voice, I can make it work."

"Huh." Lincoln leaned back in his seat, fixing his gaze on the carpeted floor of the van as he tried to think through every-thing that had been said in the house that night.

"Tell me what I'm saying," Jerek said, then went silent.

"X34D29," Mariah said. "Is that supposed to mean something?"

"Eve, could you hear it?" Jerek asked.

"I heard you mumbling something," Eve said.

"Me too," Jack said. "The hum of the engine blurred it out."

"And now you know my party trick," Mariah said.

Lincoln raked his hands over his strangely shorn, still-red hair. "We should cut her free. We can't walk her into the hotel with restraint marks on her wrists."

"Wouldn't want anyone to think I'm being held against my will," Mariah said.

"Your comfort is the least of our concerns." Eve stuck her fingers into the zip tie on Mariah's wrists, breaking it with a sharp crack.

"Ouch." Mariah gasped.

"Would you like me to break your feet off instead of the tie?" Eve asked.

"Eve," Ari warned.

"She could be useful without her feet." Eve grinned.

"We don't need to make more enemies." Ari leaned across Lincoln, her side pressing against his chest as she pulled one of the magic-made daggers from her pack.

The scent of her hair, like a fresh sea breeze, filled his lungs. He tried to hold onto the scent, memorizing it as she knelt in front of Mariah to cut her ankles free.

"You trusted me at the gardens," Ari said.

"I'm starting to think that was an appalling lapse in judgment," Mariah said.

"It wasn't." Ari set the dagger down and took Mariah's hand. "You are better off with us than trapped under LeBlanc's control. I promise you that. Please, do what we ask and help us. Give us a chance to prove to you that we are the good guys."

Ari leaned against Lincoln's knees as Jerek rounded a corner, cutting onto a road that led up to a massive hotel built in the style of a Swiss chalet.

"After I prove to you that my father isn't guilty of whatever horrible thing you think he's done, I want to know what mission you're on that makes it worth tying me up." Mariah gripped Ari's hand.

"Deal," Ari said.

Lincoln looked out the window, watching the glimmering of the pond beside the chalet.

A shameful satisfaction brushed his fatigue away as Ari sat on the seat beside him as they reached the portico and Jerek went inside to check them into another temporary haven.

54

Jack

The beds in the chalet were exquisitely soft and held a clean, fresh scent the cubby under the bench in the van never had a prayer of matching. The ceilings were high, the living room had its own fireplace, and the water pressure was divine.

But the only luxury that truly mattered to Jack were the wondrous curtains on every window in their two-bedroom suite. Heavenly blackout curtains provided by a high-end establishment accustomed to catering to hungover clientele had created Jack's vampire dream space.

Eve had moved the pullout couch to block the only exit from their fourth-story suite. All electronics, including the in-room phones, had been locked away by Ari.

If Mariah were foolish enough to attempt escape, her only choice would be to scream at the top of her lungs and hope whoever came to her rescue could make it past a very angry, just-woken werewolf.

And Lincoln was sleeping on the second couch in the living room as an extra line of defense.

There was no one to guard and nowhere to run.

Everyone else in their wayward crew had gone to sleep, leaving Jack to lie in his blissfully soft bed with no one to bother him. Or he could sit by the fireplace. Or run circles around the living room as long as he didn't mind risking waking the ragey werewolf.

So many choices for miraculously normal pleasures.

Still, Jack lay in bed, listening to Jerek's and Ford's gentle breathing as they slept.

Jerek had passed out facedown on the second bed. Ford had taken the rollaway tucked between Jerek and Jack.

Every once in a while, Ford made a tiny noise, like a failed attempt at a snore. Then his breathing would go back to normal.

Snoring. So simple and human and mundane and...wonderful.

Jack had never heard a vampire snore. He didn't know if a vampire could snore.

He imagined himself asking when he made it back to his clan in Vegas. They'd think he was strange for wondering. But lying in the dark, listening to Ford breathe, a snore seemed like too great a miracle to be ignored.

55

Ari

The timeline swirled around the living room floor, leading from the week before the Fracture all the way up to the night of the Museum of Magic opening gala. Ari had marked the places where bits of time or information were missing with miniature coffee filters, like biodegradable steppingstones bridging from one chain of facts to the next.

The crew sat on the furniture that had been pushed to the sides of the room, watching as Ari led Mariah through the information she and Jerek had spent so much time compiling before they'd even involved anyone else in their twisted mess.

"What's this one?" Mariah pointed to a twelve-page-long spreadsheet.

"Income reports from all prominent magician families," Ari said. "In most cases, at least half of their historical wealth was gone within the first year post-Fracture. A few, like the Holdens', held steady."

"But Daddy's fortune grew," Mariah said.

"A noticeable amount," Ari said.

"Having a diverse investment portfolio doesn't make you a murderer," Mariah said.

Eve growled.

"It goes a lot deeper than that," Jerek said. "Your father was in Raleigh, North Carolina when the werewolves were attacked. He was in the state the day my mother was murdered."

"Which is why I'm going to kill him," Eve said.

"Don't you dare go near my father." Mariah rounded on Eve.

"I can't rip his intestines out from a distance," Eve said.

"Both of you stop." Jack planted himself between them. "Facts first, fighting second."

"The fact is her father murdered my family." Eve reached for her pendant.

"According to Jerek," Jack said. "None of us even saw this research before the Museum of Magic. We all just assumed he was right and went along with it. I don't want to make that mistake again."

"I was right about the heliostone," Jerek said.

"That's not good enough." Jack sat on the pullout couch, which was still blocking the door.

"Jack, I helped Jerek put all these files together," Ari said. "I had my hands on all of this before we even figured out Chanler had the heliostone."

"I'm sorry, Ari. I didn't mean—"

"Don't be sorry," Ari cut across Jack. "You need to know everything we know. Just don't put Jerek's name out there without using mine. If there's blame to be had, Jerek and I bear it together."

"You bear no blame," Jerek said.

"Can I continue?" Ari made herself look his way.

Jerek sat alone in the corner, staring at the work that had eaten years of their lives. "As you wish."

Ari stepped forward to the next set of papers. "The Blood Mountain Massacre wasn't the only tragedy your father was conveniently close to. California, Massachusetts, Pennsylvania, even Ireland—every mass slaughter the feu faced in the year after the Fracture, your dad was within an hour's drive at the time of the killings."

"Daddy travels all the time," Mariah said. "My father is a humanitarian. He traveled more right after the Fracture because he was trying to help people."

"Including the Maree," Jerek said. "Your father personally funded three quests to find the source of the Fracture. All three of those quests were total losses. None of those knights ever made it home."

Tense enough to snap, Lincoln stepped forward to stare down at the rows of pictures of Knights Maree who had died trying to return magic to the world. "Why didn't you tell me?"

"And have two members of the team wanting Chanler's blood while we stole the heliostone?" Jerek said. "I needed you calm."

"You had no right to keep this from me."

A flutter of guilt-ridden relief swept through Ari as Lincoln rounded on Jerek instead of her.

"We were going to release all our files once the Fracture was mended," Jerek said.

"After you were dead?" Lincoln said.

"Ari and I had already—"

"It wasn't just the quests, Lincoln." Ari spoke over Jerek. "If you track the money, Louis Chanler played a major part in funding the Maree's retreat to Italy. He even helped enlarge the compound."

"My father is a philanthropist," Mariah said.

"Who helped 90% of America's Maree flee the country," Ari said. "Then he started collecting artifacts."

"For his museum," Mariah said.

"He created a hoard," Jerek said. "By buying up magical objects, he might as well have been stockpiling weapons."

"Artifacts aren't weapons," Mariah said.

"Want to give his stash of moonstones to my pack so we can test that theory?" Eve asked.

"Fine," Mariah said, "in the wrong hands, *some* of Daddy's collection might be considered vaguely dangerous."

"His hands are the wrong hands," Jerek said. "He profited from the Fracture. He was near every massacre—"

"You can't kill people from an hour away!" Mariah shouted.

"—and he's amassed enough power to maintain his choke-hold on the feu," Jerek finished.

"We looked for other options." Ari touched Mariah's arm, letting her attempt at comfort be cast aside when Mariah shook her away. "After the Museum of Magic, we did another round of digging."

"Did you only check magicians?" Mariah said. "What about other feu or Maree? What if a somb stumbled onto something they shouldn't have and Fractured magic without meaning to?"

"A curse caused the Fracture. A magician had to be involved," Ari said. "The only two people who fit the evidence are your father and LeBlanc."

"Then it was LeBlanc," Mariah said.

"He's not a magician," Lincoln said. "There's no way he could have done it. At least not on his own."

"Then you're missing something." Mariah backed away from the swirl of paper, staring at the mess of facts like she might be able to see something Ari had missed.

Please prove me wrong.

"It wasn't Daddy." Mariah brushed the tears from her eyes

with the sleeve of the pink shirt Ari had lent her. "LeBlanc is a controlling bastard with an awful temper. The man is a monster who's made our home hell. I can believe he had something to do with this but not my father."

"Why?" Jerek asked the question in a simple way that somehow left no room to dodge the truth.

"My mother died the day of the Fracture," Mariah said.

"In D.C.," Lincoln said. "A car accident, right?"

"I begged her to let me come with her, but she had *important business* and it was going to be a *quick trip*." Mariah brushed away a fresh batch of tears. "She was driving when the Fracture hit, she went off the road, and her car caught fire. Daddy still talks to her every night. He tells her he misses her and how sorry he is that he wasn't with her. He blames himself for not insisting she always use a driver.

"I can hear him through the wall, he doesn't know anyone is listening. If you had created the Fracture that caused the accident that killed the love of your life, would you really just be apologizing for not ordering LeBlanc to drive her everywhere in D.C.?"

"LeBlanc was your mother's driver?" Jack asked.

"Of course. He started working for Daddy as a security guard when I was little," Mariah said. "The day the Fracture happened, LeBlanc stayed behind at the Council of the Feu when Mother left. He had something else he had to do, I guess. Daddy should've fired LeBlanc for not staying with Mother, but Daddy was barely holding on after the Fracture. Feeling magic ripping away was terrifying, and then he got the call about Mother an hour later. That day...I don't think anything could ever be as bad as that day."

"I'm so sorry," Ari whispered.

"I watched the phone fall out of his hand, and he just crumpled. I'd never seen a grown-up cry like that. And the"—Mariah's breath hitched in her throat—"the nanny, she just grabbed me and carried me away. It was weeks before Daddy actually managed to look at me again. I look like my mom."

"Where was your father when the Fracture happened?" Jerek asked.

"Not in D.C." Lincoln dragged his hands through his newly returned-to-brown hair.

"He was with me," Mariah said. "We were in his office in the Newport house. I was playing at being his secretary. I used to mess up all his files, but he never complained about it."

"We were so close to being right," Jack said.

"Daddy didn't—"

"Not about your father, about LeBlanc." Jack knelt beside the spiral, staring at the very center, at the timeline of the failed mission at the Museum of Magic. "LeBlanc was in D.C. After the Fracture, he traveled with your father."

"But the Fracture was caused by a magician," Jerek said. "There's no way a person with no magic, even one who'd been trained as a Knight Maree, could've done it alone."

"He wasn't alone," Eve said. "He was with Mrs. Chanler."

"You can't accuse my mother of anything," Mariah said. "She died—"

"My mother's dead, too," Eve said. "Don't try to have a tragedy pissing contest with me. You'll lose."

"My mother died because of the Fracture." Mariah stormed toward Eve. "If she knew the Fracture was going to happen, why would it have made her wreck her car?"

"Because it didn't." A horrible, sickening weight sank into Ari's stomach. "Your mother was dead before she ever got into that car. She died creating the Fracture."

56

Ford

"How could you say that?" Mariah rounded on Ari. "You don't know anything about my mother!"

"She was in the Council of the Feu headquarters with LeBlanc." Ari held up both hands like that could somehow stop Mariah from stalking toward her. "We've found evidence that points to the curse being cast from within the CFH."

"First, your evidence points to my father and now my mother? What the hell do you have against my family?" Mariah said.

"They're murderers and thieves," Eve said.

"More baseless accusations." Mariah threw her hands up. "Do you even care what really happened, or do you just hate my family?"

"We want to mend the Fracture," Jerek said as Eve said, "I

have every right to hate your family. I lost everything in the Blood Mountain Massacre."

"That doesn't make it my family's fault!" Mariah said.

"Maybe we should all take a breath," Jack said.

"We didn't choose your family for no reason," Ari said. "Our logic is still sound. LeBlanc was working for your family."

"Staff aren't family," Mariah said.

"Wow. Never mind." Jack sat beside Eve. "Feel free to shout at the princess."

"No one needs to shout," Jerek said. "We can't afford to argue amongst ourselves. We have a mission—"

"That can't be completed without Grace." Eve leapt to her feet.

"We'll find a way," Ari said.

"Don't push a wolf's patience too far." A frightening glint lit Eve's eyes. "You're not the only one with blood-born power, and I bite."

"Back down, Gibbs," Jerek said.

"Make me, Holden."

"We're trying to save magic." Jerek dared to step closer to Eve. "This is not the time to let your temper or your wolf get out of control."

"Jerek, stop," Ari said. "You're not going to fix anything by giving a holier-than-thou lecture."

"I don't lecture." Jerek glared at Ari.

"Of course not. You just accuse innocent people of terrible crimes and murder Maree," Mariah said.

"Don't lay the blood of those Maree on us." Lincoln pushed away from the wall. "They were my brethren."

"Who you killed!" Mariah shouted.

Lincoln tipped his shoulders down, like he was about to barrel into Mariah just as a horrible growl came from Eve, Ari shoved Jerek in the chest, pinning him against the wall, and Jack leapt onto the breakfast bar with his fangs bared.

"Everybody stop!" Ford raised his hand in the air. "Quiet Coyote says lips closed!"

A strangely satisfying quiet swept slowly around the room as everyone turned to look at him and the unfortunately embarrassing way he'd made a little coyote head with his fingers.

"Right." Ford lowered his hand. "Thank you."

He made himself swallow as he stepped carefully into the center of the paper swirl.

"Now, I may not be a member of the feu, and I may not be any good in a fight"—Ford kept talking even as Eve opened her mouth—"but I am very good at conflict resolution. We have been on a difficult path, and it's normal for tensions to be high. What we need to do is remember how much we care about each other."

Mariah laughed.

"And how much we care about this mission," Ford said. "Mending the Fracture, finding the person who caused so much pain and making sure they can never hurt anyone again. We all want those things."

"But if you're trying to drag my father—" Mariah began.

"Wait, wait, wait." Ford dodged past Mariah and grabbed the first thing his hand found on the shoved-aside coffee table—a succulent in a tiny pot shaped like a bear. The green of the plant stuck out of the bear's head as though an alien had sprouted from his skull after eating his brain. "That's unfortunate."

He turned to face the rest of the group. "We need to talk through some very sensitive subjects. We're never going to get anything done if we shout over each other, so we're going to use this talking...succulent. Whoever is holding the succulent gets to talk. So let's all sit in a nice circle and have a *productive* conversation."

Jack jumped off the breakfast bar and sat without argument, even though his fangs were still out and sending just a tiny bit of blood dripping down his chin.

Ari sat beside Jack, keeping her gaze locked on the center of the spiral of truth. The others followed. Even Eve sat, though it did sound like a rumble might be coming from her chest.

Or it could have been Ford's blood thrashing through his ears as panic reminded him he'd just told six people who were very capable of killing him to sit on the floor and pay attention to the Quiet Coyote like they were a group of rowdy kindergarteners.

"Thank you." Ford's voice came out a few pitches higher than usual. "Now, who would like the first turn to speak?"

Mariah's hand shot up.

"Great." Ford pressed a smile onto his face. "Let's get this meaningful and productive conversation started."

He passed the succulent to Mariah and sat between Jack and Ari, the two people in the room who looked the least like they wanted him dead.

"My mother died in a car accident," Mariah said. "You could tell me LeBlanc was the devil himself and I'd believe you, but my mother didn't want to destroy magic. Right before she died, she spent a week interviewing new magician tutors for me. Mother was desperate for me to be a prodigy. Why would she care about my incantations if she was plotting to steal magic from the world?"

Ari raised her hand.

Mariah stared coldly at her for a moment before passing the succulent.

"Maybe your mom wasn't planning to cause the Fracture," Ari said. "Maybe she didn't even want it to happen, but is it possible that LeBlanc made her do the spell? Threatened her?

Forced her? She might not even have known what the spell was for."

"She died in a car crash," Mariah said.

"Ah, ah, ah." Ford raised his coyote hand.

Mariah gave a sigh that puffed through her nose like an angry bull.

"They found your mother's body in a burnt-out car," Ari said. "She could have been dead before the fire started."

Mariah gripped her knees.

"If we can agree that LeBlanc has replaced your father as our prime villain candidate, can we admit that, in one way or another, even if she was just LeBlanc's first victim, your mom could have somehow been involved in what LeBlanc did the day the Fracture happened?" Ari said.

Mariah stared up at the ceiling for a moment before nodding.

Jerek raised his hand.

Ari passed him the succulent.

"All of this doesn't change how the Fracture was created," Jerek said. "If anything, it reenforces the need for the items we *procured* to mend the Fracture, and confirms our fears that LeBlanc could already know what we're trying to do."

"Then let's kill LeBlanc," Eve said.

Ford held up his Quiet Coyote hand.

"You're worried he knows we're trying to mend the Fracture and will come after us before we get the chance, so let's take LeBlanc out of the picture. Eviscerating LeBlanc will only make our job easier," Eve kept talking.

"You can't just eviscerate people because you think they might have possibly been involved," Mariah said.

"Quiet Coyote." Ford wiggled his hand in the air.

"Watch me," Eve grinned.

"Just because you're a bloodthirsty—"

"Quiet Coyote! Now!" Ford's voice bounced around the room. "No one talks unless they're holding the succulent."

"I'm not holding a creepy plant," Eve said.

"It's not creepy," Ford said. "It's a talking stick."

"It's not a stick," Eve said.

"If you want to use a real stick, then go outside and find one you like," Ford said.

The room went a different, less satisfying more terrifying, kind of quiet.

"Did you just tell me to fetch?" Danger flashed in Eve's eyes as she leaned toward Ford.

"No." Ford's voice squeaked. "I'm just not strong enough to move the couch to get out of the room to fetch—I mean dig up—I mean collect a more traditional talking stick."

"Timing of the impending evisceration aside"—Ari pointed to the very beginning of the swirl—"the only way we've found to mend the Fracture takes two magicians. One to perform the incantation, one to act as a conduit."

"I'm still willing to—" Jerek began.

"Quiet Fucking Coyote, Jerek Holden," Ari said in a tone more frightening than Eve's rumbling growl. "If we're accepting that Mariah's mother was with LeBlanc when the Fracture happened and somehow became a part of the spell that began the Fracture—"

"Then the spell might have been performed by one magician," Jerek said.

"Which means there could be a one-magician way to mend the Fracture," Ari said. "We just have to find it."

57

Jerek

The layers of papers in their living room at the chalet had only gotten worse, spreading out from the carefully laid spiral to scattered stacks as everyone claimed pages to pore through.

Jerek had shifted from amused to annoyed to grateful as Ford pulled a seemingly endless supply of reams of paper and cartridges of ink from his pack to use with the printer that had joined their expedition while Jerek was unconscious after their failure at the Museum of Magic.

The comprehensive timeline had been condensed to one mountain of paper for Mariah to dig through. Lincoln, Ford, and Jack passed Jerek's journal back and forth. Eve read through printouts of all the information they'd been able to find on LeBlanc, while Ari dug deep into pre-Fracture records from feu chatrooms, trying to find a way to cheat the incantation and use one caster instead of two.

Jerek sat at the breakfast bar with his back to the wall, failing to focus on the papers in his hand as he tried not to scream.

There were only two choices he could see.

Either there was a second magician present when the curse that caused the Fracture was cast and Mrs. Katie Chanler had acted as the conduit, dying from the brute force of channeling the spell that stole magic from the world.

Or, the curse had been cast by one magician, and there was a path to mending the Fracture neither Jerek nor his father had ever found. If that were true, Jerek faced a horrible reality he didn't know how to stomach.

His father had died in vain, and Jerek had very nearly followed him.

"Are the Maree usually shit at record keeping?" Eve didn't bother looking up as she spoke.

"The Maree archives are impeccable," Lincoln said.

"Okay, knight boy," Ari laughed. "If by impeccable you mean go back really far and like to chronicle all the heroic things the Knights Maree have done, sure. If you mean accurate, I think their never acknowledging a Maree being born out of wedlock proves exactly how the Maree have chosen to paint themselves and how far from the truth their rosy little picture is."

"Are you serious?" Jack looked up from one of Jerek's notebooks.

"The Knights Maree have very strict rules about dating, marriage, and procreation." A hint of pink crept up Lincoln's neck.

"And no one's ever broken those rules?" Jack laughed. "You can't actually believe that."

"I've lived in the compound since the Fracture, and—"

"And you must have been to a bunch of shot gun weddings," Jack said.

"Of course not." The pink turned to red as it took over Lincoln's cheeks. "Duty, following rules, it's what Maree are trained to do."

"And anything that goes against those high moral standards gets tucked out of sight," Ari said.

"So what did LeBlanc do to get *tucked out of sight* for the year before he left the Maree?" Eve said. "There's a gap in his record, then an entry for his *amicable dismissal.*"

"Amicable dismissal?" Ford said. "What does that mean?"

Lincoln set Jerek's journal aside and leaned forward in his seat as though eager to discuss anything but the Knights Maree's stance on pre-marital sex.

"An amicable dismissal is a step above banishment," Lincoln said. "You've been found unfit to serve as a Maree and will suffer the disgrace of being stripped of your knighthood but haven't done anything traitorous or outright dishonorable."

"What kind of thing could he have done?" Ford asked.

"It could be anything from failing weapons training to failing to protect a member of the feu you've been ordered to guard," Lincoln said.

"I don't get it," Ford said.

"I was sent here to protect Jerek," Lincoln said.

"And what a fine job you've done," Eve said.

Lincoln's shoulders tensed, but he didn't so much as glance her way.

"If the death threats had been genuine and none of this" —Lincoln gestured to the group—"had ever happened, I would be expected to defend Jerek with my life. If six murderers broke into Holden House and managed to kill Jerek but I somehow survived, I would have failed in my sworn duty as a Maree. I would be stripped of my knighthood and given an amicable dismissal. I would be dishonored, but I would still be allowed to see my family, and my children would be eligible to swear fealty to the Knights Maree.

"Since I've disobeyed orders, stolen from the Council of the Feu, and fought against my brethren, when the Knights Maree catch up to me, I'll be banished. Stripped of my Knighthood, cast into the world of the sombs, and never be allowed to see my family again."

"That's not true." Ari reached across the coffee table and took Lincoln's hand. "We'll prove LeBlanc is a murderer who caused the Fracture. Then, when we mend the Fracture and restore magic to the world, you'll be hailed as a hero. And the official Knights Maree record will tell some wildly inaccurate tale of how they sent you on a mission to save the feu and had a hand in the whole thing."

"Probably." Mariah sighed.

"I'm fine with Lincoln not getting banished," Eve said. "But I want to know what happened to LeBlanc during his missing year."

"Did he ever mention anything to you?" Jerek looked to Mariah.

"It's not like LeBlanc and I are close," Mariah said. "The only time he speaks to me is to order me around or yell at me."

"Poor you," Eve said.

"I can try to find something in the chats," Ari said. "But he was dismissed before the feu had really gone online."

"Then I say we capture LeBlanc and beat it out of him," Eve said. "He has a blank year, gets booted from the Maree, goes right to working for Chanler, and a year later the Fracture happens."

"Which means that year is too important for us to ignore." Ari dug her fingers into her hair, leaving Lincoln's hand abandoned on the table.

"I don't like the idea," Lincoln said, "but I could try and get in touch with one of my brothers—"

"Absolutely not," Jerek said. "It's too dangerous for your family and for us."

"Everyone is in danger if we don't take out LeBlanc," Eve said on top of Lincoln's, "Martin was stationed at the museum."

"No," Jerek said.

"Please don't make the Quiet Coyote come back," Ford said.

"Or"—Mariah shouted over the chaos—"we could behave like civilized feu and just ask the archivist."

Everyone turned to Mariah.

"The who?" Jack said.

"The archivist." Mariah looked to Jerek as though seeking affirmation.

"That's not actually that helpful," Jack said.

"If anyone has a rogue copy of records the Maree wanted erased, it's him," Mariah said.

Jerek squinted at the wall, filtering the name through his memory. "I've never heard of the archivist."

"I guess that's not too surprising. The Holdens do have a holier-than-thou reputation, and the archivist isn't exactly a mainstream resource." Mariah set her stack of papers beside her chair. "His list of patrons is very exclusive. I can't imagine any of them risking the archivist's favor by telling a Holden about his collection, even in a post-Fracture world."

"Keep going." Jerek locked his gaze on Mariah's face as he tried to squash the tiny rumble of hope bubbling in his stomach.

"You have to be referred to the archivist," Mariah said. "One of his patrons tells you how to find him. Then you have to bring him collateral and an offering. A book, documents, some kind of information, and a juicy little tidbit you'd be devastated if he shared. In exchange, he lets you browse his collection."

"He's a librarian," Eve said.

"His collection doesn't have the kind of books a librarian would want to deal with," Mariah said. "It's all dark spells, centuries-old intrigue, records people have tried to hide."

"And he just has this collection?" Jerek said.

"Just because information is vile doesn't mean it should be destroyed," Mariah said. "The archivist guards the worst parts of the feu."

"That should be the Knights Maree's duty," Lincoln said.

"They're more interested in revisionist history," Ari said.

"And you think LeBlanc's important enough for the archivist to have a record of his missing time?" Ford asked.

"Maybe." Mariah shrugged. "It's the first place I'd look."

"Are we really going to take advice from a Chanler?" Eve said.

"You've just told me LeBlanc murdered my mother and burned her corpse," Mariah said.

"Or she's the monster who broke magic," Ford said.

"Mother would never have hurt anyone." Mariah stood and squared her shoulders. "But whatever happened, I need to know the truth."

Jerek laid his palms on the table the way his father used to when he was forcing his mind to stay rational and calm. His father had spent years researching the Fracture. If there really was a font of information his father had been deemed too honorable to know about...

"We need to find out what the archivist knows," Jerek said. "Even if he doesn't have information on LeBlanc, there could be something about how to mend the Fracture hidden in his files."

"Perfect," Mariah said. "If someone will lend me a phone, I'll call Daddy and have him ask the archivist to meet with me."

"Like hell," Eve said. "None of us are that stupid."

"I've just told you I want to know the truth," Mariah said.

Eve stood and rolled her shoulders back, tipping her head from side to side as though preparing for a fight.

Mariah had the sense to back away.

"We're not going to risk you calling Daddy for help," Eve said. "You're going to take us to the archivist yourself."

"I second the motion," Ford said.

"I agree," Jack said.

"This isn't a democracy," Lincoln said. "We can't just decide to go talk to someone based on Mariah's word. We don't even know if this archivist is real."

Ari dug her knuckles into her eyes. "We'll stay here for one more day. We'll rest up and keep searching. If we can't come up with a better plan, we'll head to the archivist tomorrow night."

"Where is this illusive librarian of all nasty magical secrets?" Jack asked.

"Manhattan," Mariah said. "Where else?"

58

Jack

The chalet restaurant offered a vast menu of gourmet items. Unfortunately, none of those items involved human blood.

Getting food for the rest of the crew was enough of a production—Eve had to move the couch she'd used to block the door, they had to assure the dining room that no, they didn't want room service, just six meals to go. Then they had to decide who would go down to the dining room to collect the food and how many people needed to guard Mariah.

Jack chewed on his thumbnail, stifling his need to shout that he could watch Mariah by himself and they could all go eat in the dining room if they would just stop talking about food.

But speaking would mean risking the others noticing his fangs, and no one wants to share a hotel suite with a blood-hungry vampire.

He managed to stay quiet until everyone had decided what they wanted to eat and Ari and Lincoln had been chosen to collect the food.

Ari went into the girls' bedroom to change into a shirt she hadn't slept in. Jack followed as casually as he could manage.

"Ari." He closed the door to the living room, hoping it would look like an attempt to protect Ari's modesty. "I need to borrow your phone."

"I can open my laptop for you." Ari pulled on a clean, flowing, pale pink shirt. "Just keep Mariah away from it."

"The laptop won't work." Jack grimaced. His fangs punctured his lip. "I need to use the man app. I need to find a date so I can feed."

"Oh." Ari twisted her hair into a bun. "It's been a few days since you fed on Ford. Is he still not feeling up to doing it again?"

"I"—Jack licked his blood from his lips—"I didn't ask him. The app would just be easier."

"Easier than someone who's right here?"

"If that someone is your friend's ex, then yes."

Ari watched Jack as she pulled on her shoe, waiting for him to say more.

"Feeding for a vampire, it's different than just eating." He shoved his hands into his pockets to keep himself from chewing on his thumbnail. "It's an *intimate* situation. Which is why most vampires never feed on the same human twice unless that human is their partner, which Ford isn't, and he's your ex, and it would get weird with all of us working together, and I don't want him to feel obligated to be my food source, so I think the app would be the best choice."

Ari furrowed her brow. "You don't want Ford to feel obligated to feed you?"

"Exactly." Jack put too much air behind the single word.

"Right." Ari nodded. "But you wouldn't mind feeding on him?"

"No. I mean yes, because it would get weird, and things are crazy enough around here without me adding to it."

"But if we weren't living in a hell storm of chaos, you'd be interested in Ford potentially becoming more than a onetime feeding."

"He's not into my kind of...relationship." Jack dug his hands farther into his pockets. The seams at the bottoms ripped.

"Crazy question, did Ford actually say he wasn't interested?" Ari stared dead into Jack's eyes like she was daring him to bluff.

"He didn't have to." A different sort of hollow joined Jack's hunger. "I'm not his type."

"If you're talking about the vampire thing, cryptids are exactly Ford's type."

"But I'm also—"

"A guy?" A hint of laughter lifted the corners of Ari's eyes. "Ford's Bi."

"What?"

"And don't worry about the ex thing on my end. Ford and I work way better as friends." Ari tugged on her other shoe. "So do you want the phone, or would you rather actually talk to the guy you're crushing on and see if he's interested in a second rendezvous?"

"I don't want to—"

"Hmm?" Ari leaned toward Jack.

"But it could get awkward if—"

"Sorry, what was that?"

"Okay, I'll talk to him." An odd feeling, like he should have been blushing, crept up Jack's cheeks.

"Good. If it doesn't work out, you can use the app." She headed toward the bedroom door, then turned back around. "By the way, the girls' bathroom has a bigger shower." She winked and left Jack alone to chew on his thumbnail in peace as he wondered how to ask the guy he liked to dinner, when that guy would be the meal.

59

Ari

One day to research before making their next move had seemed like a perfect plan when things were spinning out of control, but by 2 a.m. the horrible churning in Ari's gut screamed that she hadn't given them enough time.

The feu message boards were a bust. The eight references to the archivist she'd found were so obscure and ominous, breaking back into the Museum of Magic and trying mend the Fracture with a rousing round of kumbaya seemed like a better plan than going to Manhattan to find the boogeyman.

A life lived without the archivist's notice is not beyond your reach was the loving advice a mother emailed her delinquent son.

The archivist's offering must be paid. If you fail, you will forfeit more than your good name. Another email.

No official Maree references. No footnotes in the records of The Council of the Feu.

Nothing but veiled threats in emails written by magicians too clueless to realize the archivist wasn't the only one who could gather information people didn't want found.

A flicker of movement pulled Ari's focus away from her screen.

Mariah crept into the room, holding two steaming mugs.

"Anything yet?" she whispered as she closed the door behind her, leaving Eve and Lincoln sleeping in the living room, guarding the outer door.

"Nothing useful." Ari closed her laptop before Mariah could get a glimpse of the screen. "It seems like the archivist may actually exist, but there's nothing beyond what you've told us."

Mariah set a mug for Ari on the bedside table, then perched at Ari's feet. "Things are like that in our circles."

"Annoyingly obscure?"

"Secret." Mariah held her mug in both hands. "Maybe it was different before the Fracture, but everyone I know is terrified of losing everything. Their status, their money, whatever power they've managed to cling to."

"So sad to be rich and frightened."

"Not sad. More like pathetic." Mariah breathed in the steam from her tea. "Daddy was so afraid after the Fracture and losing Mother, he let LeBlanc take over our lives. I don't have a single friend I really know or trust. It's all perfect pictures and stories of dazzling success. We all know that showing any weakness could invite the piranhas who would happily eat you alive to climb a little closer to the top of the crumbling peak of feu society."

"I feel like I should say *poor little rich girl*, but it really does sound lonely." Ari lifted her mug from the bedside table, letting its warmth soothe away some of her fatigue.

"It could be a lot worse. If I ever feel too trapped, I have a lovely sailboat waiting at the pier." Mariah grinned. "If we hadn't lost Mother, and Daddy had kicked LeBlanc out of our lives, I'd say I was better off than any other child of the Fracture."

"If Eve ever asks, lead with that part." Ari sipped her tea.

"Would you really let her gut me?"

"Honestly, I don't think I'd be able to stop her. I'm a decent fighter, but I don't think I'd stand a chance against an angry Eve."

Mariah turned to sit cross-legged facing Ari. "Where did you learn to fight?"

"A perk of one of my mother's failed marriages. My favorite of the step-squad owns a martial arts studio. He still lets me train with him when I'm home."

"Where is home?"

"Vegas." Ari let herself breathe in the steam from the mug as Mariah had done. But the comfort didn't come from the soothing scent of the tea, just the promise of moisture. Even a bit of steam was better than the awful dryness of Vegas where every breath reminded her she was trapped on land.

"Did you always live in Vegas?"

"We started off in California, but Mom didn't want to raise me so close to the coast."

"Not a fan of earthquakes?"

"It's a long story."

"I don't have anywhere better to be. And I'm not just saying that because there's a werewolf guarding the door." Mariah scooted forward and leaned toward Ari, her shoulder brushing against Ari's arm as she set her tea on the bedside table. When she straightened up, her knees were only an inch away from Ari's. "So, why did your mom take you away from California?"

Ari took another deep breath of the steam. "I don't think that's something I should talk about with you."

"Too juicy?" Mariah cocked her head, a glint of teasing in her eyes. "I promise you can't shock me."

"Just too much. That story isn't the kind of tragedy I can share with you." Ari set her tea down. "I think you should sit on your own bed."

"Why?" The teasing in Mariah's eyes didn't fade.

"Because sitting together and sharing secrets feels too much like there's an *us*. And that's not going to happen." Ari unfurled her legs and stood. "It'll be better for both of us if we keep that line clear."

"What line?" Mariah stood, taking Ari's hands. "I understand that we're just getting to know each other. I'm not trying to push anything—"

"It can't happen, Mariah. I don't want to hurt you by pretending there's any chance of us becoming a thing."

Mariah yanked her hands back. "I ran away with you. I left my father."

"To escape LeBlanc."

"I trusted you."

"And I did what I promised. I got you out. I'm sorry if you thought I was offering more."

"Thought?" Mariah's shout bounced around the high-ceilinged room. "You kissed me. Were you playing me? Just string the sad little lesbian along to get her to run away from home?"

"That's not—"

"I heard them talking about you and Lincoln, but I was actually dumb enough to think they'd all misunderstood. I'm such an idiot. I got queer baited so hard I threw my whole damn life away!"

"I've never baited—"

"You kissed me!"

"You're right!" This time, Ari's shout bounced around the room. "I did kiss you. But kissing Lincoln doesn't make me any less queer and neither does not wanting to start something with you. I'm pan as hell, and that's never going to change. But I can't trust you to be alone in a room with my laptop because I don't know if you'll send a message that could get me and my friends killed."

"Ari—"

"I want you to be on our side, and I want you to be trustworthy. But I wouldn't bet my life on you. And I have a solid *don't date anyone you wouldn't trust with your life* rule. I'm sorry, Mariah, I really am. But the only thing we can be is two badass bitches saving the magical world."

"Don't say you can't trust me like I've ever lied to you, like I've ever pretended to be anything I'm not." Tears slipped down Mariah's cheeks. "I didn't break into your house, I didn't tie you up, I didn't kiss you and pretend to care when I didn't. That was you, Ari. You're the one who can't be trusted."

"I'm sorry." Ari picked up her laptop, holding it to her stomach like it could somehow shield her from the ache of knowing Mariah was right. "But I'm fighting against a murderer who broke our world. I can't be a faultless knight in shining armor if there's going to be any chance of us winning.

"I won't pretend I regret any of it, but I am truly sorry I hurt you. I'm sorry you thought there was something bigger between us."

Mariah swiped the tears from her cheeks with her sleeve.

"You should get some sleep." Ari cut past Mariah toward the bedroom door.

"I'm the only person Daddy has left. And I just abandoned him."

"Then let's nail LeBlanc and get his ass out of your house for good." Ari crept into the living room, quietly closing the door behind her.

Eve raised her head up, opening her eyes just long enough to see it had been Ari who'd entered the room before settling back down on the couch that blocked the outer door.

There were normal chairs by the breakfast bar and a fluffy chair near the TV, but Ari crept toward the second, non-pullout couch where Lincoln slept.

His mouth hung just a little bit open, like he'd been sleeping too soundly for Mariah and Ari's shouting to wake him. He was too tall to fit on the couch, so his calves rested on the arm, leaving his feet dangling in the air.

Ari sat beside him. Leaning against the warmth of his blanket, she closed her eyes, trying to think of something she'd missed.

If she'd never heard of the archivist, what other secrets were lurking in the shadows of the feu.

Too many.

A gentle touch brushed against her shoulder.

"You okay?" Lincoln whispered.

"Yeah." Ari opened her eyes, still unable to think of a new path to follow. "I didn't mean to wake you up."

"You need sleep, too." He touched her cheek.

"I have more work to do."

"You can finish in the morning."

"I won't be able to sleep until I come up with something useful."

"Can I help?"

"No." Ari leaned against his hand. "But can I sit by you while I work? I don't want to be alone right now."

"I'll stay up with you." Lincoln started to sit up.

"Don't." Ari took his hand and kissed his palm. "I just want to be near you while you sleep."

Lincoln shifted, sitting up just enough to press a kiss to Ari's temple then turning so his hand draped over her shoulder.

"Promise you'll wake me if you need anything?" Lincoln whispered.

"Promise." Ari brushed another kiss on his hand before opening her laptop and diving into secrets that had begun more than a decade before.

60

Eve

If Ari had been a member of the pack, Eve would have worried about her flaring wild and losing control of her shift. The rings under her eyes. The manic scent pouring off her.

"Drink, Ari." Ford was the first to dare to go near her. He lifted one of her hands off her keyboard and wrapped it around an iced coffee. He gently placed the straw in her mouth before slowly backing away.

"Is giving her caffeine really a good idea?" Jack asked in a low tone—not that it mattered since Ari didn't seem to be able to hear the rest of them, even when they were speaking right to her.

"She needs it. And iced coffee is the only thing I can be sure she'll drink when she gets like this." Ford hopped up to sit on the kitchen counter to finish his lunch. "I tried giving her water once, tried for an hour, and I could only get her to take a sip."

"How often does this happen?" Jack asked.

"Whenever desperation meets genius." Ford shrugged. "I've been with her for four or five of her deep dives into brilliance."

"But she'll be okay?" Jack sat beside Ford. His eyes flicked to the new pink band aid on Ford's neck before he pinned his gaze on Ari, like he was sly enough for them to not know what had happened last night.

Even a somb who'd seen horror films would be able to guess what the band aid was covering, but whether Jack was jonesing for his next meal, proud of his work, or worried about what everyone would think of him and Ford spending an hour locked in the bathroom together, that was anybody's guess.

"—depends on when she feels like she's done." Ford's voice came back into focus.

Eve rolled her shoulders, forcing herself to concentrate on the circular conversation making another lap through the group.

"We still need to be ready to leave tonight," Jerek said. "As soon as the sun is down."

"Are we sure New York is the best plan?" Lincoln said.

"Last I checked, there was no other plan." Mariah sat in a chair in the back corner of the living room, as far from Lincoln as she could manage without fleeing to her bedroom.

"We could—" Lincoln stood, angling his back to the corner, like he wanted to keep everyone in his line of sight. "I could reach out to one of my brothers."

"No," Eve said.

"I could even contact my parents." Lincoln ignored her. "I don't have to mention the Fracture or trying to mend it. My parents could have heard something about LeBlanc being dismissed from the Maree when it happened. They might know who his friends were."

"They also might give our location to the Council of the Feu and get us all captured," Eve said.

"My family wouldn't betray me," Lincoln said.

"Funny, I took a blade to the gut that says otherwise." Eve stood to face Lincoln.

"Please don't fight in the hotel room," Jerek said. "If security kicks us out, Jack will die of sun exposure."

"I'd rather not do that," Jack said.

"My brothers never betrayed me," Lincoln said. "I sent them information before I knew Jerek was right about the Fracture. I told them to get the younger ones someplace safe. They never shared any information I told them not to."

"How do you know?" Mariah asked.

Lincoln ignored her, too. "Martin helped us escape the Museum of Magic. He could help us again."

"Do you really want to risk getting him involved?" Jerek asked.

"We're Knights Maree who are sworn to protect the feu," Lincoln said. "What could be more worthy than fixing the Fracture and bringing the one behind it to justice?"

"By justice, you mean death, right?" Eve let the rage that filled her chest add a growl to her words. "Because I'm more interested in revenge. If you try to keep me from killing LeBlanc and whoever else might have had a hand in murdering my family, you'll become my enemy, Maree, and I promise you don't want that."

"Now, now, children there's no reason to fight," Ari said.

"There she is," Ford said as everyone else in the room inched toward Ari like they'd all been captured by a morbid need to make sure she really was alive.

"Are you okay?" Lincoln knelt an arm's length away from Ari.

"Of course." Ari closed her laptop and drained the rest of her iced coffee. "And the last thing we need is to get your family involved in this."

They all stayed silent as she stood. She shook out her feet, then headed toward the kitchen, cutting between Eve and Jerek like she hadn't noticed they were all watching her.

"Ari, why shouldn't we let Lincoln's family get involved?" Ford hopped off the counter, giving Ari space to grab a plate from the cabinet.

"Because the important part is what's not there. It's the beauty of missing pieces." Ari got her leftover pasta from the fridge and dumped it onto her plate.

"I don't get it," Jack whispered.

"Wait for it," Ford said.

Ari took two bites of cold pasta.

"Ari, what's not there?" Ford asked.

"Records," Ari said. "And not just LeBlanc's. I slipped into the Maree database, trying to find something, anything with LeBlanc's name on it during his missing year. There's nothing. Not a single record."

"How odd." Ford poured Ari a glass of water while she took another bite. "What else?"

"It didn't make sense," Ari said. "How could one Maree just vanish for a year? Like he was surgically removed from the records. But if they excised LeBlanc, that would leave gaps in other records. So, I started digging through other Maree's records during that time. There are gaps in other knight's files. One month here, two months there. None of them are as long as LeBlanc's, and none of them were dismissed from the Maree. But I'm willing to bet they all had something to do with whatever LeBlanc was up to."

"And what do you think that is?" Jerek said.

Ari chugged her glass of water. "No idea. I stopped looking at that."

"What? Why?" Eve said. "LeBlanc is the one who—"

Ford held up a hand, silencing her.

Eve pressed down the urge to tear his hand off.

"What did you look at instead?" Ford asked gently.

"Books," Ari said. "I love books. Books are great, but they royally screw me over sometimes. If there aren't digital copies, there's not much I can do. They just disappear. Like LeBlanc's record disappeared.

"In all the books and files I've looked through, I haven't been able to find anything about how the Fracture could have been caused or how it could be mended that wasn't included in Jerek's dad's research."

"He was thorough," Jerek said.

"For a Holden." Ari pointed her fork at him. "Mariah's right. Your dad would never have owned books about the darker side of magic, and if he tried to search for them, he wouldn't have been able to find as much as I have no offense."

She strung the last bit on quickly as though already assuming Jerek wouldn't be offended.

"And what did you find?" Jerek asked.

"Nothing." Ari chugged another glass of water, not seeming to notice everyone still staring at her.

"What kind of nothing?" Ford asked.

"The kind that would drive a research librarian crazy. I went back about twenty years and looked at all the references I could find about books trading hands. Estate sales, Council of the Feu confiscations, even an academic reference or two. Fast forward to right after the Fracture, I can't find any more mentions about half the books that focused on dark magic. Jump forward to today, boom, all of them are gone." Ari shoveled the rest of the pasta into her mouth.

Ford was ready with a fresh glass of water.

"Where did—" Jack began quietly.

"But here's the kicker," Ari said, "none of those books are listed in Chanler's personal collection *or* the library in the

Museum of Magic. Chanler spent years hoarding magical arti-facts, but the quintessential volume on manipulating the dead, not in his collection."

"Daddy never hoarded anything," Mariah said.

"Don't make me rip your arms off." Eve shot a withering glare Mariah's way.

The princess had the sense to back down.

"No books on blood magic. Not a single book on mass enchantment of sombs. We know those books exist, but where the hell are they?" Ari pressed the button on the single-cup coffee maker.

Ford grabbed a mug from the cupboard, shoving it below the stream of coffee just in time.

"So, I went through the back door and took a peek at the inventory of books held by the Council of the Feu, spoiler alert, the books aren't there and the Knights Maree don't have them either," Ari said.

"You can't keep hacking into the Maree's computers," Lincoln said.

"Then tell them not to make it so delightfully easy," Ari said. "If the books have disappeared and LeBlanc's records have disappeared, what does that mean?"

Everyone stared at her.

"Is that a real question this time?" Jack whispered.

"Why wouldn't it be?" Ari said.

"It means that a bunch of really helpful information is miss-ing," Jack said.

"Right. And?" Ari reached for the coffee.

Ford darted behind her, grabbed an ice cube from the freezer, and popped it into the coffee cup before the steaming liquid reached Ari's mouth.

"And how the hell does that much information just disap-pear?" Eve said. "The Maree records I understand. They're controlled by one group of people who care more about protecting themselves than anything else."

"That's not true and you know it," Lincoln said.

"This isn't the time," Ford said. "Don't distract."

Eve stepped closer to Lincoln, planting herself at the perfect distance to grab his arm and flip him on his ass.

Ari downed the rest of her coffee and pressed the button on the machine again.

"Okay, that's a lot of caffeine." Jack furrowed his brow.

Ford pulled out another ice cube.

"That's it? That's all you have?" Ari said. "The Maree are way too into protecting their reputation?"

"The Maree taking the books doesn't make sense," Eve said. "They'd have to manage it without any of the feu realizing what they're doing. Confiscating magical knowledge would be enough to break the treaty."

"Ding ding. Give the girl a villain to gut," Ari said. "If the Knights Maree stole all those books, it would be a conspiracy that could start the war they've been trying to avoid for hundreds of years. There's no way the knights would risk it."

"No. They wouldn't." Lincoln shifted, backing up to place himself just behind Eve.

She'd have to turn to grab him. That might give the Maree an edge.

I've been trapped in this room for too long.

"So someone—not Chanler, not the Maree, and not the Council of the Feu—has been very, very naughty. *And* the line up between the missing Maree records and the missing books is too convenient. I think the same person has been messing with the records and stealing the books," Ari said.

"The archivist," Mariah said.

"And we have another winner," Ari said. "Really, we're all massive winners right now. We should all eat cake."

"I'll call the dining room." Ford reached for the place where there should have been an in-room phone, frowning when there was nothing but a loose cord.

Jerek handed him his cell phone.

"Thanks," Ford whispered.

"Why are we winners?" Eve asked. "We already knew we wanted to go to the archivist."

"Don't taint my victory," Ari said. "We just went from a *meh, we don't have any better ideas* plan, to a *well shit, we might be looking at the path to the holy grail* plan. That is a huge step up. All signs point to the archivist not only having the book with the spell that caused the Fracture—"

"But also knowing what happened during LeBlanc's missing time," Jerek said. "If we can find those records—"

"We might be able to find irrefutable, would hold up in a somb court, proof that LeBlanc helped cause the Fracture." Ari finished her second cup of hot coffee. "Proof of LeBlanc's guilt and a shot at finding a way to mend the Fracture without needing a sacrificial lamb all in one place."

"But you were railing about how my mother died when the Fracture was created," Mariah said.

"When LeBlanc had his hands in the incantation," Ari said.

"My father found a way to mend the Fracture without any of the resources the archivist has—" Jerek said.

"And there's not a chance in frozen, ice dancing hell that LeBlanc is as good as we are," Ari said. "If we can accomplish all we have with nothing but three notebooks and a dream—"

"What can we do with actual information?" Jerek sank down onto the couch.

"The limit does not exist." Ari pressed the coffee button again. "We've spent years mining for scraps, and now we've found a nefarious diamond mine. All we have to do is dive in."

"I don't want to kill the excitement, but how do we dive in?" Jack said.

"I'm still working on that part," Ari said. "But we've broken into places before."

"We can't steal an entire library's worth of books and records. Even I'm not that good," Jack said. "We'll have to know exactly what files and what books we need."

"Then we make the archivist tell us." Eve shrugged. "If he's been hiding proof that LeBlanc had anything to do with the Blood Mountain Massacre, our questioning him will be the least of his worries."

"Go to New York, break into the archives, question the archivist, find the spell that caused the Fracture, formulate our own spell to mend the Fracture that doesn't involve anyone dying, get the records about LeBlanc's missing time, figure out who helped him, let Eve have her own special kind of party with them as honored guests, then we have our own fabulous afterparty to congratulate ourselves for saving the magical world and stopping some evil killers." Ari beamed at them all.

"Sounds...easy." Mariah looked halfway between terrified of Ari's plan and nauseous at the thought of Eve getting the vengeance she'd craved for so long.

"We'll need to book a place to stay in New York," Jerek said. "Would midtown be ideal, Mariah?"

"Upper West Side," Mariah said.

"We need to scout the archives," Jack said. "Security systems have never been on my list of specialties."

"We'll find a way in," Eve said. "Even if I have to smash through the front door."

"Discretion would probably be better." Ari sipped her coffee and sank down into one of the kitchen chairs. "The last thing we need is to end up fighting Maree again. We just have to...have to slip in and out."

Ari's eyes fluttered shut.

"And she's spent," Ford whispered. "Welcome to hibernation mode. I'll put her in bed."

"I've got it." Lincoln cut around Eve to stand by Ari's chair, facing Ford like he was ready to fight for the chance to carry the completely unconscious Ari.

"Sure." Ford stepped back, plastering himself to the fridge to move out of Lincoln's way. "Make sure you put her under the covers. When she's been on a tear like this, it wipes her out for a while. Her heart slows down, and she gets cold. The coffee helps keep her heartrate up a little bit, but it's not enough. She still needs layers to keep warm. If she starts shivering, it's hard to get her to stop."

"I'll put extra blankets on her." Lincoln scooped Ari into his arms. She hung completely limp.

"Put some socks on her," Ford said. "Her feet go white and blue."

"Right." Lincoln looked down at Ari for a moment before holding her tighter. "I'll layer those, too."

He carried her into the girl's bedroom.

"Shouldn't we be worried?" Mariah said. "Her feet turning blue? Her heartrate slowing down? She's had enough coffee her heart should be racing."

"That's funny." Eve gave a low, dry laugh. "Keep worrying about that caffeine consumption."

"Nobody has to worry," Ford said. "I already ordered the cake for when she wakes up."

61

Jack

The van jostled with a thump as Jerek hit another dip in the mountain road.

Jack gasped, clinging to Ari's laptop, keeping her precious pink device safe. He waited a moment to make sure the danger had passed before loosening his grip and going back to work.

"Since we're going to be checking in after midnight, there are limited options for housing." Jack clicked over to the hotel's homepage, scanning the details of the available rooms before continuing. "The best I can find is a two-bedroom suite in a boutique hotel. There are enough beds for all of us, and no windows in the sitting room, but the price is...panic-inducing."

"It's fine," Jerek said. "Get the Milton Rayburn card out from under my seat. They won't be able to trace that one."

"But is the credit limit high enough?" Jack carefully passed

Ari's laptop to Eve before crawling forward to dig under Jerek's seat.

"He's a Holden," Eve said.

"The Rayburn card can take a hundred thousand," Jerek said.

Ford whistled.

Jack flicked through the credit cards and IDs in the box. "I never thought of housing as being the most expensive part of planning a heist or saving the magical world. Fancy equipment, plane tickets, hush money—but never housing."

"If it's getting too rich for Holden's blood, I can tap into my trust," Mariah said.

A growl rattled in Eve's throat.

Jack snapped the box of cards shut and scrambled back toward Eve, snatching Ari's laptop away from the hazards of Eve's rage.

"You can't tap into your trust," Lincoln said.

"I assure you, I can," Mariah said. "I gained access to the money Mother left me when I turned sixteen."

"And what about Daddy Dearest's money?" Eve asked.

"That comes in stages." Mariah smiled at Eve, like she knew how badly Eve wanted to rip her apart and was having fun tapping on the glass. "I'll get part on my eighteenth birthday, part when I finish whatever educational path I choose, part when I marry, and the rest when I have my first child."

"Getting paid to breed." Eve leaned forward in her seat.

"In my circle, we call it continuing the family line." Mariah winked. "Somebody has to protect Daddy's legacy."

"We are all set to check into our hotel upon arrival!" Jack shouted before Eve could leap across the van to kill Mariah. "I don't know how Ari manages all this."

"Carefully," Jerek said.

Jack looked to where Ari slept on one of the two benches

running along the sides of the van, waiting for her to sit up and say something witty about being brilliant, but she didn't move.

Lincoln had folded up one of Ford's shirts for her to use as a pillow and draped one of his own over Ari's shoulders like a fairly useless blanket.

Everyone but Jerek rode in the back of the van as they headed toward Manhattan.

Lincoln sat on the floor by Ari's head, bracing her with a hand on her side every time they hit a bump.

Mariah had been placed on the backseat, across from Eve, who sat next to the van's double doors watching Mariah as though waiting for an opportunity to murder Chanler's precious heir.

Ford sat on the bench opposite Ari, in his own world as he typed furiously, his brow furrowed like he was trying to syphon the information out of the internet and right into his brain.

Jack sat beside Ford, trying to feel like booking their hotel somehow made him useful.

The rumble of the road changed as Jerek steered them onto the highway.

"Not good enough," Ford muttered to himself, jabbing the delete key as though it had somehow personally disappointed him.

"Do we want to try street parking for the van, or should I look for a garage?" Jack asked.

"Garage," Jerek said. "I don't want the van on the street. We should keep her out of sight."

"You got it."

I'm a valet. I started as a thief, and now I'm dealing with parking places and check-in hours.

"You're sure the archivist is on 87th?" Ford whipped his head toward Mariah, who had the sense to shy away.

"I told you it was," Mariah said.

"Where?" Ford slid down the bench, knocking his knees against hers.

"I don't know the address," Mariah said. "I only saw the place once."

"Show me exactly which house." Ford turned his laptop toward her. He'd pulled up a street view map, showing all the houses in real, if slightly distorted, detail.

"White with black trim. Bay windows with iron detailing along the top. A little gate that blocks the front steps..." Mariah clicked west along 87th street. "There. That's the one." She tapped on a house that matched her description.

"Are you sure?" Ford asked.

"Yes," Mariah said.

"Really sure?" Ford asked.

"Yes," Mariah said.

"Shit." Ford slumped in his seat.

"What's wrong?" Jerek looked at them through his rearview mirror.

"If you're looking for a secure place to hide questionable feu information, nothing." Ford closed his laptop and set it aside. "If you want to break in, there's a lot lacking."

"Like?" Eve said.

"There are no connecting cellars on that block, no subterranean points of entry at all." Ford dug his fingers into his soft, blond hair. "There are also no fire escapes in that part of town."

"Is that legal?" Jack asked.

"Of course," Mariah said. "They changed the law when they realized rusty fire escapes are tacky."

"Not quite how it happened," Ford said, "but the outcome is the same. There's no way to come up from under and no fire escape to get in on a higher floor."

"Don't forget the security system," Mariah said. "Someone like the archivist has got to have an amazing security system."

"Are you aware you're not helping?" Ford asked. "Or is tossing problems at people how you show support?"

"What about blueprints?" Lincoln said. "Can we find out what the archivist's security system looks like?"

"Blueprint maybe," Ford said. "Security system? Probably not."

"Then we'll do it the old-fashioned way," Eve said.

"Stake out the house and search for weak points?" Ford said.

"Bust in and take out whoever gets in our way," Eve said.

"We can't storm in," Lincoln said. "If this man has all the books Ari thinks he does, breaking through his front door could easily be a death sentence."

"Then I'll go through a window," Eve said.

"We already almost lost you once," Jack said. "I don't think any of us want to go through that again."

"We're not going to find a risk-free plan," Eve said.

"But we can be smart about it," Lincoln said.

"I'm not going to take advice from a Maree," Eve said. "Waiting and cowering aren't my specialties."

"And alarm systems aren't mine," Jack said.

"Ari might be able to figure it out." Ford said. "If we wait until she wakes up, then—"

"Or we could just ask Daddy to walk us in." Mariah spoke over the growing chaos.

"What?" Eve said in a tone a reasonable person would have recognized as dangerous.

"Daddy is a patron of the archivist," Mariah said. "We picked Daddy up after one of his meetings with the archivist, that's how I know where the house is."

"You've never been inside?" Ford said.

Mariah didn't bother glancing his way. "If I get Daddy to come to New York, he could just walk in. He could give me his recommendation as a new member and introduce me to the archivist himself."

Eve sprang up, moving so quickly it was hard to tell how she'd gone from sitting on the floor to being in a crouch, poised to attack. "There is not a chance in hell you and Daddy Dearest are waltzing into that house."

"Daddy's been in the archives before. He could help," Mariah said. "If LeBlanc really was involved in my mother's death, we have just as much a right to vengeance as you do."

Eve launched herself at Mariah.

Mariah had the sense to scream as Jack dove toward her, using his body as a shield to keep Eve from murdering her.

"Both of you stop!" Lincoln bellowed as Jack swept his arm down, trying to knock Eve off her feet.

But she was too fast. She got a hand behind Jack, laying him out face first on the carpet in a single blow.

"Do not hurt the van!" Jerek didn't bother pulling over as Lincoln grabbed Eve's arm, buying Mariah a split second to dive into the safety of Jack's cubby.

62

Eve

The way Mariah winced as she walked gave Eve a soothing sense of satisfaction. Even precious *Daddy's* money couldn't protect her when a fight broke out. If they hadn't been in Jerek's van, and Ari hadn't been passed out on the seat, and they hadn't needed Mariah's knowledge of the archivist, Eve could've slashed Mariah's throat open. Or, broken her neck if cleanup was an issue.

Plotting Mariah's death added beauty to the day as she followed Jerek, Lincoln, Ford, and Mariah along 86th Street, heading toward the archivist's multimillion-dollar lair.

"We should take turns doing surveillance," Lincoln said. "Five of us loitering in an upscale neighborhood could draw attention."

"I'll stay with Princess Chanler." Eve grinned as Mariah's shoulders tensed.

"No thank you," Mariah said.

"I'm not sure you're allowed to make choices like that," Ford said in such a calm, blunt way Mariah didn't try to argue with him.

"We can keep switching groups," Jerek said. "I'll pair with Eve first then Lincoln can do a pass with Mariah."

"Are *you* allowed to make decisions like that?" Ford said. "I thought Ari banned you from—"

"But he's right," Lincoln said. "They're less likely to catch on if we're passing with different people."

"As long as I'm not the one who has to tell Ari that Jerek was making decisions while she was resting." Ford stopped at the sidewalk seating in front of a coffee shop that promised the best pastries in Manhattan. "Give me a minute to test my connections for special super stealth operations..." He flipped open his laptop, furrowing his brow while he checked something that looked far more complicated than a normal internet login. "We...are...good!"

"Perfect," Jerek said.

Ford pulled out his tablet, tossed his backpack into one of the chairs, and settled himself at the table. "We'll be up and running in two and can someone grab me a coffee so I don't get kicked out?"

"I'll go," Mariah said.

"Don't—" Eve began.

"I'll watch her." Lincoln held out his hand, accepting cash from Jerek.

"In case of emergency, the code word is *butterscotch*." Ford didn't look up from his tablet.

"I'm not using a code word." Eve strode down the street, leaving Jerek running to catch up to her.

"It's a decent code word," Jerek said as they waited for the crosswalk light to turn. "Coming from Ford, it's quite respectable."

"Nothing about walking laps in front of a house when the person inside might know who murdered my family is respectable, Holden," Eve said.

Jerek didn't respond until they'd crossed the street and put distance between themselves and the New Yorkers who'd been waiting for the light.

"We're not making laps," Jerek said. "We're doing surveillance."

"Like I said, walking laps."

"We'll be doing more than that soon enough."

Jerek slowed as they reached the white house with black trim. The building looked the same as it had on the internet except for two massive urns of flowers flanking the front door.

"We're only going to get one shot at this." Jerek leaned against a tree catty-corner to the house. "We need to know if there's anyone inside besides the archivist. Any hint as to what kind of security system he has would be useful as well."

"I know what we're looking for." Eve glared at Jerek even as she tried to match his relaxed stance.

Cross the street, hop the gate, smash through a window. I'd be inside in twenty seconds max.

"I want you to come in with us," Jerek said.

"What?" Eve's attention snapped away from wondering how fast the somb police would come if an alarm went off.

"Having backup on the street may be comforting, but if things go wrong, I want you inside the house," Jerek said.

"I'm sure the archivist won't mind a werewolf tagging along," Eve said.

"There are skylights in the master bedroom on the fourth floor." Jerek nodded to a passing man, even smiled at his two chihuahuas.

The dogs growled, then yipped, then headed straight for Eve.

Damn.

"Sorry." The man scooped one dog under each arm. "Sorry, they get feisty sometimes."

"It's fine," Eve said.

"Thanks." The man carried the dogs away. "Francis, Bacon, if you can't learn to behave, you're going back to doggy school."

"If you can get to the fourth-floor balcony, you can come in through the skylight," Jerek continued as though they hadn't been interrupted. "Those glass panels aren't meant to open."

"So they shouldn't have an alarm on them." Eve shut her eyes, picturing the few images of the back of the house Ford had managed to find. "I can get up there."

"Good." Jerek turned his back on the house, letting Eve get a clear view of the place over his shoulder. "Get in, stay quiet, be ready if I need you."

"And if Ari doesn't want me breaking in?"

"Then she can be furious with us once our work is done."

"We're not telling her?" Eve cut around to Jerek's side, leaning against the tree so he could take a turn watching the house.

"Ari's brilliant, but it's different for her than it is for us. I trust her with my life. I trust you to get justice for all we lost."

"And Mariah?"

"If she becomes a problem, handle her."

The hunger burning inside her brought a genuine smile to Eve's lips. "Gladly."

63

Jack

"Shoes with lifts, check. Suit, check. Wig, check." Jack sat on the floor in the sitting room—an aptly named place for those who weren't out casing the archivist's house—ticking his way down the list he'd scrawled on the hotel notepad. "Dress, check. Trouble dealing with the reality of how I got myself into this, check."

He closed his eyes, trying to picture the perfect accessories for the newly ordered outfits without letting his mind wander to wondering what trouble the rest of the crew might be getting themselves into out in the sunlight where there was shit he could do to save them.

"I'll need sunglasses, earrings, cufflinks—"

"Don't put Jerek in a tie," a rasping voice said.

Jack leapt to his feet and reached Ari's side in three long strides.

"You're awake." He knelt next to the couch, placing an arm

behind Ari's back and propping her up to lean against his shoulder. "Ford said to give you water as soon as you woke up."

"Thanks." Ari let him lift one of the three waterglasses Ford had prepared to her lips. She took three big gulps. "How long was I out?"

"About a day."

"No wonder I feel like ass." She finished the glass and reached for the next on her own. "Where are we?"

"Four blocks from the archivist's house. Everyone else is out doing surveillance."

"Mariah's with them?" Ari furrowed her brow and shifted to sit up on her own.

"She demanded it, and Lincoln didn't want her to stay here with you. It was actually kind of cute. Aside from the implication that I wouldn't be able to protect you from Mariah, I think he didn't like the idea of Sleeping Beauty waking up to Mariah watching over her instead of him playing the role of the handsome prince."

"Great." Ari started on the third glass of water.

"It's sweet." Jack poked Ari's leg. "Watching him try not to fall for you has been very entertaining."

"Glad to bring joy to your life." Ari tossed back her blanket.

"Sorry to have to steal joy from yours."

Ari froze with one foot on the ground.

"They've already decided on a plan to get into the archivist's house. They're going in tomorrow morning, and I don't think there's anything we can do to change their minds."

"Great." Ari stood.

Jack gripped her arm as she swayed.

"It gets worse," Jack said. "You and I aren't invited to the party."

64

Grace

The booming thunder shook Grace's bones as though the Florida storm were warning her exactly how much trouble she was in. Another streak of lightning split the sky, reminding her that hiding at the bus stop three blocks from her house was not only a bad idea during a storm this big, it also wouldn't make her fathers any less mad when she eventually had to knock on their front door.

My front door. My home.

I'm going home.

Grace chewed on her bottom lip, trying to think of something to say that would make her parents any less likely to insist on knowing exactly what the hell had happened while she was gone.

"Dammit, Ari." Grace bounced in place as the rain pounded down on the plexiglass roof of the bus stop shelter.

Ari pretending to be Grace and telling her dads she was doing a fancy internship in New York might have been Ari's idea of a good plan, but Grace didn't know anything about Manhattan.

The story would crumble as soon as they started asking questions.

"Hi Dad, Pop. Sorry I ran away. It turns out I'm a magician, and I got mixed up with some people who kill people sometimes, but I left them and came home and I promise I won't catch the house on fire again."

Grace stared at her hands for a moment, making sure sparks hadn't started leaping from her fingers.

"Even if I leave the killing people part out, they're going to think I was hallucinating the whole time I was gone. This is bigger than therapy, Grace." She dragged her fingers through her too-short hair. "I'll be living the inpatient treatment life by the end of the day tomorrow."

She kept chewing on her lip as she watched the rain pound down on the dark street. She swayed from foot to foot, trying to convince herself to move.

"My parents love me." She nodded to no one. "Unconditional love. Whatever the punishment or closely supervised treatment, I can make it through, and then I'll get my life back. Step one is knocking on the door."

She walked out into the rain. Locking her gaze straight ahead, she focused on keeping her feet moving.

A car passed, sloshing water onto the sidewalk and over Grace's feet.

A shower waited inside her house. Clean, dry clothes waited inside her house.

Hot food, her bed.

Her family.

Just get through the door.

Another car passed. Grace didn't bother dodging the sloshing rainwater.

"Hi. I'm home and I'm cold, and I really just need you to tell me everything is okay."

Hot tears streaked through the rain streaming down Grace's cheeks. That was the best, most honest thing she'd been able to come up with.

"Hi. I'm home and I'm cold"—Grace stepped out onto the last cross street before her house—"and I really just need you to tell me everything is okay."

A van cut in front of Grace, stopping in the crosswalk.

She veered sideways to cut behind the van. "Hi. I'm home and—"

Arms wrapped around her waist, lifting her into the air.

"Stop!" Grace kicked back. Her foot made contact, but before she could try to break free, a bright, blue-white light flashed to life beside her.

Silver glinted in the corner of her vision as the light wrapped around her like a rope, binding her arms to her sides with a vicious, buzzing sting.

"Let me go!" Grace tried to kick again, but her captor tossed her through the side door of the van.

A woman dressed in black knelt inside the van, holding a silver dagger whose tip gleamed as it fed the light that bound Grace.

A man jumped into the van and the driver sped away. The man slammed the side door shut before looking down at Grace. He raised his wrist to his mouth.

"The fox has caught the rabbit." The man gave a satisfied grin. "The hunters are coming home."

65

Ari

"Have I mentioned how much I hate this plan?" Ari asked.

"Multiple times." Jerek adjusted the screen of the laptop Ari very graciously held beside the mirror, giving him a clearer view of the face he needed to copy.

"Then don't go," Ari said. "We don't have to get into the archivist's house today. We can take more time to—"

"If you really thought we had time to create a better plan, you would have banned me from going into the archivist's house." Jerek dragged his pointer fingers along his chin, giving himself a better-defined jawline.

"If I told you not to go into what is quite possibly a trap, would you actually listen to me?" Ari asked.

"Of course." Jerek brushed his fingertip against his irises, changing their normal sea blue to a honey brown that matched Mariah's.

"Then don't go." Ari tipped her laptop so Jerek couldn't see the screen.

"Are you giving that order as the de facto leader of this world-saving adventure?"

"I'm asking as a panicked friend. I already came too close to losing you, Jer Bear."

"You really want me to give up the best plan we have when I could finally find out who murdered my mother and find a way to mend the Fracture that doesn't involve sacrificing a life?"

Ari shut her eyes, banishing her tears as she searched for the strength to say yes.

"I'll be fine, Ari." Jerek touched her cheek. "You have my word as a Holden. I have every intention of making it out of that house alive."

"Is that supposed to be comforting?"

"Yes." He kissed her forehead. "Trust me. I'm going to be all right."

"Okay." Ari opened her eyes, wishing she could see Jerek's real face instead of the tan, forty-year-old man who gave her a comforting smile. "You should make your teeth perfect, creepy white."

"And the rest?" Jerek studied his false face in the mirror.

"Ask Mariah," Ari said. "She knows her father's face better than we ever could."

Ari closed her laptop and slid it into her backpack. She'd already tucked her clean socks and underwear into the bag, along with the chargers for all her electronics.

In case we're not done running.

"We'll get through this." Jerek placed his too-tan hand on her shoulder.

"I really want to believe you."

He took her arm, turning her around so he could wrap her in a tight hug. "Tomorrow morning, you and I are going to brunch. *We* are going to sit and eat and be annoyingly proud of how far we've come."

Ari buried her face on his shoulder.

"You can pick any restaurant you want," Jerek said.

"Promise?" She looked up at him.

"On my father's legacy." He tucked her hair behind her ear. "Which is why I need you to trust me."

She backed away from him.

"Ari."

"Don't do this, Jerek."

"Do what?"

"Whatever it is you're about to talk me into."

"I need my ring." Jerek tapped the bottom of her sternum, right where she'd pinned his red-stoned ring to the center of her bra.

66

Jack

With the amount of buzz in the sitting room of their suite, a somb might have assumed Jerek and Mariah were a bride and groom instead of an heiress and her imposter father getting ready to wheedle their way into a townhouse filled with magical secrets.

"Daddy would never wear his hair like that." Mariah batted Jack's hands away from the wig he'd been so carefully placing on Jerek's head.

"Did you really just do that to a vampire?" Jack's fangs grew, piercing his bottom lip.

Mariah ignored him. "The front needs more volume, and the sides shouldn't be as harshly slicked."

A warm hand slipped into Jack's, gently guiding him away.

"Let her primp," Ford whispered.

"It's my only job," Jack whispered back.

Ford let go of his hand.

A weird tremble of embarrassingly desperate abandonment tightened Jack's throat. Before he could berate himself for being a ridiculous sap, Ford touched the small of Jack's back, steering him into a chair beside Ari, who also looked like she was about to jump out of her skin.

Keeping her gaze fixed on Jerek, Ari took Jack's hand, threading her fingers through his, locking their hands together.

"We're all going to be nearby." Lincoln paced in front of the door that led to the hall. "If anything goes wrong, we'll be right there."

"Nothing is going to go wrong." Mariah fussed with Jerek's collar.

"I pressed that shirt," Jack said.

"And you did an acceptable job." Mariah shot him a smile too quick to be anything but dismissive. "Daddy never lets his collar hang that far open."

"If the archivist is worried about your father's collar, then my speaking voice will already give us away," Jerek said.

"Sunglasses and a gravel to his voice are common morning problems for Daddy." Mariah ran a comb through Jerek's wig. "Wince whenever there's a sound and you'll be fine."

Ari tightened her hold on Jack's hand.

"The car is going to be here in five minutes," Ford said. "Have them take you—"

"Down past the southern end of the park, then loop north to the archivist's house," Mariah said. "It's like you all think I don't listen." She brushed off the shoulders of Jerek's jacket. "Your pants aren't hanging right." She reached for Jerek's thigh.

"That's enough." Jerek stepped away.

"My turn?" Ford leapt to his feet.

"Please." Jerek dodged as Mariah reached for the back of his wig.

"An earpiece for you both." Ford placed one of the smaller devices in each of their palms. "*Hopefully*, the surrounding buildings won't interfere too much and we'll be able to clearly hear everything you're saying."

"*Hopefully* is so comforting." Mariah fitted the device in her ear.

"If something goes wrong, just shout *butterscotch* really loud, and I should be able to hear you," Ford said.

"We've moved up to *should*." Mariah fixed her hair in the mirror.

"Shoes, Jerek." Ari didn't let go of Jack's hand.

Jerek sat to put on his shoes. The lifts weren't quite large enough for him to match Louis Chanler's exact height, but even Mariah had the sense not to fuss as Jerek stood and brushed out the front of his pants.

"If my gut instinct to attack you is right," Eve said, "no one will guess you're not Chanler."

"Daddy is a victim, too." Mariah handed Jerek his sunglasses. "Now, try a nice hungover gravel."

Jerek cleared his throat. "I'd like to introduce you to my daughter Mariah."

"Better than I thought it would be." Mariah pursed her lips.

"The car is here," Lincoln said.

"Let's get this over with." Mariah grabbed the clutch Jack had chosen for her, striding past Lincoln and out into the hall without so much as a thankful backwards glance.

Jerek made it to the doorway before hesitating.

"I'll see you all in a bit." He looked right at Ari. "I promise."

A hitched breath like swallowed tears came from Ari as Jerek-made-Chanler followed Mariah down the hall and out of sight.

"We need to get into position." Eve grabbed her earbuds from the table.

Ari gave Jack's hand one last squeeze before letting go. She ran her fingers over her pockets, like she was making sure she hadn't forgotten something, before taking Lincoln's arm and steering him into the hall. Eve followed, leaving Jack and Ford alone.

"See you in a bit." Ford swung his backpack on.

"Be careful, okay?" Jack stood, taking Ford's hand before he could walk away. "If something goes wrong, if anything happens to any of you...I'm trapped in this room. There's nothing I can do to help."

Ford twisted their joined hands so he could kiss the back of Jack's hand.

A tiny flutter rippled through Jack's panic.

"I'll be back soon." Ford let go of Jack and stepped toward the door.

Jack grabbed Ford's wrist, pulling him in, wrapping his arms around his waist.

"If anything goes wrong, I'll never forgive myself." Jack rested his forehead against Ford's. "Don't make me live with that kind of guilt."

"I wouldn't dare." Ford brushed his lips against Jack's, giving him a kiss far too brief to satisfy the longing that overwhelmed Jack's reason as Ford went into the hall and closed the door behind him, leaving Jack alone, useless, and trapped in a hotel room on the Upper West Side.

67

Jerek

The sounds of the city filtered through the blood pounding in Jerek's ears, muddying his thoughts in a panicked way he could never bear to admit.

Mariah ordered the car to make a downtown loop in a brisk tone that would have earned a lecture on appreciating the work of others from Jerek's father.

Breathe, Jerek.

Following Mariah's lead, he waited for the driver to come open his door before stepping out of the car, then walked straight to the archivist's house without acknowledging the driver with so much as a nod.

A bit of rudeness is the least of your worries.

Jerek opened the wrought iron gate in front of the archivist's house, bowing Mariah, his daughter, toward the front steps.

The panic in his chest buzzed even harder when the scent

of the flowers in the two massive urns on the stoop surrounded them as they stood at the front door.

Jerek stared at the painted white wood.

"I'm so excited, Daddy." Mariah gripped his arm a bit too hard. "I've been begging to play a larger role in curating your collection for so long."

"It's not my collection we're here for," Jerek said in a gravelly voice as he rang the doorbell.

He faked a wince as a cheerful, chimed tune carried through the front windows, but the quickening of his heartbeat was genuine.

It couldn't be the overzealous doorbell that was frightening him. Or diving into a dangerous plan.

He'd walked into the Museum of Magic with no intention of coming back out. Giving his life to mend the Fracture had been his goal.

An electronic hum came from the right of the door as a small camera focused on Jerek's face, the sound almost painful against the pounding in his ears.

The hum came again. Mariah turned toward the camera, giving it a little wave as though she felt none of the panic that threatened to drown Jerek.

The humming stopped, but the door didn't open.

Jerek stared at the lock.

Hundreds of years' worth of feu secrets waited just beyond the door. If the archivist didn't answer, if he wasn't home, they could break into the house. Take the information they wanted without ever having to speak to the archivist at all.

The lock turned with a heavy thunk.

An odd and overwhelming sense of calm smothered Jerek's panic as the doorknob turned.

"I expect your most charming behavior, Mariah," Jerek said. "You only get one first impression."

"Are those the wise words that won you your fortune?" the archivist said as he opened the door.

He smiled at Jerek, or Jerek-made-Chanler, in a friendly way that didn't fit the dark persona Jerek had imagined for the keeper of dark secrets. Near forty, with receding but well-trimmed hair, he wore a cardigan over his t-shirt. His eyes didn't seem to hold any malice as his gaze shifted to Mariah, just a wanton hunger obvious enough to spark anger in Jerek's gut.

"My fortune was won with much more mundane words," Jerek said. "Generational wealth and profitable investments."

"And will your fortune survive to be passed on to your daughter?" the archivist asked.

"His fortune and his legacy will." Mariah let go of Jerek's arm and stepped forward, giving a sly smile as she presented her hand to the archivist. "Mariah Chanler. It's a pleasure to meet you."

"And do you know who you're meeting?" The archivist bent to kiss her hand, lingering a bit too long with his eyes level with her breasts.

"Vaguely," Mariah said. "Daddy likes to keep his secrets."

"I've come to recommend my daughter as one of your patrons," Jerek said.

"That's not how this works, Louis," the archivist said. "Or have you forgotten the rules?"

A cool laugh rumbled in Jerek's throat. "Not forgotten, no. But current circumstances require a more expeditious path."

The archivist stared at Jerek.

"It will be worth any inconvenience you might suffer," Jerek said.

"I'll be sure to tell my other patrons that when they want your blood." The archivist stepped aside, letting them into his house.

"Why would they want Daddy's blood?" Mariah latched

back onto Jerek's arm, clinging to him as though they were entering a dungeon instead of a well-decorated home.

The walls had been painted a light, gentle color, giving the entryway and staircase that swept up to the second floor an airy feel, despite the rows upon rows of bookshelves lining the walls.

"Membership to my archives comes with very strict rules, Miss Chanler." The archivist shut the door behind them. The inside of the door had been reenforced with metal and closed with seven locks that could deter any somb thief.

"I envy your battleworthy door," Jerek said. "That many locks in my home, and rumors of my paranoia would spread like wildfire."

"Even after Maree were murdered in your little basement museum?" The archivist unlocked a drawer in the bureau beside the door.

"Especially now," Jerek said. "I can't afford to show any sign of fear."

"Yet you bring your daughter to me." The archivist held out a thick, black bag.

"What's that for?" Mariah said, quickly enough to spare Jerek from guessing.

"It's a faraday bag. I can't risk recordings of my treasures leaking out into the world. This bag prevents that. Phones, watches, any other electronics you have with you must be placed inside. And don't try to cheat. I scan all my guests, Miss Chanler. I would hate to have to search you in front of your father." The archivist winked.

"Daddy and I don't keep secrets from each other. May I?" Mariah stepped behind the archivist to set her clutch on top of the bureau. She brushed her hair back, letting her right hand linger by her ear for a moment as she opened her bag with the left. "You still haven't explained why anyone would want Daddy's blood."

"Do you know what this place is?" the archivist said.

"Some kind of old boys club desperately in need of an infusion of interest from a new generation of magicians." A hint of something shiny and tan caught Jerek's eye as Mariah tucked her phone into her clutch. "Ugh. Can I just put my whole clutch in your Faraday bag? I really don't feel like carrying it. I hate the texture."

"The texture?" The archivist turned to Mariah.

Jerek slipped his earpiece out, palming it as he pulled his phone from his pocket.

"Just because a bag is designer doesn't mean the leather is soft," Mariah said.

"Keep my phone with yours, dear." Jerek slid his phone and earpiece into Mariah's clutch.

"Worried you'll lose it again?" Mariah shook her head and gave a sighing laugh. "You are positively helpless, Daddy."

"Which is why you're here," Jerek said.

Mariah dropped her clutch into the faraday bag and ran her hands over her hips. "That's all I have."

"Good." The archivist closed the bag, folding over the top to secure the metal clasp. He placed the bag in the drawer and locked it with the key from his pocket.

"Can we get back to the blood bit?" Mariah said.

"My collection contains information many would die to possess and more would die to keep hidden." The archivist opened another drawer, pulling out a black baton much like those Jerek had been probed with by sombs at airport security.

Jerek made himself breathe as the archivist swept the baton up one side of his body and down the other.

"Membership to my archives is available only to a very exclusive and elite selection of individuals. Even then, an applicant must be presented with the recommendation of a current member." The archivist ran the wand up the front of Mariah's body, taking extra time as he neared her breasts.

"I have Daddy's recommendation." Mariah's words came out a bit too crisp.

"And did you bring your offering and collateral?" He let the baton slide over the curve of Mariah's buttocks.

"Daddy's the one in charge of the money." Mariah turned to face the archivist, knocking his baton away with her hip.

"Not money." The archivist placed the baton back in the drawer. "I require a much more particular cost of entry for new patrons. One item to grow my collection, and one piece of information that would see you ruined if it ever leaked out of these walls."

"I'm afraid my daughter doesn't have any secrets dark enough to satisfy you." Jerek took Mariah's arm, guiding her back to his side.

"And you've dared to recommend her?" The archivist's lips curved in a satisfied frown. "You've brought her into my home knowing she does not meet the requirements of patronage. A heavy price must be paid to restore—"

"Surely, an exception can be made," Mariah said.

"Her knowing of the existence of the archives endangers all my patrons," the archivist said. "If they found out what you've done, Louis, they would demand the release of your collateral, and then where would you be?"

"Are you trying to blackmail my father?" Mariah yanked free from Jerek's grip and planted herself in front of him.

"I am reminding him of the oath he gave." The archivist's smile didn't falter as he bowed. "I can't be blamed for your father forgetting his end of the bargain."

"I haven't forgotten anything," Jerek said. "My oath holds value, but I have to protect my family. I am being accused of murder. There are rumors of my somehow being responsible for causing the Fracture."

"Such interesting whispers." The archivist's smile stayed.

"I am prepared to provide the offering and collateral on my daughter's behalf," Jerek said.

"How generous."

"My legacy is being threatened," Jerek said. "There is nothing I wouldn't do to preserve the Chanler name."

"Then to the parlor we shall go." The archivist bowed in a deferential way, stepping aside to allow Jerek to lead.

Mariah pulled free from Jerek, looped her arm through the archivist's, and headed down the hall. "How many people's deepest darkest secrets are hidden in this house?"

The archivist steered her toward the stairs instead. "The information in my collection could collapse feu society or create a king."

"How about a queen?" Mariah said. "I look dazzling in a crown."

68

Lincoln

The sunlight-filled morning held a sweet promise in the air. A new day with a mission already underway. A chance to move forward in their quest to mend the Fracture.

That vague, fragile hope settled in Lincoln's chest, adding weight to his every breath. A wrong move, a wrong word, and that hope would crack like a barely frozen lake, leaving him to flounder and drown, trapped in a prison from which he'd never break free.

"We all want coffee, right?" Ari was the only one in their group who managed to look at the menu as their server stood beside their table, giving them a panicked sort of smile Lincoln should have felt sympathy toward.

But the weight of sympathy might break the ice.

"We'll take four coffees," Ari said. "Four croissants for

here—two chocolate, two plain—and two more plain in a to-go box."

"Great." The server fled back into the overcrowded interior of the café.

"I hope that's what everyone wanted," Ari said.

"I'm not eating," Eve said.

"Perfect. More for me." Ari pressed on her ear like she was making sure she hadn't lost her earpiece.

"They aren't at the house yet." Ford kept his gaze locked on the tablet in his hand. "Sounds like they'll be there in a minute."

"Turn on our earpieces," Eve said.

"As you wish." Ford tapped on the tablet.

"I can't hear anything," Eve said.

"They're not talking." Ford shrugged.

"A silent car ride is a great start," Ari said.

"At least their channels are coming in clear," Ford said. "The sound levels would be a lot easier to manage if we were back in a garden instead of surrounded by buildings."

"We should be closer to the archivist's house." Lincoln's leg began bouncing. He dug his heel into the ground to stop the movement.

"We're close enough." Ari laid her hand on his thigh.

The warmth of her touch sent tiny cracks through the ice.

"This is the closest public place we can wait, and lurking on the street would be risky for everyone." Ari left her hand on his leg, as though it were natural for her to maintain physical contact with him.

"I'm so excited, Daddy." Mariah's voice sounded tinny in Lincoln's ear. "I've been begging to play a larger role in curating your collection for so long."

"It's not my collection we're here for." The gravel of Jerek's voice shot another crack through the ice.

Calm, Lincoln. You're a Maree. You're trained for combat.

Ari squeezed his leg.

Then why does this feel worse than charging into a fight?

"Four coffees." The server appeared by their table. She set the coffees down and went back inside, completely unaware of the voices chirping in her customers' ears.

"I expect your most charming behavior, Mariah," Jerek said. "You only get one first impression."

"Are those the wise words that won you your fortune?" An unfamiliar voice spoke.

"The archivist," Ari whispered. "Can you bring up the mics?"

"A bit." Ford tapped on his tablet.

"Here are your croissants." The server placed four plates on the table. "I'm not sure which is for who."

"Doesn't matter." Ford waved the server away.

"Thank you." Ari shot the server a smile.

"They're inside the house." Ford spoke in a tense whisper as the server walked away. "They're actually inside the house."

"That was the plan," Ari said.

I should be there. I should be playing Chanler. I should be protecting Jerek.

"You okay?" Ari leaned toward him.

Lincoln shook his head.

"Why would they want Daddy's blood?" Mariah said.

"What's wrong?" Ari turned toward him, taking both his hands.

"I was sent all the way from Italy to protect Jerek," Lincoln said. "I've defied the Maree, I've fought against fellow knights. If anything happens to Jerek—"

"It won't," Ford said.

"But if it does," Lincoln said. "I will have failed in every way."

"No, you won't," Ari said. "You are fighting to protect the

feu. That is the purpose of the Knights Maree. Everything we're doing, right down to helping Mariah escape LeBlanc, all of it has been to defend the feu and put our world back to the way it should be. The Knight's Council not knowing what you're doing doesn't make your work any less important or noble."

"Some kind of old boys club desperately in need of an infusion of interest from a new generation of magicians." Mariah's microphone popped.

Lincoln winced at the noise.

"What was that?" Ari let go of Lincoln. She stood and cut around behind Ford to stare at his tablet.

"I'm not sure," Ford said. "The channel looks fine."

Lincoln stood, wanting to see the tablet even if he couldn't help, leaving Ford as the only one sitting at the table.

"—with yours, dear." Jerek's words came out muffled.

Lincoln scanned the crowd. Customers at tables. A couple passing on the sidewalk.

"Where's Jerek?" Ari gripped Lincoln's hand. "I can't hear him. I can't hear Mariah."

"I don't know." Ford dragged his fingers up the bars on his screen. "They're gone. Both of their feeds are gone. Maybe they ditched their earpieces."

A pair of white earbuds lay on the café table.

"Their mics were in the earpieces," Ford said. "They both knew that."

"Eve's gone." Lincoln stared at the fourth seat at their table.

"What?" Ari looked to Eve's empty chair.

"She's gone." The ice in Lincoln's chest shattered.

69

Eve

Her fingers itched to flip open the pendants around her neck, not because she needed to defend herself from the New Yorkers who walked at a fast enough pace to suit her long legs, just to feel the power of her transformation tear through her veins, jolting her in a way that could prove this wasn't a dream.

Half-a-block north of the café, Eve turned down the alley that cut behind the archivist's house. It wasn't even really a house. Not by pack standards.

It was a mansion. The archivist lived in a mansion in Manhattan.

Not all rich folk are monsters. The Holdens aren't evil. Gran's voice soothed Eve's rage. *Not all money was gained with blood.*

I know, Gran. I know.

Eve squeezed around a dumpster and the person sleeping beside it.

But if the archivist is the devil…

She stopped just shy of the white-painted backside of the archivist's lair.

When Maree slay monsters, they call it noble. I can't let the knights have all the fun.

She touched the pendants at her neck, making sure her mother's moonstone was still safely hanging next to hers, before taking two long strides and jumping for the archivist's second-floor balcony.

Grabbing the railing, she pushed herself up and over, landing on the deck with barely a sound. She froze for a moment, listening for any hint of an alarm. Taking a step forward, she peered through the balcony doors.

Shelves lined the walls of the room, and in the center, a glass case, like a person-sized terrarium, held even more books.

But there was no movement in the space. No hint of the archivist.

Eve turned, jumping up onto the railing, then jumping again, rotating midair to grab the rail on the third-floor balcony.

She repeated the same process on that level, listening, peeking through the door. That room had glass cases along the walls, filled with artifacts like an exhibit in Chanler's precious Museum of Magic. A hulking statue of a badly carved man took up the back left corner, but there still weren't any signs of living people.

The fourth-floor balcony was only half the size of the lower two, but it didn't make the jump any more difficult. The room that opened out to that balcony wasn't filled with books or relics. An unmade bed and a pile of clothes in the corner made the bedroom look almost normal, like the archivist might be an actual person with a life beyond their hoard.

Eve took a running start and jumped up onto the roof of the archivist's house.

From above, the view of the alley and packed-together houses made the street look more like a line of kennels trapping their owners than mansions fit for the power-hungry elite.

"Who the hell would want to live like this?" Eve whispered.

The siren of a passing ambulance screamed its reply.

Shaking her head, Eve crept to the row of three skylights set into the roof. She knelt beside the glass and ran her hands along the edges. None of the windows had a latch or any way to be opened, just layers of silicone weatherproofing holding the glass in place.

"Great." Eve pressed her palm to her pendants. "Hope nobody's watching."

She flipped open her mother's moonstone.

The blissful thrill of power surged through her as her nails lengthened into claws.

Ignoring the unnatural texture, she scraped her claws through the weather proofing around the glass, peeling the shiny silicone out one strip at a time.

70

Ari

"Where the hell did she go?" Ari stood on her seat, searching the other diners for any hint of a ginger werewolf.

"Bathroom?" Ford said.

"Really?" Ari jumped off her chair and pulled her phone from her pocket.

"I can't get Jerek's and Mariah's feeds back," Ford said.

"Why would she leave?" Lincoln stepped out onto the sidewalk, like they might've missed a six-foot tall redhead.

"Shit." Ari rammed her fingers into her hair.

"What?" Lincoln dodged back to the table.

"Still nothing." Ford swiped open a new page on his tablet. "It's not even interference. Their feeds are just gone."

"And Eve left her earbuds," Ari said. "Not that she would listen if we asked her to come back."

Lincoln dragged his hands over his face. "What the hell is she doing?"

"Shit." A sense of cold, heavy panic started in Ari's feet. "Jerek asked me for his ring. The one with the red stone. He said he needed it in case he had to defend himself."

"Could the ring stop my feeds?" Ford asked. "Giving the archivist their phones wouldn't have affected the sound."

"If he's planning something—"

"And he's got Eve in on it." Lincoln held Ari's gaze.

"He said he wasn't going to do anything stupid." Ari pulled up the hotel's number. "He promised."

The hotel's phone began to ring.

"If you know your party's room number, you may dial at any time."

Ari punched in 302.

"They wouldn't have actually given the archivist their earpieces," Ford muttered. "Tell me you still have your earpiece, Jerek."

"We need to find Eve," Lincoln said.

"And do what?" Ari said. "If she and Jerek are working together, there's shit we can do to stop them without tipping off the archivist."

"Hello?" Jack answered the room phone.

"Jack, can you get to Jerek's pack?" Ari said.

"Sure," Jack said. "It's in the sitting ro—"

"Are the heliostone and Blood List still in there?" Ari asked.

The line went quiet.

Ford stared at Ari. Lincoln tucked his hands behind his back. Both looked tense enough to explode.

"The stone and Blood List are gone," Jack said. "There's nothing in the safe, either."

"Shit." Ari scrunched her eyes shut.

"What's happening?" Jack asked.

"Jerek must have taken them," Ari said.

"But he wasn't carrying anything when he left the hotel," Ford said.

"It doesn't matter," Ari said. "He found a way to sneak them out."

"What can I do?" Panic filled Jack's voice.

Ari ran through the images of the house in her mind. A locked front door. Unknown security system. If Eve had figured out a way in, Ari wouldn't be able to use it.

The ring, the stone, the scroll.

Jerek, Mariah, Eve.

Jerek promised he was coming back out of that house alive.

There could be another reason he took the Blood List and heliostone. There had to be.

"Nothing," Ari said. "There's nothing we can do but hope Eve and Jerek really do have a plan."

Ari hung up.

"Ari." Lincoln reached for her arm.

She ignored him, pulling out enough money to pay for their food and tossing it onto the table. Grabbing Eve's discarded earbuds, she headed out onto the sidewalk.

"Where are you going?" Ford chased after her, tablet in hand.

"Close enough to hear the screams from the archivist's house when shit goes wrong."

71

Jerek

Mariah stayed on the archivist's arm as he led them up the staircase, down a small hall, and into a room lined with more books.

A table with a decanter of brown liquor and a book that had been left open as though hastily set aside sat next to a high-backed chair that appeared to be the most comfortable seat in the room.

The few other seating options were either tucked between shelves or blocked by a stepping stool just tall enough to reach the highest books.

A tingle of fear crept up Jerek's neck even though there were no swords, knives, clubs, or ropes in the room. The only weapons the space presented were the shelves upon shelves of books.

Jerek tucked his hands into his pockets, barely resisting the urge to pluck a book off a shelf and see what secrets or horrors it contained. If all the books on all the shelves held information members of the feu wanted to hide…

We know nothing about our own people.

The archivist led Mariah to a small, antique sofa flanked by two shelves.

Not penned in. Not with my back to the wall.

Mariah sat without complaint.

Jerek meandered to the far side of the room, examining the shelves he passed.

"I must admit, I didn't think this day would arrive so quickly." The archivist sat in the highbacked chair opposite Mariah.

"Hmm." Jerek kept looking at the books, his mind racing through what he as Chanler was and wasn't supposed to know.

The archivist poured two drinks from the decanter.

"So sorry," Mariah said, "but what day didn't you think would arrive so quickly?"

"Your visit." The archivist held a glass out to Jerek. "From everything I've been told, your father didn't wish you to meet me. At least, not until you'd joined the family enterprise."

"Circumstances have changed." Jerek reached for the glass from the archivist.

The archivist held onto the drink a moment too long, staring into Jerek's sunglass-shielded eyes.

Jerek stared straight back.

"Cheers." The archivist finally let go but didn't raise his own glass to toast with Jerek.

"The Museum of Magic is attached to our home." Mariah sat forward on the sofa. "Criminals invaded the museum, Knights Maree died. I don't even feel safe in my own room anymore."

A heavy tone filled Mariah's voice, as though this, of all the things she'd said in Jerek's presence, were the most inarguably true.

"There's a reason for the fiends' intrusion," Jerek said. "There's a reason there are whispers about blood on my hands, about my being connected to the beginning of the Fracture."

"And why has that led you to my door?" The archivist sipped his drink.

"I want to know where these rumors began, and who is responsible for the vile acts I find myself accused of," Jerek said. "And once I've discovered the truth, I want the villains who have sullied my name brought to justice."

A wrinkle pinched between the archivist's eyebrows as he set his drink aside.

"Do you have all that information?" Mariah said.

"Such a funny thing for you to ask." The archivist leaned back in his chair, tipping his head as he studied Jerek.

"Is the truth amusing?" Mariah said.

"More than you know." The archivist clasped his hands together and looked to Mariah. "But first, your collateral and your offering. Which shall I have first?"

"The collateral," Jerek said.

"Perfect." A hungry smile lit the archivist's eyes. "Letters, diaries, bank records?"

"Nothing quite so...flammable," Jerek said.

The archivist frowned.

"Daddy, don't be coy. Mr.—" Mariah looked to the archivist. "Sorry, what's your proper name?"

"The archivist," the archivist said.

"Mr. *The Archivist* may not appreciate your witty brand of charm," Mariah said.

"My apologies." Jerek nodded to the archivist. "The collateral doesn't come with such defined documentation."

"Then sit and explain yourself." The archivist nodded back, gesturing for Jerek to sit beside Mariah.

Jerek glanced toward the other seats in the room. All of

them were placed to the side or behind the archivist at too odd an angle for Jerek to choose another chair without seeming suspicious.

"Come, Daddy." Mariah patted the seat beside her on the sofa.

"It must be difficult when the child begins to shepherd the parent," the archivist said.

"More than you know." Jerek raised his glass to his lips, letting the liquor barely seep into his mouth as he sat beside Mariah.

"Now tell me your lurid tale that has no paper trail before I get bored and toss you out," the archivist said. "Then your lovely daughter couldn't become a patron, and I'd have to let the other members know that you had allowed an outsider to follow you into the place where all their best secrets are hidden. If I sent your secrets out into the world, how long would it take for the Chanler legacy to collapse?"

"Such dire words from a glorified librarian," Mariah said.

"Hush, dear." Jerek gripped her wrist. "There is no need for hostility between friends."

"Of course not." The archivist set his drink down on the table beside his high back chair. "But even between friends, there are limits to patience."

"Of course," Jerek said. "The tragic truth that I offer as collateral is that I've made enemies of the werewolves in North Carolina."

The archivist froze.

"After the Fracture, the butcher attacked the pack that lives on the Holden family's mountain." Jerek held the archivist's gaze. "I knew the lives lost in the bombing would tear the pack apart, I knew orphans had been made, and yet I did nothing to help, though I fully anticipated how desperate things would become.

"I tracked the pack's money, watching, waiting for them to have their electricity cut because they couldn't pay the bill. Kept tabs on who had dared to venture to the sombs' food pantry. And when I knew they were desperate enough to sell their treasures, I descended, preying upon their shattered lives, paying them a pittance to gain symbols of the werewolf legacy that never should have left the pack."

"But you paid them." Mariah pulled her wrist free. "The wolves agreed to give you their trinkets, and you gave them the money you promised."

"Does that make me any less of a monster?" Jerek looked to Mariah. "The museum I claim to be so proud of was built on the pain of the Fracture. I targeted those most wounded by the tragedy that struck the feu. If people knew how I had plotted against the weak and needy, the Museum of Magic could never again be called a bastion of knowledge and history. The feu would see it for what it is—a hoard gained by a grave robber."

"You're wrong." Tears brimmed in Mariah's eyes.

"Your father knows the penalty for attempting to insert falsehoods into my collection," the archivist said. "Louis Chanler would never dare do such a thing."

"No." Jerek held Mariah's gaze. "I wouldn't."

"But the truth of your...less than noble collection is hardly fitting collateral," the archivist said.

"Understandable." Jerek glared at Mariah, trying to act cold, disapproving, and disappointed in a way he'd never been treated by his own father.

Mariah's breath hitched. She flinched and looked up toward the corner of the ceiling, turning her face away from Jerek in a way he took to imply some success.

"However," Jerek pressed on, "my offering is exceptional. I don't think any feu alive would be willing to turn down this treasure."

The archivist circled his hand, gesturing for Jerek to continue.

Holding his breath, Jerek reached into his jacket pocket and pulled out the heliostone. He held the massive diamond forward, allowing it to catch the light.

"What is it?" Mariah whispered.

"The heliostone," Jerek said.

The archivist shifted forward to perch on the very edge of his seat.

"A magical object that could, in the wrong hands, topple kingdoms," Jerek said. "Or even cause the Fracture."

"Where did you find this?" The archivist reached for the stone.

"A treasure hidden within a treasure"—Jerek wrapped his fingers around the diamond, not allowing the archivist to take it—"its true nature concealed in such a way, I must believe the ones who hid it hoped it would never be used again."

"But you say it caused the Fracture?" The archivist stared at Jerek with a darkness in his eyes that extinguished the last ember of Jerek's guilt.

"No, no." Jerek chuckled. "Until a few days ago, the heliostone was trapped within the Caster's Fate. The stone had been completely unusable for centuries."

"Then what does it have to do with the Fracture?" Mariah froze for a moment before adding, "Daddy?"

"I have been accused of murder. I have been accused of causing the Fracture, and in my hand, I hold the means to commit those very atrocities," Jerek said.

"You are wise to leave such a powerful object in my care," the archivist said.

"I didn't bring the stone to you because I fear it," Jerek said. "It is my daughter's offering. She will become one of your patrons."

"A generous contri—"

"And you will provide her with every scrap of information you have on the missing files of the Knights Maree," Jerek pressed on.

"An interesting inquiry." The archivist stood and looped around to stand behind his chair.

"LeBlanc's file is missing a year," Mariah said. "He lives in our home. I want to know what he did that's terrible enough for the Knights Maree to hide it."

"It is such an interesting tale," the archivist said. "Dark for such a young, innocent creature."

"You will provide the information." Jerek stood, making his gaze level with the archivist.

"I don't abide by demands, Louis." The archivist bowed. "You are my patron, not my master."

"You will also dig up every scrap of information you have regarding the genesis of the Fracture." Jerek held out his hand, placing the heliostone in the sunlight peering through the window, making the diamond gleam in an intoxicating way.

The archivist didn't hide his hunger as he stared at the heliostone.

"Will you provide the resources we need to prove my innocence?" Jerek said. "Or should I take my diamond and my search elsewhere?"

The archivist closed his eyes for a moment, giving a little nod as though confirming his own thoughts.

"There is a heavy burden that comes with being the keeper of such powerful secrets," the archivist said. "And deadly consequences for those who would try to steal them."

The archivist cocked his finger.

"Your dedica—"

"No!" Mariah grabbed Jerek's wrist, yanking him sideways as she threw herself to the ground.

Pain ripped across Jerek's ribs as he landed face-first on the floor beside her.

He stifled a scream as he rolled onto his back, ready to spring to his feet.

Mariah planted her hand on Jerek's chest, shoving him back to the ground as a silver disc flew over them, slicing into the wall above the couch with a ringing thud.

"It's a pleasure to meet you, Mariah." The archivist strolled slowly toward them, his finger still cocked. "I'm sure Mr. LeBlanc will be relieved when I call to inform him the wayward Chanler has been found."

"I will not—"

"Please don't." The archivist smiled down at Jerek. "If you truly think your sad imitation of Louis Chanler was enough to fool me, I don't want to waste my time bantering with you."

"No banter then." Jerek shifted, easing his weight off the wound on his side. "But my offer for payment still stands. The heliostone in exchange for all the information you have on the genesis of the Fracture."

"Pity you didn't do more research before your failed portrayal of Louis. It would have saved you a great deal of pain." The archivist held out his hand. "Now give me the heliostone, and I'll keep you comfortable while we wait for LeBlanc to collect you."

"Gladly." Jerek opened his fist but kept his hand just above his chest.

As the archivist reached for the treasure, Jerek kicked out, catching the archivist behind the knees.

The archivist stumbled.

Mariah yelped and rolled away as Jerek reached for the archivist's ankles, trying to pull him down. But a blur soared over Jerek's head, knocking the archivist to the ground with a teeth-rattling thud.

72

Lincoln

"We should have invested in a parabolic mic." Ford paced between two trees, keeping his gaze locked on his feet, as though not looking up might somehow stop anything horrible from happening inside the archivist's home. "We need to be able to hear. We need to find a way to get them out."

"We don't know that anything's wrong." Ari leaned against a tree, her palms pressed to the bark. "Jerek promised he was coming back. I looked him in the eye, and he promised."

"Was Eve in on that promise?" Ford shook his head, still looking at his feet. "Did he make that promise before or after he took the heliostone and Blood List into the archivist's house?"

"Unless you can think of a way to help that doesn't involve putting Jerek, Eve, or Mariah in more danger, then please shut the hell up." Ari shuddered. Droplets of water ran down the backs of her hands. "Sorry, Ford. I'm sorry. I just can't—god, I'm such an idiot."

"You're not." Lincoln dared to step closer to her. Gently, he placed his hand on the back of her waist, ready for her to shove him away.

She sagged against his side, resting her head on his shoulder.

He slid his hand out to her hip, letting himself take comfort in the feel of her weight pressed against him.

"Tell me they'll be okay and mean it," Ari whispered.

Lincoln opened his mouth to speak but couldn't make himself form the words.

"Pizza!" Ford shouted. "We need to order a pizza."

73

Eve

If she hadn't already seen Chanler's hoard in the Museum of Magic, Eve might have been astounded by the cases of artifacts that filled the rooms on the third floor of the archivist's house. Weapons, chalices, jewels, even a display of four intricately carved wands.

She crept through the rooms, peering into the corners, searching for any hint of people lurking inside the house. But the corners just held more relics of the feu, and the only sounds came from the floor below.

Testing each stair, Eve crept down to the second floor where shelves of books took the place of the cases of artifacts.

A glass-fronted cabinet filled with scrolls had an electronic panel on the front, monitoring the humidity inside the case. Some of the scrolls looked old enough to have been written before the first packs came to America.

A profoundly tempting curiosity begged Eve to smash

through the glass front of the case and see exactly what secrets the scrolls contained. But the hum of voices came from the front of the house, and the scrolls were all too old to hold the information Eve truly wanted.

She crept slowly toward the voices, trying to hear what they were saying.

The crackling voice was Jerek's, the girl's voice was Mariah's. A third voice for the archivist. No fourth voice.

"No!" The shout came from the room up ahead.

Eve reached the door in two steps. Before she could turn the handle, the calm voice of the archivist spoke.

"It's a pleasure to meet you, Mariah. I'm sure Mr. LeBlanc will be relieved when I call to inform him the wayward Chanler has been found."

"I will not—" There was a hint of pain in Jerek's voice, but not fear.

Patience, Evelyn, Gran whispered.

Eve kept her hand on the doorknob, careful not to let her claws clack against the metal, as she angled herself to watch the stairs.

"—heliostone in exchange for all the information you have on the genesis of the Fracture," Jerek said.

"Pity you didn't do more research before your failed portrayal of Louis. It would have saved you a great deal of pain," the archivist said. "Now give me the heliostone, and I'll keep you comfortable while we wait for LeBlanc to collect you."

Give it to him, Holden. Eve gripped the doorknob. *Let him bring LeBlanc here.*

"Gladly," Jerek said.

A thud and a grunt came from inside the room. Then a yelp.

"Dammit, Holden." Eve threw open the door and charged into yet another room filled with books.

Jerek and Mariah were on the ground. Jerek gripped the ankle of the man standing above them.

Eve charged the man, ducking low to smash her shoulder into the small of his back, bringing him down with a satisfying crash. She jammed her elbow between his shoulder blades, keeping him pinned down.

"The archivist?" She blew her curls out of her face.

"Get off me!" the man shouted.

"He is." Jerek began to stand.

"No!" Mariah grabbed the neck of Jerek's shirt, yanking him back to the ground as a silver disc shot out of nowhere and lodged itself in the wall just behind where Jerek's jugular would have been.

"What the hell was that?" Eve raised the archivist's chest six inches off the ground and slammed him back down.

"I can hear a click in the wall just before they shoot out," Mariah said.

"How are you doing it?" Eve asked.

The archivist laughed.

"How?" She slammed him down again.

"Have you ever heard of a little thing called *magic?*" the archivist said in a tauntingly matter of fact way.

"Hurling objects across the room would take more than a bit of trace magic left behind by the Fracture," Jerek said.

The archivist chuckled. "Such a clever man. The real Chanler would benefit from your ability to reason."

"Don't insult my father," Mariah shouted.

"How are you doing it?" Eve leaned close, whispering in the archivist's ear. "Tell me, or I'll start breaking bones."

The archivist's laughter grew.

Eve twisted, angling her foot above the archivist's calf. She stomped down, not bothering to hide her smile as she broke his leg with a satisfying crack.

"Do you know what happens when you make a werewolf mad?" Eve spoke over the archivist's shouts of pain. "Instinct starts to take over and we tear our prey apart."

"I don't"—the archivist panted—"I don't have to launch the discs. I only need enough magic to trigger the springs."

The archivist twitched his finger.

A disc flew from the top of the far wall, cutting down toward the base of the couch beside Mariah.

Mariah screamed as the disc sliced into her arm.

"No more." Jerek smashed the heliostone down on the archivist's hand.

The archivist's scream joined Mariah's.

"Pin his hands," Jerek said. "We need to get the hell out of this room."

"Great." Eve grabbed the archivist's wrists, mashing his hands together hard enough to make him scream again. She pulled backward, flipping him up and over, letting his weight hit his broken leg. "Where to?"

"The kitchen." Jerek pushed himself to his feet. Blood seeped through the side of his suit jacket.

Eve dragged the archivist toward the door. "Do you have a first aid kit in the kitchen?"

"Go to hell." The archivist tried to pull free.

Eve swung him into the hall, smacking him against the wall. "I *was* going to be gentle with you on the stairs."

The archivist spat blood onto the polished, wooden floor. "Let me go."

"How original." Eve dragged him down the stairs, enjoying his tiny yelps that came with each step. She flung him against the wall at the bottom of the stairs for good measure.

"Don't knock him out," Mariah said. "We still need him to talk."

"What could the runaway Chanler, a wolf, and an imposter

want from me?" the archivist said. "Steal whatever you came here for and get out of my house."

"We didn't come to rob you," Jerek said. "All we want is the information we've already asked for."

"Why the hell do you care how the Fracture happened? It's done."

Jerek got in front of Eve, opening a door on the right that led to a dining room with a table even bigger than Gran's. He left that room and went to the swinging door at the end of the hall, which opened into a kitchen with pale wood, white tiles, and a glass door that led out to the fenced-in patio.

"Duct tape, rope, anything we can tie you up with?" Eve asked.

"I'm not helping you," the archivist said.

"Do you want me to get creative?" Eve asked.

"There's tape in the drawer on the left side of the sink," the archivist said.

"See how easy that was?" Eve said.

Jerek pulled a roll of silver duct tape from the drawer.

Eve pinned the archivist's palms together and held him in place as Jerek bound his hands with layers and layers of tape.

"Jerek, we're both bleeding." Mariah leaned against the doorjamb, her hand pressed to the wound on her arm.

"Towels?" Jerek looked to the archivist.

"Drawer to the right of the fridge."

Eve lifted the archivist into a chair, using more tape to bind him in place.

"There's a hospital not far from here," the archivist said. "It looks like you both need stitches."

"You might get us to consider taking you in for x-rays of your broken leg, too." Eve sat on the table. "But no one is going anywhere until you give us the information we want."

"The start of the Fracture, proof of Chanler's innocence."

The archivist spat blood onto his white floor. "Only a fool would make such a request."

"Only a fool would bother stalling," Eve said. "I have spent years waiting to find out who murdered my family. I'm done waiting. You're going to tell me who caused the Fracture. You're going to tell me who killed my family."

"Proof of Chanler's innocence." The archivist locked his glare on Mariah.

"I don't give a shit about Chanler's innocence." Eve flicked open her mother's pendant, letting her claws grow. "I want the truth, and you're going to give it to me."

"There are some truths better left hidden," the archivist said.

"Unacceptable," Jerek said.

Eve leaned down and slashed her claw across the archivist's shin.

The archivist screamed.

"Who caused the Fracture?" Jerek wrapped tape around his own chest, binding an already bloody towel to his wound.

"What is done is done," the archivist said.

Eve slashed her claw across the archivist's shin again, earning a satisfying gasp and whimper.

"We can mend the Fracture," Jerek said. "We are going to bring magic back into the world. Tell us who created the Fracture, and you may live long enough to enjoy having your full powers restored."

"The Fracture cannot be mended," the archivist said.

"Sure it can." Eve reached for the archivist's uninjured leg.

"I mean it shouldn't!" the archivist shouted. "Magic was not removed from this world for the sake of a petty vendetta. What was done was done to protect us all, feu and somb alike."

"What the hell are you talking about?" Eve said.

"The Fracture caused catastrophe and death," Jerek said.

"The Fracture saved more lives than it cost," the archivist said. "Every shelf in my collection contains tales of horrors committed in the name of magic. Silencing sombs, sacrificing Maree, magicians abusing their power as though the world is their playground and everyone in it nothing more than ants to be tormented.

"It was only a matter of time before a catastrophic use of magic drew the attention of the sombs. How many lives would be lost to gain magicians power over the somb population? Losing magic was an unpleasant inconvenience. Allowing magicians to continue on their dark path would have caused a massacre."

"You can't know that," Mariah said.

"Read every book I have read, and you will agree. The Fracture is necessary."

"Then you're the one who did it?" Mariah grabbed a knife from the counter. "What did you do to my mother? Why was she—"

"I know nothing about that!" the archivist shouted as Mariah held the knife to his throat. "I don't know why your mother was with them. I didn't create the Fracture. I only helped them with research."

"Them?" Jerek's voice was completely calm.

"No." The archivist shook his head, wincing as his throat brushed against Mariah's blade. "I've told you enough, now let me go."

"Not gonna happen." Eve slowly pressed her claw into the archivist's thigh.

He panted through his scream.

"Who caused the Fracture?" Eve said.

"No." Sweat and tears dripped down the archivist's face.

"Who caused the Fracture?" Eve crooked her finger, letting her claw find a new angle in the archivist's flesh.

His scream pounded around the kitchen. She waited for him to stop, her claw still in his leg.

"Who caused the Fracture?" Eve whispered.

"If I tell you, they'll kill me." The archivist's voice cracked.

"If you don't tell us, *I'll* kill you." Eve straightened her finger.

The archivist whimpered. "This is bigger than you know. There are some forces you can't stand against."

"Try me," Eve said.

"Go home," the archivist said. "I'll forget you were ever here."

"Who caused the Fracture?" Eve wiggled her finger. "Tell me, or I'll actually try to hurt you."

The archivist scrunched his eyes closed for a moment before nodding. "I will never betray them. Just kill me. You've left yourself no other choice."

"Don't be so bleak," Jerek said. "Hours, days, weeks—we can keep working on you. I've spent years researching the cause of the Fracture. I've learned quite a bit about patience."

"Being tortured by you is better than the punishment I would receive for my betrayal," the archivist said. "If you wish to mar your souls playing with torture, so be it. I can patiently wait for death."

Eve pulled her claw from the archivist's leg and drove it into a new hole.

The archivist tipped his head forward, leaning into Mariah's knife as he tried to swallow his scream.

Mariah yanked her knife away and forced the archivist's chin up to see his throat. "He's not bleeding too badly. I don't think he nicked anything important."

"Just kill me and end it," the archivist said.

"Who caused the Fracture?" Eve swirled her finger. She shouted over the archivist's scream. "Who are *they*?"

"No!"

"Who did you help?" Eve drove another claw into his leg. "Who caused the Fracture? Who caused the Blood Mountain Massacre?"

"Me!" The archivist screamed through his sobs. "*I* told them to attack the pack."

Eve yanked her claws out of the archivist's leg as a wave of child-like terror broke through her rage.

"You set the bombs?" Jerek's tone was too calm, too distant. "You murdered my mother."

"I didn't set the bombs. I don't leave Manhattan. I don't know who they sent to do the wetwork." The archivist sat up straight. A glint of pride shone in his eyes. "A strong pack backed by the Holdens was too dangerous to be allowed. The threat had to be stopped."

"My mother was never a threat to anyone," Jerek said.

"The wolves needed to be exterminated!" the archivist said.

"You're a murderer!" Eve leapt to her feet, landing a punch in the archivist's ribs.

"I only regret that some of the vermin survived." The archivist coughed out the words.

"Eve, he—"

The archivist shouted over Jerek, "At least we killed some of the pups."

The world went quiet as Eve slashed her claws across the archivist's stomach.

Jerek

The archivist's scream sliced fear through the calm Jerek had been so desperately clinging to.

A fine spray of blood spattered the floor as the archivist coughed.

"My brother was not vermin. He was just a kid." Eve pulled her hand back to strike again.

"Eve, no!" Jerek grabbed her arm, but she didn't seem to notice as she swiped her claws across the archivist's chest.

"Stop!" Jerek shouted over the archivist's scream. "We still need him!"

"Too late." The archivist spat blood onto Jerek's shoe, choking on his laugh. "I'll be dead soon enough. You can't scare me into talking now."

Eve backed away from the archivist, staring down at the red coating her claws.

Jerek grabbed more towels from the kitchen drawer.

"Unless you're going to call a somb ambulance, you might as well cut my throat. Make the end a bit faster." The archivist coughed up more blood.

"The spell," Eve said. "The healing spell you did with Grace, can't you—"

"I can't do that kind of incantation alone." Jerek pressed the towels to the slices on the archivist's stomach.

The archivist smiled through his scream.

"Then use your fancy string," Eve said. "We need to find out who planted the bombs."

"They'll find you." The archivist spoke between shaky breaths. "They'll kill you. They'll know my sacrifice...sav—saved us all."

"You're nothing more than murdering scum," Mariah said. "Everyone will know that we have your collection because *you gave it to me.* You sold me your books, and artifacts, and secrets and fled the country."

The archivist's blood leaked through the towel.

"That's what every one of your patrons will believe," Mariah said.

The blood stained Jerek's hands, tainting his red-stoned ring.

"They...won't..." The archivist dragged in a breath. "They won't believe you."

"Of course they will." Mariah grinned as she leaned close to the archivist. "The living control the narrative, asshole. You don't get to be a martyr. Just filth that will soon be forgotten."

"No, you..." The archivist leaned forward, like he was trying to break free. "I've served my cause. I die for my...my cause."

"Traitor," Mariah whispered in his ear.

The archivist gave a gurgling whimper.

"Jerek, do something," Eve said.

"I can't replace blood." Jerek kept pressing the soaked towel to the archivist's wounds. "I can't save him."

"Good." Mariah patted the archivist's cheek. "He deserves a meaningless death."

Jerek closed his eyes, clawing through his memory to find a spell that might help. A healing incantation would close the wounds, but that wouldn't be enough. In all the incantations his father had taught him—

"Not meaningless." Jerek tossed the towels aside and raised his pants leg. "His death won't be meaningless. Mariah, have you ever piggybacked a spell?"

"What? No." Mariah stepped away.

Jerek unfastened the belt he'd used to secure the Blood List to his calf. He placed the scroll on the kitchen table.

"Why do you have that, Holden?" Eve said.

"Get this between his hands." Jerek pulled the heliostone from his pocket and tossed it to Eve.

"What is...what..." The archivist barely managed to lift his head as he tried to fight against Eve ramming the heliostone between his hands, ripping part of the tape that had bound him. "What are you..." His head slumped forward.

Jerek pulled the wound-up golden cord from his pocket and tossed it to Mariah.

It landed on the floor.

"Pick it up." Jerek pulled the red stone from his ring, nicking his own finger on the sharp end, and drove the point into the center of the archivist's chest.

He grabbed the cord from the floor, smacked one end into Mariah's hand and closed her fist around it.

"Jerek, what are you doing?" Mariah didn't drop the cord.

"Don't worry about what I'm doing. Just focus on funneling your magic into the cord."

Jerek unrolled the Blood List on the kitchen table. Three names written in blood showed on the parchment.

Richard Holden

Risa Holden

Jerek Holden

"What is that?" Fear widened Mariah's eyes. "Is that the Blood List?"

"*Allarium finastra dothhartra.*" Jerek began the incantation. "*Imarta hontorat fini.*"

He kept his eyes open as he spoke the words that had killed his father, had almost killed him. "*A colminna entresa.*"

Heat filled Jerek's body. The names on the Blood List began to shine, as though his parents were urging him to keep speaking the words.

The archivist gasped as the gem Jerek had pressed into his chest began to glow. The red light bursting from the gem joined with the glow of the heliostone, igniting with a power that sent fire racing through Jerek's veins.

"*Fai atsu albretsa maeartanu.*"

In a surge that nearly knocked him off his feet, a new power, Mariah's power, raced into Jerek's body, blurring his thoughts with the blinding weight of magic.

"*Allarium finastra dothhartra. Faitet lardum meino sacrificium.*"

A scream echoed from far away, too far away to break through his dire need to continue speaking.

Finish the incantation. It was the only thought he could cling to. Finish the spell.

"*Infarso LeTurtso Malisco Maleficium.*"

White hot fire surged through Jerek's chest, sending him into blackness.

75

Eve

Light poured from the heliostone, and Blood List, and golden cord, and red gem Jerek had stabbed into the archivist's chest.

Eve stood beside the table, frozen with a helpless sort of fear she'd never felt in a fight.

"Fai atsu albretsa maeartanu."

The archivist arched back. A horrible scream ripped from his throat, but Jerek kept speaking. The light of the spell grew brighter as it spread across the archivist's chest.

The light would consume him. Tear through him.

"Allarium finastra dothhartra."

Jerek swayed as he spoke, his shoulders sagging like the weight of the spell was crushing him.

"Faitet lardum meino sacrificium."

The archivist's scream stopped as a look of pure terror twisted his face.

"Infarso LeTurtso Malisco Maleficium."

With a bright flash, the light disappeared.

Jerek tipped toward the floor.

Eve lunged forward, catching Jerek while Mariah crashed to the ground.

"Jerek." She laid him on the blood-speckled kitchen floor. "Jerek!"

He didn't speak. Didn't flinch.

He was still breathing. Slowly. Maybe too slowly. But his heart was beating. She could hear it beneath the racing of her own heart. Mariah's, too.

Two slow, steady heartbeats.

"You're okay, Holden." She grabbed the last of the towels from the drawer and tucked them beneath Jerek's head. "You're going to be okay."

A sickening stench caught in Eve's nose as she took a ragged breath.

Singed flesh.

She sprang to her feet and vomited into the kitchen sink.

She'd caught that scent before. When she'd smelled her family burning.

She pushed down her sob and made herself turn back toward the three magicians.

Mariah lay on the floor like Jerek. Unconscious but breathing.

Swallowing the sour in her throat, Eve looked at the archivist.

He'd gone well past breathing.

His hands and arms had been charred black by the heliostone. The skin around the red gem in his chest had gone an awful, deadly shade of white, like the power of the gem had sucked the life right out of him.

His head had tipped back, his eyes blank, though terror still twisted his face.

Eve turned to the sink and vomited again.

When she'd finished, Jerek and Mariah still hadn't moved.

Eve closed her pendant, letting her claws shrink back into normal fingers. She scrubbed the blood from her hands and splashed cold water on her face.

There were no more towels in the drawer. She had blood on her shirt.

She dried her face with paper towels.

She needed to...

Needed to do something.

She could sit. Wait for Jerek to wake up. He could pry the heliostone out of the dead man's charred hands.

She dry-heaved over the sink. Pounding rattled through her thoughts. An irregular rhythm. Not her heartbeat.

The sound came from the front of the house.

She pressed her palm to her pendants, like a child checking they hadn't lost their blankie, as she followed the pounding to the front door.

The person knocked different rhythms, like they were trying to entertain themselves.

Eve shook out her shoulders and raised her chin.

I'm a Gibbs. I'm a Gibbs.

I'm a wolf. I'm a predator. Not prey.

She peered through the peephole.

Ford stood on the front steps, holding a stack of pizza boxes.

Eve turned the seven locks on the door and flung it open.

"Hi I'm here with your—Eve?" Ford took a step back, his eyes wide with fear like the charred archivist had opened door. "Why is there blood all over you?"

Eve looked down at her clothes. The blood stains were worse than she'd thought.

"Come in." She stepped aside. "Leave the pizza here. You don't want to take it into the kitchen."

76

Ari

Ari didn't fight Lincoln as he wrapped his arm around her waist. She didn't have enough left in her to pretend she didn't need him to hold her up. "Did it work?"

"I don't know." Eve stayed by the kitchen door, like she needed to be ready to run. "I didn't think it could without Grace."

"Jerek and I, w—we thought there might be a chance with piggybacking," Ari said. "Jerek said it was too risky. We couldn't gamble with mending the Fracture, and Grace was the only sure bet."

"If it's anything like after the Museum of Magic, we need to find Jerek and Mariah a safe place to rest while they sleep it off," Ford said. "Can we get them back to the hotel?"

"Maybe once it's dark," Lincoln said. "We could carry them. Make it look like they're passed out drunk."

"And what about the archivist?" Eve said. "We can't just leave a corpse in Manhattan. There are too many somb police."

"I can—" Ford looked around the kitchen like he was searching for suggestions. "I can look online. See what the best ways to dispose of a body in Manhattan are."

"You'll have to look up how to clean blood, too," Eve said. "And fingerprints. We're not going to have a flock of Maree making sure the sombs don't find out someone died."

"Okay, we'll get things cleaned up and get Jerek and Mariah out of here and then get out of town." Ford pulled out a kitchen chair. Speckles of blood stained the seat. "I can work standing." He took his tablet to the kitchen counter.

"We can't leave town." Ari slid away from the comfort of Lincoln's support. She dragged her fingers through her hair, yanking it back. "I don't even think we can abandon this house."

"We have to leave," Eve said.

"This house holds all the information powerful feu don't want out in the world," Ari said. "Some of it may be stupid family secrets—"

"But the incantation that caused the Fracture could be here, too," Lincoln said.

"We can't risk that information ending up with one of the archivist's patrons," Ari said.

"Or whoever caused the Fracture in the first place." Eve sat on the floor just inside the kitchen door. "He kept talking about a *them*. *They* caused the Fracture. *They* would do horrible things to him if he talked."

"And you didn't find out who the *they* was?" Ford asked.

Eve gripped her pendants as she shook her head. "We tried. But he said he'd sent the butcher after my pack. He said he'd caused the Blood Mountain Massacre. It was his fault my family died. And I just..." Tears slid down Eve's cheeks. "I slashed him and he was going to die, so Jerek did the spell."

"Maybe it worked," Lincoln said. "It never occurred to me that we wouldn't know right away."

"But what if the archivist was lying?" Eve swiped the tears from her cheeks. "He wanted us to kill him so we couldn't ask more questions. And I did. I tore into him and—"

"Don't." Ari sank to the ground to sit beside Eve. "You can't blame yourself for the work of demons."

"I could've gotten him to tell me who planted the bombs," Eve said. "I failed my family."

Ari dared to wrap her arms around Eve. "You didn't fail anyone."

"We're in an archive of magical secrets owned by a man who, if he wasn't responsible for the massacre, at least knew who was." Ford kept tapping away on his tablet. "If nothing else, we're a hell of a lot closer to knowing who murdered your family and Jerek's mom than we were this morning." He glanced over his shoulder and shot Eve a tight smile. "Think of it like that. We've made a huge step forward and it's not even time for dinner."

"Thanks." Eve pulled away from Ari. Not rejecting her concern, more like her physical contact quota for the year had been met.

"How would we feel about relocating the archives? I can get four moving trucks here by six if we can get rid of the body before then," Ford said.

"Chanler may have been willing to sell a story about LARPing to somb caterers at the Museum of Magic opening, but I don't think we can risk bringing sombs in here. One stolen book and we could expose the feu," Ari said.

"Not to mention the booby traps," Eve said.

"I'm sorry what?" Ford said.

"Then we hunker down," Lincoln said. "Secure the house,

barricade ourselves in, and be ready to defend the archives if any of the archivist's patrons show up."

"I hate that plan," Ari said. "But I don't have anything better."

"There are bedrooms on the fourth floor." Eve stood. "I'll carry Holden. You carry Chanler."

"I'll let Jack know what's happening," Ford said. "Maybe he has some ideas for body disposal."

As the others kept moving forward, finding something useful to do, Ari stayed sitting on the kitchen floor staring at the archivist's corpse, waiting for the ground to shake as magic screamed its presence to the world.

77

Jack

The chill of the night air did nothing to temper the stench of the city. The dumpsters in the alley behind the archivist's house needed to be emptied. The smell of car exhaust seemed to cling to the buildings themselves.

But as Jack sat on the roof, missing the fresh air he'd grown accustomed to since joining Jerek's crew, all he could feel was grateful for not having to smell the corpse they still hadn't managed to get rid of.

"Anything your way?" Ford asked from the far side of the roof where he'd been stationed to watch the front of the house.

Jack peered down into the alley four stories below. "Three oversized rats."

"I don't think they'll try to break in," Ford said.

"I hope not. I may have spent a lot of time underground in Vegas, but I'm still not fond of rodents."

Ford gave a little chuckle.

Jack's mind whirled as he tried to think of something witty or funny or smart to say.

Underground. Secrets. Secret romance. Romantic tryst. Underground tryst interrupted by rodents and secrets.

He had nothing.

The rats fled as a drunk stumbled down the alley.

"The..." Ford shuddered.

Jack should have remembered to bring a blanket for him.

"The charred *trouble* in the kitchen," Ford said. "I don't know what we should do."

"Me neither."

"When our guard shift is over, I don't know if I can sleep with it still here. Does that make me a coward?"

"Not even a little."

"I'm going to have to sleep though. I'm not like you. I've been up for twenty hours. I'll pass out whether I like it or not. But can you...will you stay with me while I sleep? Is that too weird?"

"I'll stay with you." A hint of joyful sorrow swept through the swirling in Jack's mind. "I won't let anything happen to you. I promise."

"I know you won't." A hint of a smile colored Ford's voice. "That's why I want you with me."

78

Lincoln

Her blond hair cascaded over her pillow, laid out behind her in a way that tempted Lincoln to touch it. Just graze his fingers across the strands to see if the texture really was as soft as his memory swore it to be.

She'd wanted to sleep downstairs, near the front door in case anyone came seeking the archivist. Eve was watching Jerek and Mariah on the fourth floor. Ford and Jack were on the roof. Lincoln couldn't let Ari sleep on the first floor by herself. Not when there was a corpse in the kitchen.

At least, that was the excuse Lincoln had given when he'd hauled down the queen size mattress from one of the four bedrooms upstairs.

He was going to sleep on the floor, leaving the last available bed for Ford when he finally dropped from exhaustion. But Ari had insisted Lincoln share her mattress, threatening to sleep on the floor herself if he wouldn't stop fussing over not wanting to sleep beside her.

After all, the mattress left a whole foot of space between them.

But Lincoln couldn't sleep. Not with Ari so close by. Not with her scent surrounding him and her hair glistening in the light creeping in through the windows.

Not with every warning about women his parents had ever given him screaming in his head.

A sound, like the engine of a garbage truck, rumbled down the street.

Ari stirred, starting to wake up at the sound.

"Shh." Lincoln hushed. "It's just a truck. You're okay."

"Mmkay," Ari murmured.

She rolled over and nestled herself against him, her head on his shoulder, her hand lying on his chest. She squirmed for a moment, locking her body even closer to his, her ankle crossing over his.

She gave a contented sigh. Her breathing went back to a slow, steady rhythm.

Lincoln wrapped his arms around her, holding her tight, allowing himself to live in the fantasy that she might truly be his to protect.

79

Ari

Beep. *Beep. Beep. Beep.*

The sound yanked Ari out of sleep more efficiently than an ear-splitting scream could have.

A heavy, warm weight blocked her as she tried to dive across the mattress for her phone.

"Shit." Ari shoved the weight away and scrambled to the far side of the makeshift bed.

"What's wrong?" Lincoln threw back the blanket and sprang to his feet, facing the front door.

"It's an alert." Ari grabbed her pink phone and swiped it open. "I've set them up on Jerek's bank accounts, the Holden House security system"—she tapped the red flashing button in the middle of the screen—"shit."

A wave of cold dread crushed that last bit of sleepy warmth.

"What?" Lincoln knelt beside her.

"An email." Ari scanned the message once, letting her heart

have a moment to shoot into her throat before she read aloud. "Jerek, according to recent reports, Lincoln is still traveling with you. Even if he isn't, I need you to get a message to him. Don't let him come back to the compound. Don't allow him to contact the Council. Fighting between Maree broke out during the night. A faction is trying to seize the compound. I got Mom and Dad out."

Lincoln gasped in a shaky breath.

Ari took his hand.

"I got Mom and Dad out. The bottom five are already at the bay. No word on Martin. With all the incidents flying through the news, if the Maree don't act quickly, centuries of work will be destroyed. I have to stay at the compound. We have to stop the uprising and stifle the surge of magic before it's too late.

"Tell Lincoln I'm sorry I can't be there to protect the family. This fight is bigger than the Martels. I can't run when there's still a chance to save the Knights Maree and the feu. Tell Lincoln I'll contact him through you when I can. Keep my brother safe. Keep him away from the Maree. Fredrick."

Ari held her phone out to Lincoln. He didn't take it.

"What does he mean *uprising?*" Lincoln's face was cold and blank. "How could there be an uprising? It's just knights. It's all Maree in the compound. There's no one to fight against."

Ari pulled her laptop from her bag, flipped it open, and began entering the series of passcodes.

"He got Mom and Dad out?" Lincoln said. "Fredrick's not even supposed to be in the compound. He's stationed in Paris."

Ari clicked open a news site.

"I wanted all the younger siblings sent to the bay. The bottom five are just kids, they shouldn't be anywhere near a fight," Lincoln said. "But Mom and Dad leaving the compound? I don't understand."

Ari only had to scroll halfway down the first page for her heart to leap back up to pummel her throat.

"It worked." She forced the words out. "The incantation worked."

Boxes of cereal floating off the shelves on Long Island. The lights in Times Square flickering as though mirroring a heartbeat.

She pulled up a page of national news.

The cages in a Florida pet store all opening at once. A single street icing over in Arizona.

"It actually worked." Ari sat back, leaning against Lincoln as the hallway started to spin. "We actually mended the Fracture."

"Then why are the Maree fighting? This is what we lost so many knights trying to achieve."

"I don't know." Ari threaded her fingers through his, anchoring herself to his steady warmth. "I'll tap into feu chatter. See what I can find."

Beep. Beep. Beep.

The alarm on Ari's phone sounded again.

Lincoln peeled his hand away from hers to wrap his arm around her waist, keeping her close as she opened her phone.

"Florida news alert." Ari's voice sounded hollow to her own years. "An unexplained fire consumed a warehouse. A female suspect was caught on a security camera fleeing the scene."

Ari scrolled down to the photo.

Flames leapt high into the air as a girl with black hair and terror on her face fled the scene.

"Grace," Lincoln whispered.

"Shit."

———

At long last, the Fracture has been mended and magic has been restored to the world.

But was the archivist right? Was the world better off without magic? Find out when *The Bloodbound Knight* releases August 22, 2023.

Thank you for reading *The Oathbound Blade*. If you enjoyed the book, please consider leaving a review to help other readers find this story.

As always, thanks for reading,
    Megan O'Russell

Never miss a moment of the magic and romance.

Join the Megan O'Russell Readers Community to stay up to date on all the action by scanning the QR code below with your smart device.

HOW I MAGICALLY MESSED UP
MY LIFE IN FOUR FREAKIN' DAYS

We walked uptown toward my dad's. I don't know if it was instinct, habit, or the fact that my keys to Mom's place had been melted by a fire. Either way, Le Chateau seemed like the best bet.

A cab would have been faster, but since I smelled like a barbeque gone wrong, I figured it was better to walk.

Devon started by giving me a blow-by-blow of what the firemen had been doing: running in and out and a lot of hauling hoses mostly. "And then Linda May, sweet little Linda May, was so terrified she needed comfort, and of course she ran to me. I'm telling you man, the fire made 8th Ave crazy."

"You do remember I was there, right?" I asked, trying not to sound snarky even though I was tired enough to curl up on a subway grate and sleep. "I was the one who saw the fire start and pulled the alarm to get everyone out."

"Really?" Devon asked, looking surprised for a second but trying to cover up his shock by punching me in the arm. "Good for you, man! Elizabeth must think you're a hero. This could be the break you've been waiting for. Did you ask her out?"

"What? No, I didn't ask her out!" I ran my hands through my hair. It was gritty from the smoke and orange paint.

Devon grimaced and shook his head, looking down at the sidewalk.

"What?" I asked again, trying not to get angry. "What did you want me to do? Was I supposed to look down, see a fire, and stop on the way to the alarm to ask Elizabeth to be my girlfriend?"

"I mean, *girlfriend* might have been pushing it, but it would have been better than nothing," Devon said.

"Sorry, I was trying to make sure everyone didn't burn to death."

"What about when you two were talking once everyone was out of the theatre then?" Devon said, nodding and winking at a random dog walker.

The poor girl had two mastiffs, three Chihuahuas, and one drooling pug. Their leashes had all gotten tangled, and one of the Chihuahuas was dangling over the bigger mastiff's back. Being a dog walker was on my top ten list for jobs I never wanted in Manhattan.

"I don't know how many more chances you can hope to get with Elizabeth."

"I've never had a single chance," I said as we turned onto Central Park West, "and now she probably thinks I'm a freak, so...." I was screwed. There was something about knowing she thought I had magically started a fire with a cellphone and was now afraid of me that made it seem more true than years of her never speaking to me ever had. My stomach felt heavy and gross.

"Why does she think you're a freak?" Devon asked. "I mean, you just saved the whole theatre class."

I pulled the little black demon out of my pocket.

"She's thinks you're a freak because you forgot to return the phone? Which, by the way, is not cool, man. You don't leave a guy phoneless in Manhattan."

"If you remember, before you *had* to tell me all about how you made out with Linda May while our school was on fire, Elizabeth wants me to get rid of the phone." I slid it back into my pocket. Somehow having it out in my hand made me feel exposed, like a big eye in a creepy tower was watching me as I ran toward a pit of lava.

"So then let's get rid of the phone," Devon said. "We'll take it to the purple restaurant and make it their problem to find the vampire dude, and you can tell her you did what she wanted."

"She doesn't want me to return the phone," I sighed, knowing full well Devon was going to laugh at me. "She wants me to throw it into the Hudson to destroy it. She thinks the phone started the fire."

I started counting to three in my head. Before I got past two, Devon had tossed his head back and roared with laughter. People stared as they walked by.

It took Devon a full minute to speak. "I'm sorry." He wiped the tears from his eyes. "Was there a stray ray of sunlight you reflected off the screen to ignite the mounds of dried grass in the set shop?"

"No." I pushed Devon in the back to make him start walking again, and he promptly skidded on sidewalk goop. "There's an app on the phone, and she thinks I started the fire with it."

"An app. She thinks you started a fire with an app on a phone you can't even open?"

"I did open the phone," I said, "and a fire app thing."

"How did you open the phone? It should have a password." Devon turned to me, his laughter fading a little. "Do you have like post-traumatic stress or something from the fire? Because I mean, we could call your mom."

"I don't have traumatic stress." I pulled Devon into the

shade of a coffee shop awning. The place smelled like vegan food and almond milk. "And I didn't use a password." I glanced around before pulling the phone back out of my pocket. I didn't know what I was looking for. No one seemed to care about the two teenagers hanging out by the vegan coffee shop. But I still couldn't shake the feeling that someone was following me. Or that the evil eye was gazing down at me from the Empire State building. "I used my thumbprint." I pressed my thumb to the button, and the phone opened, showing the same funny symbols as before.

"Whoa!" Devon took it from me, but as soon as it left my hands, the thing turned back off. "Aw, come on." He pressed his thumb to the sensor, but the screen stayed dark. "Damn. Battery must have died."

I took the phone back and pressed my thumb back on the button. The screen popped back up. Devon grabbed the phone again, and it was the same thing. Him—phone off. Me—phone on.

"Bryant." Devon's voice was barely above a whisper. "Did you buy a phone and rig it to do that to freak me out? Because I mean, good for you, but that's a lot of trouble for a prank."

"You found this in the cab. And I would never prank you. I know better." And really I did. Devon would take any reason to punk you. If you were five minutes late when you were supposed to meet him, you had to spend the next week wondering what his revenge would be. Pulling a prank on him would be the worst idea anyone in Hell's Kitchen had ever had. Except maybe the next thing I did. That may have been the worst idea anyone in New York had ever had.

Devon was still giving me the *I don't believe you* stare with his eyebrows raised and his arms crossed. And Elizabeth thought I had a possessed phone, and my mom's theatre had burned down, and I had sort of had enough.

"Fine." I dragged him over to a trashcan by the side of the street, then tapped on the app that showed the picture of the fire. There it was—the still flames with the bar below balancing perfectly centered. I held the phone out like I was going to take a picture of the can and tapped the bar, tipping it all the way to the right.

Big mistake.

Flames shot out of the can and flew ten feet into the air like the sanitation department had decided collecting trash was too hard and installing a giant blowtorch was a better use of resources.

People behind us started to scream. Devon cursed and backed away. I stood there, frozen by the sudden heat. I couldn't move. I mean, I know I had gone to the fire app to prove to Devon that I wasn't wandering the city in some PTSD haze. But finding myself in front of a ten-foot-tall pillar of fire, holding a possessed cellphone in my hands, I sort of felt like maybe I had lost my mind. Maybe this wasn't even New York and I was locked in a cell. Or even better, and less scary maybe, I was still in bed, and this whole thing was a dream. I hadn't even gotten out of bed yet, and soon I would wake up with cat ass on my face.

I squeezed my eyes tightly shut and opened them again. There was still a fire right in front of me. No padded white room. No stinky cat ass.

I tapped the left side of the bar and pulled it all the way down. Just like it had sprung up without warning, in an instant, the fire disappeared with nothing but a melted trashcan to show for itself. Well, that and the sour, nose hair-burning stench of flaming crap.

I turned to Devon who stared, petrified, at where the flames had been.

"See? Not a prank."

"What the hell?" he muttered. "Not okay. That is definitely not okay. Burning trashcans is not okay."

The rubberneckers behind us chattered noisily. One woman shouted into her cellphone, "The fire's gone out, but I think it's a gas line!" She paused for a second. "Back away. 9-1-1 says everybody back away."

People immediately scurried down the street or hugged next to the building, still transfixed in fascinated horror.

"You need to move, boys!" the cellphone lady shouted at us as sirens echoed between the buildings.

"Go!" I pushed Devon so hard his feet finally started to work again. I grabbed his arm and dragged him onto a side street out of view of the fire trucks as they pulled up to the melted trashcan.

Two run-ins with the fire department in one day is not a good thing. Especially not when you might have caused the fires. Even if it was by accident.

We cut back around the block and to my dad's building. The fire trucks had parked down the street, but from here we couldn't even see what all the firemen were staring at.

Drake was behind the desk like always. "Mr. Adams." He smiled. "I wasn't expecting to see you here today."

"Yeah." I tried to put my thoughts into an order that didn't involve a possessed demon phone with the ability to make things spontaneously combust that was currently burning a hole in my back pocket. Not literally. I hoped. "There was a fire at school. Everybody's okay, but I lost my house key, so I'm gonna hang out here until my mom gets home." If my mom still had a house key.

"Of course, Mr. Adams." Drake unlocked the safe beneath the desk. "I would be more than happy to let you into the apartment. I am so relieved you're safe. Have you called your father?"

Drake led us to the elevator and turned the key to go up.

"No." It hadn't occurred to me to call my dad. I mean, how could he be worried about me when he didn't even know my school had been on fire? Never mind the fact that the more time passed, the more convinced I was that I had caused the fire in the first place. But Drake was still looking at me all concerned, so I said, "Not yet. I'm going to call before I shower." And I did need to shower. Even though the elevator was a big one, it was still small enough to trap in the horrible smoke and burning trash smell that was stuck to me.

The door opened to my dad's apartment, and Drake waved us in. "Shall I call for a pizza?"

"Two." Devon half-stumbled into the apartment.

"Very well." Drake closed the elevator doors and was gone.

Devon walked into the living room and collapsed onto the couch. I followed him, a little afraid he might be panicked enough to start throwing up onto the carpet. And having to call the cleaning lady to tell her you got puke in the carpet was never a fun time.

I sat on the metal rim of the glass coffee table and stared at Devon, waiting for him to speak. If he could still speak. I wasn't too sure about that.

"The fire," Devon said finally, his hands shaking as he dragged them over his face. "The phone started the fire."

Elizabeth had been right. She had seen it right away.

"Both fires. And the one at school didn't go out till I put it out with the app."

Devon scrunched his face and let out the longest string of muttered curses I had ever heard. "We have to get rid of it."

"Same thing Elizabeth said. I can take it down to the restaurant and leave it with them."

"No way in *Hell*!" Devon shook his head, looking as pale as I had ever seen him. "You just burned down half the school with that thing. You can't keep it. It's arson evidence, Bry."

"So we give it—"

"We are not giving the damn phone to people who might want to do more damage with it than you've already done! That guy we saw looked evil. He looked like a vampire or demon or something. We can't give an evil dude something this danger-ous. What if he lights us on fire? Or decides to take out Times Square. I can't have that on my head, man."

"So, we do what Elizabeth said and dump it into the Hudson," I said, wondering if I could convince Drake to find a guy to take the phone to the river.

No, it couldn't be trusted to a courier. I mean, who wouldn't want to open a package they had been hired to dump into a river. We'd have to do it ourselves.

I turned my wrist over, making my watch blink on. Nearly seven PM. "If we head to the water in a few hours, we should be able to find a place to dump it without getting noticed."

"No way." Devon pushed himself to sit up. "The river's way too risky. What if it washes up and someone finds it?"

"It's a phone. It'll be dead from the water."

"A demon phone that starts fires, and you think water is going to hurt it?" Devon stood up, color coming back into his determined face. "We have to destroy it ourselves. It's the only way to make sure it's done."

Order How I Magically Messed Up My Life in Four Freakin'
Days *to continue the journey!*

ABOUT THE AUTHOR

 Megan O'Russell is the author of several Young Adult series that invite readers to escape into worlds of adventure. From *Girl of Glass*, which blends dystopian darkness with the heart-pounding danger of vampires, to *Ena of Ilbrea*, which draws readers into an epic world of magic and assassins.

With the *Girl of Glass* series, *The Tethering* series, *The Chronicles of Maggie Trent*, *The Tale of Bryant Adams*, the *Ena of Ilbrea* series, and several more projects planned, there are always exciting new books on the horizon. To be the first to hear about new releases, free short stories, and giveaways, sign up for Megan's newsletter by visiting the following:

https://www.meganorussell.com/book-signup

Originally from Upstate New York, Megan is a professional musical theatre performer whose work has taken her across North America. Her chronic wanderlust has led her from Alaska to Thailand and many places in between. Wanting to travel has fostered Megan's love of books that allow her to visit countless new worlds from her favorite reading nook. Megan is also a lyricist and playwright. Information on her theatrical works can be found at RussellCompositions.com.

She would be thrilled to chat with you on Facebook or Twitter @MeganORussell, elated if you'd visit her website MeganORussell.com, and over the moon if you'd like the pictures of her adventures on Instagram @ORussellMegan.

ALSO BY MEGAN O'RUSSELL

The Girl of Glass Series

Girl of Glass

Boy of Blood

Night of Never

Son of Sun

The Tale of Bryant Adams

How I Magically Messed Up My Life in Four Freakin' Days

Seven Things Not to Do When Everyone's Trying to Kill You

Three Simple Steps to Wizarding Domination

Five Spellbinding Laws of International Larceny

The Tethering Series

The Tethering

The Siren's Realm

The Dragon Unbound

The Blood Heir

The Chronicles of Maggie Trent

The Girl Without Magic

The Girl Locked With Gold

The Girl Cloaked in Shadow

Ena of Ilbrea

Wrath and Wing

Ember and Stone

Mountain and Ash

Ice and Sky

Feather and Flame

Guilds of Ilbrea

Inker and Crown

Myth and Storm

Viper and Steel

Tower and Grave

The Heart of Smoke Series

Heart of Smoke

Soul of Glass

Eye of Stone

Ash of Ages

Fracture Pact

The Cursebound Thief

The Oathbound Blade

The Bloodbound Knight

Sorcerers of Ilbrea

Spell and Secret